W9-AWC-569

Zero hour was approaching . . .

"We'll be gunned down or kidnapped when we step outside this tour bus," Andrea whispered. She thought of her shock at seeing the open doors of their limo just moments ago. Someone inside had been dead and either she or Philip had been the intended target.

"They'll kill us in the town of Agra." In spite of the danger, Philip's voice was a velvet murmur. He pulled her close. "I want to leave you in this bus."

"I'd never stay behind," Andrea protested.

His level gaze met hers. "You'd risk your life for me?"

"I already have." *And she had risked her heart.*

The tour bus turned off the crumbling road and entered through a high iron gate. It stopped. Then the driver pulled a lever and the door slid open.

Andrea grasped Philip's hand, then hit the ground running.

Zero hour was here. . . .

ABOUT THE AUTHOR

Vickie York has served as a commissioned officer in both the U.S. Army and U.S. Air Force. After an assignment to the Defense Language Institute in Monterey, California, where *School for Spies* is set, Vickie served as an intelligence officer for the rest of her military career. She was awarded a Bronze Star for service during the Vietnam conflict. Beginning with the publication of *The Pestilence Plot* in 1982, in hardcover, her novels have been based on her intelligence expertise. Vickie has traveled extensively and now makes her home in Tacoma, Washington, where she was born. She enjoys riding ferries on Puget Sound with special friends, singing in the church choir and taking long walks with her German shepherd. To help with the writing of *Abandoned*, Vickie took a research trip to India and Nepal.

Books by Vickie York

HARLEQUIN INTRIGUE
  43–A TOP SECRET AFFAIR
  73–MORE THAN A HUNCH
178–SCHOOL FOR SPIES
211–LIAR'S GAME

Don't miss any of our special offers. Write to us at the following address for information on our newest releases.

Harlequin Reader Service
901 Fuhrmann Blvd., P.O. Box 1397, Buffalo, NY 14240
Canadian address: P.O. Box 603,
Fort Erie, Ont. L2A 5X3

Abandoned

Vickie York

THOMAS HACKNEY BRASWELL
MEMORIAL LIBRARY
ROCKY MOUNT, NC 27804

Harlequin Books

TORONTO • NEW YORK • LONDON
AMSTERDAM • PARIS • SYDNEY • HAMBURG
STOCKHOLM • ATHENS • TOKYO • MILAN
MADRID • WARSAW • BUDAPEST • AUCKLAND

If you purchased this book without a cover you should be aware
that this book is stolen property. It was reported as "unsold and
destroyed" to the publisher, and neither the author nor the
publisher has received any payment for this "stripped book."

For Virginia,
who shared India and Nepal with me

Harlequin Intrigue edition published June 1993

ISBN 0-373-22231-9

ABANDONED

Copyright © 1993 Betty Ann Patterson. All rights reserved.
Except for use in any review, the reproduction or utilization of
this work in whole or in part in any form by any electronic,
mechanical or other means, now known or hereafter invented,
including xerography, photocopying and recording, or in any
information storage or retrieval system, is forbidden without
the permission of the publisher, Harlequin Enterprises Limited,
225 Duncan Mill Road, Don Mills, Ontario, Canada M3B 3K9.

All the characters in this book have no existence outside the
imagination of the author and have no relation whatsoever to
anyone bearing the same name or names. They are not even
distantly inspired by any individual known or unknown to the
author, and all incidents are pure invention.

® are Trademarks registered in the United States Patent and
Trademark Office and in other countries.

Printed in U.S.A.

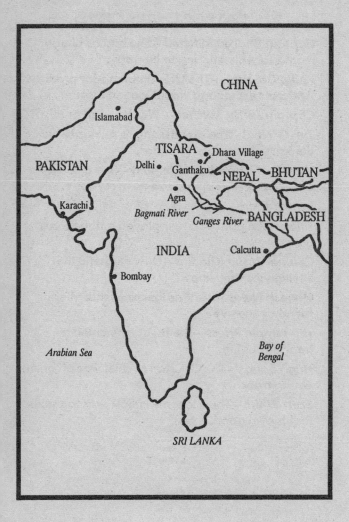

CAST OF CHARACTERS

Captain Andrea Mitchell—She had an ulterior motive for volunteering to be a spy.

Philip Dorough—The U.S. ambassador predicted Andrea's espionage would lead to disaster.

Captain Jeffry Mitchell—Was he dead or alive?

Jan O'Neal—The ambassador's secretary was determined to protect her boss.

Warrant Officer Sam Connelly—The embassy's chief of security kept an eye on everybody.

Dass Verma—Was he human?

Tulak—The paid informer played a dangerous game.

Colonel Ratna Khadka—How much did the intelligence chief know?

Ganesh Nakarmi—Was the minister of interior friend or enemy?

The Temple Priest—The fat gardener led a treacherous life.

Hugh Boggs—The CIA station chief was off on the wrong track.

Scott White—The economic officer was too sexist for his own good.

Chapter One

The interrogator loaded six cartridges into his revolver and pointed it straight at Andrea's head. She flinched. Suddenly, the bright overhead lights felt unbearably hot. Her mass of fine blond hair was damp with sweat, her gray prison smock wet with perspiration. The heavy material covered her tall slender form from neck to midcalf, but nothing could hide the shock she felt at seeing the loaded weapon.

"Confess or die." His voice, a gutteral whisper, held a trace of an accent. He was straddling a chair opposite hers. Frowning, he tipped it toward her, his bright red uniform contrasting starkly with the narrow room's sterile white walls.

Stolidly, Andrea forced herself to repeat the words she'd already said at least fifty times. "I am Andrea Mitchell, a citizen of the United States. I demand to talk to somebody from the U.S. Embassy."

The interrogator sneered, his lip a twisting ugly line. "How many time do I have to tell you, Captain Mitchell, your embassy will not help you. Your government wants no connection with a military officer who masquerades as a civilian to spy on our kingdom." He pulled back the hammer on the revolver with his thumb. "We know you're not a civilian secretary. If you want to leave this room alive, confess."

This can't be happening, she thought, feeling an unwelcome spurt of adrenaline. *He wouldn't dare hurt me.* She stuck her chin out. "I am a citizen of—"

"You're not playing the game, Captain." Her tormentor's black eyes narrowed to slits. With a barely discernible movement, he turned the hand holding the gun slightly to his right. The weapon fired with a loud cracking sound. Andrea felt the air stir as the bullet passed her cheek. It crashed into the wall behind her head, shattering the plaster.

Her hands clenched in her lap, and her heart pounded. If she'd jerked her head even slightly, she'd be dead now. She felt the blood drain from her face.

"Ah, I have your attention at last." The interrogator's mouth curved into a sarcastic smile. He inched his hand to its former position, with the gun pointed straight at her head. "Now, I'll ask you again, Captain Mitchell. Whom do you report to? What is the name of your superior?"

Andrea took a deep breath and swallowed, hard. "I've already told you." She couldn't keep the quaver from her voice. "I'm the secretary to the U.S. ambassador. *He's* my superior."

The interrogator sighed. The look in his dark eyes turned lethal. "You're still not playing the game, Captain Mitchell. You know precisely whom I'm talking about. Your superior is not the U.S. ambassador. Your superior is the intelligence agent who controls you in the United States. I'm sorry to have to do this..."

He uncoiled himself from the chair he'd been straddling and stood up. He was stocky, with dark straight hair cut short. A ghoul of a man.

Horrified, Andrea watched him aim the gun once again at her forehead, watched his finger tighten on the trigger. In her heart of hearts, she knew he wouldn't kill her. But that didn't stop her from throwing her hands over her face.

"No!" she screamed at the top of her lungs.

The weapon fired again, its noise deafening in the small interrogation room. For an instant, Andrea sat there stunned, unable to breathe. Then reality seeped in.

I'm okay, she told herself. *He doesn't dare hurt me.*

Shaking, she jerked her hands away from her face. Slowly, she folded her arms across her chest. "I am a citizen of the United States," she repeated in a loud voice. "I am not a spy. I demand to talk to someone from the U.S. Embassy."

Her tormentor returned to his chair. "Very good, Captain Mitchell." The gutteral sounds of his accent disappeared. Before her eyes, Andrea watched him turn into a human being. "The exercise is finished." His smile was warm, his twisting, sarcastic leer gone. "You passed with flying colors."

For a second, Andrea was tongue-tied. Was the exercise really over or was his reassurance some sort of horrid test? After two hours of intense pressure, she didn't dare relax. Anxiety spurted through her like blood squirting from a slashed artery.

When she finally spoke, her words were halting. "You're sure this isn't some kind of—ah—trick to get me to say something I shouldn't?"

He laughed heartily. "I'm positive." He stuck the revolver in a holster at his side.

Andrea forced a weak smile. What had she gotten herself into by volunteering for this undercover assignment as a military attaché? Would she end up disappearing mysteriously on some mountain slope, the way her husband, Jeffry, had? Was this the right way to go about finding him?

"Are you all right?" The interrogator sounded concerned. "If you need to use the bathroom, there's one adjoining the dressing room where you changed."

Andrea clasped her hands in her lap to keep them from shaking. "That would be nice." She was pleased to note her voice was steady. The disturbing flutters in her stomach were diminishing.

He nodded approvingly. "My office is across the hall. As soon as you freshen up, come on over, and we'll talk." He stood up and started toward the door, pausing as he reached it. "Since we're going to be working together, we might as well be on a first-name basis. I'm Tom, Andrea."

Working together. Andrea sank back down on the chair. Was this awful man going to be her controller? Lord, she hoped not.

He was eyeing her speculatively from the door. "Are you sure you're okay?"

Andrea managed a smile she hoped was convincing. "I'll be fine after I've had a couple of minutes to catch my breath. The past two hours weren't exactly a tea party."

"It was a necessary part of your training." He didn't return her smile. "We'll talk in my office."

A HALF HOUR LATER, dressed in the plain brown dress she'd worn that morning, Andrea knocked on the door across from the interrogation room. A sign identified the room's occupant as Tom Nolting, Colonel, U.S. Army.

"Come in." The voice sounded like her interrogator's.

She thrust the door open, took one look at the man sitting behind the desk and knew she'd made a mistake. This man wore horn-rimmed glasses, had iron-gray hair and looked close to fifty. His eyes were blue and he was wearing a rumpled business suit that made him appear heavier than the interrogator who'd tormented her for the past two hours.

"Excuse me." She started to close the door.

"Hold on, Andrea," he said, rising. "You've got the right office." He waved his hand at the chair beside his desk. "Come in and sit down."

As Andrea crossed to his desk, she noticed a framed picture on top of it. Two young blond children smiled back at her. *Grandchildren.* She was amazed that this horrid man could have something so ordinary as grandchildren.

Sinking into the chair, she folded her hands in her lap and waited nervously for him to begin. After seven years in the Air Force, she knew better than to open an official conversation with a superior. It was up to him to say the first word.

He eyed her with an amused expression. "So, Andrea, what's your honest opinion of our test exercise?"

She took a deep breath, biting her tongue so she wouldn't spit out the angry words she was thinking. She *was* angry, she realized suddenly. Angry at this school for permitting such frightening tactics. Angry at this middle-aged man for scaring her half to death.

She'd been told the exercise situation would be realistic. But she'd had no idea somebody would point a gun at her head and actually pull the trigger.

Nolting's expression turned demanding. "I'm serious. I'd like to know your opinion."

She stared at his blue eyes, hidden now behind thick eyeglasses. How had they changed to light blue? Contact lenses, probably. And the brown hair had obviously been a wig.

"You're a good actor—ah—Tom," she said, swallowing the "sir" that came automatically.

"I try to make my scenes with my people realistic." His expression didn't change. "As you see it, what was the point to the whole thing?"

To scare the bejesus out of me, Andrea thought, her anger threatening to spill over. She took a long breath to steady herself. "To test my response, should I get caught by the Tisarans."

He shook his head. "We could have accomplished that with a little playacting." He leaned toward her expectantly, egging her on. "What were you thinking when I put the bullets in my revolver?'' His voice sharpened, grating on her nerves.

He wants my honest opinion, does he? Andrea's anger surged to the surface. ''If you must know, I thought it was a damned dirty trick. Firing a loaded weapon at a student's head has got to be illegal.''

''Just a minute,'' he shot back. ''What makes you think anything we do around here is legal?'' He folded his arms and examined her critically. ''That's the whole point. You'll be involved in espionage. That's very illegal—and very dangerous.''

Her cheeks burning, she glared at him. ''Nobody has to tell me how dangerous this assignment is. But what I just went through was nothing but a damned exercise. What if I'd moved when you fired?'' Andrea felt her voice rising. She made no attempt to lower it. ''Or is it considered line-of-duty around here if a nervous student gets killed?''

He leaned back in his chair. ''You were never in any danger. Those were blanks in the revolver, and it wasn't pointed directly at you either time I fired.''

She blinked. ''The bullet crashed into the wall behind me. I felt it go by my head.''

''You imagined what you felt.''

''I didn't imagine the bullet hitting the wall.''

''There was a charge in the wall set to go off when I fired the blank.'' He nodded smugly. ''We're good at that sort of thing here. You ought to know that from your six weeks of training.''

Andrea *did* know that. One entire section of the course had been devoted to explosives. Another, to listening devices. Still another dealt with photography, using tiny cameras not much bigger than a thumbnail.

''So what was the point?'' Andrea's anger began to dissipate. Maybe there was a good reason for this phase of the training after all.

Tom Nolting stood up and walked to the window. It was barred, as were all the windows in this old army fort near Baltimore, Maryland.

Bright sunlight reflected on the late-winter snow outside. Inside, the heating system purred efficiently.

Without turning, Nolting spoke again. "Your danger is twofold. You've been told this before, but it bears repeating."

Andrea tensed, aware of a threatening new dimension in Nolting's tone. She could feel her pulse at the base of her throat. She took a deep breath, and was relieved when the throbbing stopped.

"I think I know what the dangers are, Colonel Nolt...Tom," Andrea began. She wasn't sure she wanted to hear what Nolting was going to say. For the umpteenth time since she'd volunteered for this assignment, she questioned her good sense. If she were caught, she wouldn't be treated as a prisoner of war. No indeed. Nothing so respected as the Geneva Convention would protect her.

Just the opposite. Military people pretending to be civilians were automatically assumed to be spies. And that's what she'd be doing in Ganthaku, Tisara's ancient Himalayan capital, pretending to be Ambassador Dorough's secretary when she was really a captain in the Air Force. Spying.

Nolting turned to face her. "Everybody's aware of the danger from the host country if you're caught, but that's not the most frightening thing about this assignment."

How quaint to call it the "host country," Andrea thought. The term made her feel as if she were being sent to somebody's house as a guest to steal the family silver.

"No," Nolting went on, "the most frightening thing about an espionage assignment is that you're *totally on your own.*" His expression turned sympathetic. "If you're caught and taken into custody, the best we can do for you is stick with your cover story, deny you're a spy and try to get you out as a U.S. citizen—all in one piece, if possible.''

Andrea shifted uneasily on her chair. ''I was aware of that when I volunteered for this assignment. It wouldn't make sense for our government to admit it sent me to Tisara to spy on a top secret biological warfare facility.''

''There's more to it than that.'' Nolting returned to his desk and sat down. ''If you're caught, there'll be no behind-the-scenes maneuvering to get you out. No deals.''

What was she letting herself in for? Could she possibly end up a captive in some hellhole of a prison? A familiar jittery feeling raced down her spine at the thought. As always, she forced herself to ignore it.

His eyes bored into hers. ''If you want to back out, now's the time—before you hear my briefing.''

Andrea looked away. Ever since she'd come up with her theory that the Tisarans were producing biological weapons, she'd been determined to do everything she could to prove that theory right. This assignment was her big chance. It was also the best opportunity she'd ever have to find out what happened to her husband. An Air Force pilot on an official flight to India and Tisara, he'd vanished—along with nine others in his trekking party—on an overnight stay in the latter country thirteen months ago.

Jeffry was still alive. Deep inside, she knew it. She had to find him, had to give him the chance he'd asked for to work out the trouble between them. She couldn't let a little smoke-and-mirrors exercise scare her off.

She lifted her eyes and stared at Nolting with a steadfast gaze. ''Let's get started, Tom,'' she said, leaning toward him.

But in spite of her brave words, Andrea had never felt quite as alone as she did at that moment. A terrible sense of inadequacy swept over her. Would she be strong enough to complete the herculean tasks that lay ahead?

IN THE NEXT half hour, some of Andrea's doubts were dispelled. Most important, Nolting gave her the names of several local people who could help her get into the temple where she believed she would find Tisara's biological warfare laboratories.

"Don't expect any support from Ambassador Dorough," Nolting added grimly. "He's going to make your job as hard as possible." He handed her a sheet of paper. A biographic sketch of the U.S. ambassador to the Himalayan Kingdom of Tisara, it was classified *Secret* and marked *Limited Distribution* in red capital letters.

From her previous assignment as Tisaran desk officer at the Pentagon Intelligence Agency, Andrea knew the U.S. ambassador's name—Philip Rupert Dorough III, but she had never seen his biography.

Interested, she focused first on the picture inset at the left side of the page. He had large features, she noted. A deep chin, strong nose and bushy eyebrows with dark eyes and hair. His charismatic smile, showing even white teeth, beamed at her from the black-and-white print.

Overall, he had a compelling face full of strength and good humor. Andrea was surprised to notice in the descriptive text that he was only five feet ten, barely an inch taller than she. Somehow, from his picture, she'd have thought him taller.

The first line in the summary paragraph at the top of the page caught her eye. Dorough was a political appointee to the ambassador's post.

She glanced at Tom Nolting. "If he's only thirty-six, this must be his first diplomatic assignment."

"Right," Nolting affirmed. "Young as he is, he's a big man in California politics. Insiders in the administration credit him with winning the state for the President. That's how he got this appointment—sort of a reward for his help in the election."

Reading on, her heart sank as she scanned the rest of the information in the neatly printed paragraphs.

Dorough had high political aspirations. That meant he would probably be more interested in media reaction than in doing what was right. She couldn't stand people like that. Also, he was from a wealthy publishing family located in Santa Barbara, California, so he'd have little in common with Andrea, whose father was a machinist in the Vallejo Naval Shipyard north of San Francisco.

What's his wife like? Andrea searched the page. "Single," read the text.

Her gaze focused on the last part of the sketch:

Ambassador Dorough is firmly opposed to the assignment of a military undercover agent to replace Colonel Donald G. Butler, U.S. defense attaché declared *persona non grata* by the Tisarans. Dorough agreed to Captain Mitchell's assignment only after considerable pressure by the executive branch. The ambassador is convinced that the Tisarans are NOT, repeat NOT, hiding a biological warfare laboratory in the Ishwaranath Temple compound as claimed by the Pentagon Intelligence Agency.

Captain Mitchell should be warned that the ambassador will resist the operation. As much as possible, it should be conducted without involving him.

Andrea handed the page back to Nolting. "Sounds like he's going to be a problem."

"If he interferes with what you're doing, let me know," Nolting said. "We'll get the administration to put on more pressure."

Doubt nagged at her. How could she possibly accomplish her mission with the U.S. ambassador against her?

Andrea shifted nervously in her chair. "He's probably afraid I'll rock the boat, the way Colonel Butler did." She straightened, resolved not to let a tinhorn politician frighten her before she'd even met him. "By fighting me, he's protecting his own tail section."

Nolting nodded. "You've got the ambassador sized up pretty well. It's to his advantage to maintain good relations between Tisara and the United States. The sooner you find out what's in that temple compound, the better."

A few minutes later, Andrea left Nolting's office with the distinct impression that her primary obstacle wouldn't be the Tisarans involved in biological weapons research.

The biggest obstacle she faced in this impossible mission was the U.S. ambassador, Philip R. Dorough.

PHILIP DOROUGH SAT in the shadows behind his desk, his arms folded across his chest, waiting. A powerfully built man who took good care of himself, he slouched comfortably in his chair, facing the big window that dominated one wall.

Outside, the sun cast dying rays on magnificent Laigsi Peak, highest of the mountains northeast of Ganthaku, Tisara's capital. A crumbling, ancient city, Ganthaku nestled in a valley between the mighty Himalayas and the tropical plains of northern India. Now the tips of the jagged peaks were bathed in dull rose-red light. Philip stared sightlessly at the fading aura, his mind concentrating on the coming confrontation.

Inside the huge library-like room where he had his office, it was nearly dark. He didn't bother to get up and turn on the lights but waited in the gloom with the patience of a predator.

What would Andrea Mitchell be like, this woman-spy the Pentagon insisted on sending? How could he get her to quit and go home, before she ruined the fragile friendship he'd established with Tisara's young king? The deposed attaché's foolish antics had almost destroyed the relationship

Philip had worked so hard to build. He couldn't let anything like that happen again. The stakes were too high.

Located between India and China, Tisara functioned as a buffer between the two most populous countries in the world. Both were nuclear powers who had traded threats in recent months. War between them was a horrifying possibility that could engulf the earth. Above all, the United States needed Tisara for a listening post and a platform for maintaining peace.

For a moment, Philip allowed himself the luxury of feeling anger toward Don Butler, the Army colonel who had served as his defense attaché. What had the fool been thinking of? Disguised as a beggar, he'd managed to get inside the guarded inner court of the temple to the Hindu deity, Ishwara, an incarnation of the god Siva. The Tisarans had caught him snooping in their sacred shrine.

I should have let him rot in prison, Philip mused, angry at himself for not ordering the attaché to stay away from the temple. He'd never dreamed Butler would take such a risk. *I won't make that mistake again,* he thought grimly.

Now Philip had an even worse problem on his hands: Andrea Mitchell, a female spy who was actually a captain in the Air Force. He didn't want to think about the trouble this woman could get herself into—and the embassy, too.

Philip groaned. On top of everything, this was her first undercover assignment. If the brass at the Pentagon Intelligence Agency wanted to plant a spy to replace Butler, why hadn't they sent somebody experienced? Philip wouldn't rest easily until he got rid of her. Since her cover assignment was as a civilian secretary in his office, at least he'd be able to keep a close eye on everything she did.

A close eye. That reminded him that he hadn't yet told his secretary to bring the woman back here from the airport.

Philip pressed a button on his intercom. "Would you come in, please, Jan?"

A moment later, the door opened. His secretary, Janice O'Neal, stood framed in the doorway, the light from the outer office behind her. A petite, softly rounded woman in her late forties, she combined efficiency with mature good looks.

"It's dark in here, sir," she said. "Shall I turn the lights on?"

"Go ahead." He squinted as two enormous lead crystal chandeliers bathed the big room with light.

"Sit down." Philip motioned toward the chair beside his desk. Thoughtfully, he watched her walk toward him.

A highly efficient person who liked working alone, Janice O'Neal could be counted on to make life unpleasant for the new woman. She'd already voiced her strong opinion that there wasn't enough work for two secretaries. Furthermore, she'd claimed, living in the same house with the other secretary would be a strain on both of them since they would be together all day in the office.

Janice lived in a three-bedroom house rented from the Tisarans by the U.S. Government, so there was plenty of room. Philip suspected sharing it would be a strain more because Janice wanted privacy than because she and the new woman worked together all day. But if her resistance meant she'd pressure Andrea Mitchell to quit and go home, so much the better.

"I'd like to ask a favor, Jan," Philip said, getting right to the point.

"Anything short of suicide, sir," she returned, smiling.

"Would you bring the new woman back here from the airport so I can meet her before you take her to your house?" He felt a little hard-nosed for demanding an immediate audience. After Captain Mitchell's long flight to Delhi and then to Ganthaku, she would probably appreciate a good night's sleep before meeting him. But if he wanted to catch her off guard, what better time than this?

Janice smiled smugly. "She's not going to like that."

"I know." He shrugged off his guilt. "Do it anyway."

Her smile broadened with approval. "We'll be back here an hour or so after her plane lands." She started to get up.

Philip motioned her back to the chair. "There's one other thing, Jan. Keep an eye on her the next few weeks. I want to know what she does, where she goes, whom she sees."

"Sounds like you think she's up to something." Janice's eyes glinted with interested curiosity.

"Not at all." Much as Philip wanted Andrea Mitchell to quit, he couldn't risk exposing her cover. "Keeping an eye on her is more of a protective measure. She's young and inexperienced. Until she knows her way around, let's make sure she doesn't get herself into trouble."

Janice lifted an eyebrow. "At twenty-eight and a widow, she's hardly a babe in arms."

Philip felt like frowning. He forced himself to smile instead. "Humor me on this, Jan. After the problem I had with Colonel Butler, I want to be sure she doesn't set foot anywhere near the Ishwaranath Temple compound."

Her expression lightened. Philip was pretty sure she'd accepted his explanation. After all, it was partly the truth.

"Do you want me to have Sam...er...Mr. Connelly put the word out to his people?" Sam Connelly was the warrant officer Jan was dating. A Marine, he was in charge of security, including the embassy's detail of Marine guards.

Philip shook his head. "It's not that big a deal, Jan. I just want to keep her out of trouble. Whatever information you can give me about her comings and goings for the next few weeks will be appreciated."

"You can count on me, sir." From the way she said the words, Philip could tell she was delighted to comply.

THE WOMAN who met Andrea inside Ganthaku's square brick terminal made no attempt to be friendly.

"I'm Mrs. O'Neal, the ambassador's private secretary," she informed Andrea in a haughty tone. "You'll be working for me while you're here."

"Thanks for meeting me." Andrea did her best to sound congenial. The trip from California, where she'd spent a week with her family, had taken more than thirty hours. She was exhausted.

"Don't thank me," the other returned. "Ambassador Dorough asked me to come. He wants to see you right away at the embassy."

Andrea couldn't believe her ears. "Right now?" To her, her voice sounded like a croak. Her knees felt so weak she wasn't sure she could make it outside, let alone through an interview with her new pretend-boss.

"That's what he said." The woman's tone held a note of smug satisfaction. It didn't take a genius to figure out she resented Andrea's presence.

Outside the terminal building, they were quickly surrounded by urchins, each holding out a hand and crying, "Allo, madam. Allo. Allo."

"Don't give them anything or we'll be overrun," Mrs. O'Neal warned.

Andrea looked down into six pairs of wide brown eyes and wished she'd taken the time to change some cash into the local currency when she was inside the terminal.

A black car drove up. The driver loaded Andrea's bags in the trunk.

Mrs. O'Neal gestured toward an open rear door. "Get in."

Andrea sank against the back seat with a grateful sigh. *Ganthaku.* She'd arrived at last. From her research and what her husband, Jeffry, had told her about the city, Andrea knew it was a place of colorful temples, square brick buildings and people who laughed a lot. She'd heard about the holy men with snakes around their shoulders, and about the open-air markets where the ground was covered with heaping baskets of carrots and cabbage, mangoes and oranges.

But nothing had prepared her for the poverty she saw from the car window. Though it was after dark, Andrea got a vivid look at the ragged robes on the crowds lining the hilly streets, the waist-high piles of dirt that seemed everywhere, the people squatting around open fires. The car windows were closed, but she smelled the acrid smoke and realized it was from dried burning cow dung.

Finally, the car turned into an area protected with concrete walls and iron fences. The embassy was hidden behind an eight-foot-high wall made of brick and painted white. Only the glassed-in guard post was visible. There was no vehicle entrance from the main street, only a small pedestrian passage alongside the guard post.

The car swung around a corner, finally stopping before a solid-looking iron gate off a side street. A Tisaran guard hurried to unlock it and swing it open. Inside, strategically placed bushes blocked Andrea's view of the compound.

Circling around, they neared several square buildings constructed of brick and painted white like the outside wall. The largest, with pillars in front and a big semi-oval porch, was undoubtedly the embassy.

A well-kept lawn surrounded the buildings. Even in the deepening darkness, Andrea could make out the blooming rhododendron bushes dotting the grounds.

"We'll have to go in the front door," Mrs. O'Neal announced. "The staff entrance closes at seven."

When the older woman got out of the car, Andrea followed. Not for the first time that evening, she was aware of her unstylish low-heeled walking shoes, her faded jeans and the baggy turquoise sweatshirt she wore over a pink short-sleeved blouse with a Peter Pan collar. She'd known the long trip would be tiring and had worn the most comfortable clothes she owned.

She hadn't counted on reporting in to the ambassador in them.

Chapter Two

Mrs. O'Neal banged the embassy door with the knocker, a monstrous lion's head with its tongue hanging out.

The door swung open. A young freckle-faced Marine corporal stood inside, his uniform immaculate, his mouth set in an appealing smile. "I thought it might be you, Mrs. O." He focused on Andrea, his smile broadening. "This must be the ambassador's new secretary." He opened the door wide.

Stepping inside, Andrea took a look around. The floor was marble. Wood-paneled walls of polished teak rose to an embossed ceiling. Off to one side, a wide stairway curved upward.

"You knew very well this is Mrs. Mitchell, Billy." Mrs. O'Neal's voice turned affectionately patronizing. She smiled mischievously. "Why else would you trade duty with Jim Snowden?"

The corporal's cheeks flamed pink, dulling his carrot-red hair. "There's no crime in wanting to meet a pretty lady, Mrs. O." The Marine stuck his hand out. "Bill Stoakes, Mrs. Mitchell."

Andrea shook the hand he offered and gave him her widest smile. "I'm pleased to meet you, Bill Stoakes." Apparently, there weren't many young American women working at the embassy. Stoakes appeared to be at least eight years younger than she and fully three inches shorter. But that hadn't dampened his eagerness.

"The sign-in book is right here." Stoakes pointed toward a desk off to one side of the big foyer and guided Andrea to it. "You can use my chair."

She smiled at him before bending over the desk. "After the past two days, the last thing I need right now is a chair." She swung the book toward herself and began signing her name. Behind her, she heard Mrs. O'Neal's heels clicking on the marble floor as she started slowly for the stairs.

Andrea sensed rather than heard the change in the atmosphere. Mrs. O'Neal stopped walking. Beside the desk, Stoakes straightened. Andrea took a quick glance at the Marine's face. He was looking toward the staircase with an expectant expression.

She followed his gaze. Coming down the stairs was an athletic-looking man who carried himself with the balanced precision of a marathon runner. Even across the big foyer, she could see his commanding expression, could feel the penetrating depth of his dark eyes. With his large features, his face was arresting, the kind of face she'd liked sketching when she was an art student at the University of California.

Andrea felt a nervous flutter. If Philip Dorough had looked formidable in his picture, he seemed doubly so in the flesh.

Smiling, Stoakes walked toward him. "Good evening, Mr. Ambassador. We were just going to escort Mrs. Mitchell up to your office."

"That won't be necessary, Corporal Stoakes." The ambassador's voice was mellow, but deep at the same time, a rich male voice that commanded attention. He approached the desk where Andrea was standing. "I'm Ambassador Dorough, Andrea."

She stuck out her hand, and he took it. His grip was gentler than she expected from such a powerfully built man.

"I've been looking forward to meeting you, Mr. Ambassador."

"And I, you." He searched her face with an intensity that made Andrea want to look away. She didn't. He mustn't know how tired she was, or how wobbly he made her feel.

The ambassador turned to his secretary. "Jan, have the driver take you to your house and unload Andrea's bags. Then send him back here to pick her up."

"I'd be glad to wait, sir," Mrs. O'Neal offered. "That would save a trip for the car and driver."

The ambassador waved his hand to dismiss her. "We may be awhile. There are a couple of things I want to go over with Andrea tonight first thing."

Mrs. O'Neal smiled slyly, as though she knew what the "couple of things" might be.

Not possible, Andrea thought. *Unless he's told her something to throw her off the track so she won't suspect I'm working undercover.*

"Then I'll see you later tonight, Mrs. Mit...er... Andrea." Her high heels clicking, Mrs. O'Neal left the foyer.

When Stoakes had returned from locking the door behind her, the ambassador placed a big hand on the Marine's shoulder. "Take my calls down here in the lobby, please, Corporal."

"I'll see you're not bothered, sir." The young Marine was dwarfed by the broad-chested man beside him.

"Good." The ambassador smiled down at the enlisted man. Andrea could sense the smile's warm effect from the pleased expression on the corporal's face.

The ambassador's gaze swept down Andrea's slender form and back to her eyes. For an instant, she thought she saw a masculine gleam of appreciation in his look.

Wishful thinking, she thought wryly. For one of the few times since she'd been a teenager, Andrea wished she'd inherited her mother's pretty face and well-rounded figure instead of her dad's angular frame and plain features. Then maybe she'd have seen real admiration in this man's eyes.

My God, what am I thinking? She forced herself to stare at him, eyeball to eyeball. She held his gaze, trying to ignore the uncomfortable tightness in her throat.

A muscle twitched at the corner of his mouth. "We'll talk in my office, Andrea. It's on the second floor." He turned and started toward the staircase.

Andrea drew a deep breath and squared her shoulders. She forced all thought of tiredness from her mind, then, with all her senses on full alert, she fell into step beside him. The battle was about to begin.

AT LEAST SHE'S no weakling, Philip thought, noticing that he didn't have to shorten his stride so Andrea could keep up. She was tall for a woman—almost as tall as he—with slim hips and long legs to match.

Was he being hasty in his decision to get rid of her? Perhaps he should get to know her before putting the screws to her. Maybe she wouldn't be as much trouble as he imagined.

Don't go soft, he warned himself. With her mass of blond curls and startling blue eyes, Andrea Mitchell would stand out among the darker, shorter Tisarans like a swan among ducks. And she carried herself regally, like a princess. He'd already noticed that she hadn't backed down under his penetrating stare. This woman would do whatever she pleased, whether he liked it or not.

No, he'd have to get her out of the country and on her way home as soon as possible—no matter how dedicated she was or how hard she tried to convince him that the Tisarans were manufacturing biological weapons to sell to the highest bidder.

Philip took a deep breath as he started up the stairs. In a way, it was too bad. A woman willing to take the kind of risks she'd volunteered for had to have a lot of nerve. She might be worth knowing better.

"My office is down the hallway to the left," he said, without glancing at her. As he turned toward it, he could hear her striding along beside him, her rubber soles squeaking on the highly polished hardwood floor. He'd set a deliberately quick pace up the long staircase to tire her, but there was no sound of heavy breathing. Apparently, she was in good physical condition.

Philip pushed open the main door to his suite. Like the rest of the woodwork in the building, it was teak. He flicked a switch. Light flooded the large wood-paneled anteroom outside his own office. It was occupied by two desks and a row of chairs along one wall. One of the desks, much larger than the other, was positioned at the room's center. The other stood inconspicuously in the corner.

"This is where you'll be working." He didn't bother pointing out which desk was Andrea's, assuming she'd know it were the smaller of the two. She looked relieved.

"Thank goodness I won't be in a prominent spot." Her voice, low and musical, sent a ripple of awareness through him. "That way it won't be so obvious that I'm gone a lot." She sounded as though an important problem had been solved.

"You won't be away from your desk often," Philip corrected smoothly. Might as well get her straightened out right now. "As long as you're assigned as my secretary, you'll put in eight hours a day, just as Jan O'Neal and the rest of the staff do."

He paused to watch her reaction. She was pretty good at covering her emotions, but Philip caught an instant of surprised disappointment before her expression became unreadable.

Good! Pour on the pressure until she quits. Instead of the exhilaration he usually felt at besting an adversary, the thought left him with a hollow, empty feeling. She had dark shadows under her eyes, he noticed. How long had it been since she'd slept? He forced the thought from his mind. He had to get rid of this woman, and there was only one way to do it: by being as hard-nosed as he knew how to be.

Just the same, Philip felt an uncharacteristic urge to explain himself. "Your cover as my secretary won't be believable if you take a lot of time off during regular business hours. You'll have to do your snooping on your own time."

He saw the wheels turning in her mind. "It was just a thought, Ambassador Dorough," she said. "Forget I mentioned it."

He examined her face through narrowed eyes. There was no trace of anger or disappointment. She recovered quickly. He'd have to give her that much.

The door to his own office was on the opposite side of the secretaries' anteroom. Pushing it open, he escorted Andrea inside the large room, lined with books on floor-to-ceiling shelves. Then, leaving her in darkness near the big window behind his desk, he switched off the light in the anteroom and returned to her side.

In the glow from the three-quarter moon, the snow-capped mountains were dimly visible, floating high above the lights of the ancient city. The sight never failed to impress Philip. He moved a step closer to Andrea.

"It's incredibly beautiful," she said, her voice taking on a breathiness that made the air around her seem electric.

Frowning at his own empathetic reaction, Philip forced himself to return to the task he'd set for himself. "When you're out snooping around, remember that the view from Slonpo Prison isn't the same as what you're seeing here."

She turned toward him, her face an oval splash of whiteness in the moonlight. "What do you mean, Mr. Ambassador?"

Philip heard the exasperation in her voice.

"I'm sure you already know the risks involved," he warned, "but you need to be aware that there's not much I can do to help if the Tisarans get wise to you."

"If you had me brought here directly from the airport to tell me that, you're—" She stopped abruptly. Philip guessed she was about to tell him he was wasting his time.

"That's not why." He strode to the door and switched on the lead crystal chandeliers.

The teak-paneled room sprang to life. The world outside the big window turned dark. Moving quickly, Philip closed the vertical blinds, shutting out the blackness beyond. For security reasons, he usually kept the blinds drawn when the lights were on.

He watched Andrea glance around the room. She took in the American flag behind his desk, the huge globe of the world near the window, the woolen Indian carpet on the floor. Its dominant red color matched the brocaded sofas and a number of easy chairs.

Philip didn't suggest that they sit down on one of the sofas. The more uncomfortable she was, the more likely she'd be to fly off the handle and let him know what she was thinking.

"I wanted to talk to you right away so I could get one thing across to you." He injected authority into his voice. "I don't want any more military people causing problems between this embassy and the Tisarans."

Examining her face, Philip could find no trace of defiance. She had an arresting, irregular face with a square chin and wide mouth. She stood facing him in a relaxed position, her arms folded across her chest, her leather shoulder bag hanging at her side. Grudgingly, he admired her poise under stress.

But that didn't mean he intended to ease up on her. "If the Tisarans catch you snooping around and find out you're a military officer—an intelligence officer, in fact, who's an expert on this region—I have no doubt that they'll sever relations with the United States."

"I won't get caught, sir. And even if I did, I wouldn't talk." Andrea spoke confidently, holding his gaze.

"You'd talk." Philip forced himself to ignore the tiny worry lines that had formed on her forehead. She had to be more concerned about getting caught than she pretended.

"But that's not the point," he went on. "The point is that we need this embassy. We can't afford to be kicked out of this country because some inexperienced espionage agent screws up."

"You don't have to worry." Andrea thrust her chin out at his patronizing tone. "I've had the best training available."

"But absolutely no experience." With his dark eyes flashing and his face lit up with a crusader's inner passion, the ambassador oozed power.

Andrea felt engulfed, like a rowboat caught in a mighty current. She wished she weren't so tired. He'd never have an impact like this if she were rested.

"Maybe I don't have much experience," she conceded, "but I'm going to do the job I came here to do. I'm going to find out if the Tisarans are manufacturing biological weapons for either India or China—or both."

"They're not." His jaw tensed, but his eyes darkened with certainty.

"How can you be so sure?" She leaned toward him, not masking her doubt.

He smiled knowingly. "I looked for myself."

She stared at him in disbelief. "You can't mean you saw the temple's inner courtyard on the other side of the river. It's guarded twenty-four hours a day to keep out nonbelievers."

"The guard looked the other way when he saw I was with Interior Minister Nakarmi."

"If you and the interior minister had an appointment, somebody had time to sanitize the area." Andrea didn't try to keep the skepticism from her voice.

His face went grim. "That doesn't make sense. Nobody could remove an entire lab with only a few hours notice."

"I'll have to check out the temple compound myself, using my own sources," she returned, confident of her authority.

"How do you intend to do that?" His voice was deceptively mild.

Andrea hesitated only a moment before answering. The less she told the ambassador about her plans, the better.

"I'll check out my theory by asking a few questions, talking to some people," she replied, deliberately vague.

His heavy eyebrows drew together. Andrea took a quick breath. Promptly, she added, "I'm sure you know that's how intelligence agents get their information. We ask questions and talk to people."

"Fine," he said. "Talk to as many people as you like, as long as you don't go anywhere near the Ishwaranath Temple compound."

"I beg your pardon?" Andrea tried to keep her consternation from showing.

"You heard me. Stay away from there." He studied her with a commanding expression that made her see red.

"Ambassador or not, you can't order me to do that!" She spat out the words. "I've got military orders to find out what's going on inside that place."

"Sorry, Andrea." There was a steely firmness in the ambassador's voice. "You'll have to find out without going near it. I won't jeopardize the mission of this embassy to satisfy the curiosity of some Pentagon general."

To satisfy the curiosity of some Pentagon general? Was that what he thought she was risking her life for? Andrea swallowed her harsh words before they could escape. Arguing with this man would do no good.

Well, she'd follow Nolting's order, not the ambassador's. Nolting was her boss until she finished this operation. And *nobody* was her boss when it came to tracking down her missing husband. Philip Dorough could take his ridiculous command and stick it in his ear.

"One other thing." His voice was calm, his gaze penetrating.

Andrea got the uncomfortable feeling that he'd figured out what she was thinking.

"If I catch you within a block of that place, you'll be out of this country so fast, it'll be months before your belongings catch up with you." The ambassador's lips twisted into a cynical smile. "I've got eyes and ears all over Ganthaku. If you go near Ishwaranath, I'll hear about it."

Andrea felt her face flush. If he had her watched, she'd be hamstrung. She had no doubt that he'd do what he threatened—throw her out of the country—if he caught her disobeying him.

"Then you must be paying Tisaran spies to keep an eye on Americans!" As soon as she'd flung the words out, Andrea was sorry she'd said them.

Surprisingly, he didn't seem angry at her comment. "The Tisarans are watching the temple, not the Americans who work here at the embassy. But if anyone on my staff goes near the place, I'll be informed."

Deliberately, Andrea walked over to the brocaded sofa and sat down. He might be in charge of the embassy, but he certainly wasn't in charge of her.

"I'll protest your order through official channels." Considering how tired she was, she was pleased at her reasonable tone and the steadiness of her voice. "You must know you'll be required to rescind your order in my case."

He eyed her for a moment from the center of the room and then walked toward her. Andrea was struck by the surefooted way he moved, like a trained athlete. He stopped in front of her but didn't sit down.

"Maybe yes, maybe no. Until I get a direct order from the State Department, don't go near Ishwaranath Temple compound." He folded his arms across his chest. "Is that clear, Andrea?"

"Very clear, sir." She managed a small, tentative smile. "If there's one thing we learn in the military, it's to obey direct orders from your commander."

Only you're not my commander, she thought, determined not to let him stand in her way.

"Good." Eyeing her with a critical squint, he sat down next to her on the sofa. He wasn't touching her but was close enough for her to feel the heat from his body. He was wearing a well-fitting tailored silk suit. But for some reason, she was uncomfortably aware of his muscular leg so close to hers, of his arm extended across the back of the sofa behind her. Twisting, she moved as far from him as she could.

He offered her a forgiving smile. "Now that we've got that bit of unpleasantness squared away, I hope you'll agree to call me Philip."

Andrea felt her jaw drop. "Philip?" To her embarrassment, her voice broke.

"I'm on a first-name basis with the professional staff," he explained. "Since you're a commissioned officer serving as my defense attaché, you rank with the professional staff."

"But nobody knows I'm an officer except you," she gasped, still startled by his quick change in attitude. "I'm supposed to be a secretary. Won't it give away my cover if I call you Philip in front of someone—even a professional— and none of the other secretaries do?"

Andrea caught a glint of amusement in his dark eyes. He was teasing her, she realized suddenly. Well, two could play at that game. She'd bet a month's pay he had no intention of letting her call him by his first name under any circumstances.

"I'll tell you what, Mr. Ambassador," she said, keeping her face sober. "I'll call you Phil, and you can call me Captain Mitchell. But only when nobody else is in earshot. That way we won't give away my cover."

He stared at her with such a surprised expression that she couldn't help smiling.

"No deal." His voice was harsh. Had she gone too far?

His tight expression relaxed. He leaned back, an amused smile on his lips. "I've got a better idea. When nobody's around we'll be Andrea and Philip. It'll be our secret. If anybody's in hearing distance, you'll have to call me Ambassador Dorough to protect your cover."

Andrea caught her breath. She'd been wrong. He obviously *did* want her to call him Philip, at least when they were alone. Had she also been wrong about her antagonistic first impression of him, when she'd read his bio in Tom Nolting's office? Maybe the ambassador wasn't quite as hostile as she'd thought.

FOR A LONG TIME after he'd taken Andrea downstairs and seen her into the waiting car, Philip sat alone in his darkened office. With the lights off and the blinds raised, he again surveyed the scene outside his window.

Why had he encouraged Andrea to call him by his first name? For her own safety, no one must suspect that she was anything other than what she was pretending to be. If someone accidentally overheard her call him Philip, would she be put at risk?

No, he told himself. A casual observer hearing her call him by his first name would suspect a personal relationship between them, not that she was a spy.

The real problem was that this made him less a threat to her. If he wanted to get rid of her, he had to maintain his distance.

Then, why had he done it?

Finally, he acknowledged the truth he'd been avoiding. She interested him. More than any woman he'd known in many years. He felt a quickening in his loins and cursed.

Philip stared out the window toward the mountains. The jagged peaks were bathed in light from the unseen moon, now riding high beyond the frame of his window.

Ah, the silent mountains. If only he could achieve the peace in his own life that he felt in those majestic peaks.

THE STREET in front of Jan O'Neal's house was blocked by a humpbacked cow wearing a necklace of marigolds around its scrawny neck. From Andrea's background on Tisara, she knew the animals were sacred. This one must have missed the evening roundup by its owner. Behind the embassy car, a crowded bus pulled up and stopped, also waiting, its exhaust belching clouds of black smoke.

Finally, the cow sauntered away and the driver parked the car as close to the yard's iron fence as he could, taking up most of the dirt strip in front that passed as a sidewalk. With a loud bleep of its horn, the bus swerved into the right-hand lane to pass.

Waiting for the driver to open the rear door, Andrea caught the scent of night-blooming jasmine through her open window. The jasmine, along with wine-red bougainvillea, tumbled over the fence near a cluttered pile of dirt and loose bricks.

Through the fence, she could make out a square two-story house of red brick with a pagoda-like roof. The place didn't look half-bad. Not until the driver had unlocked the gate and led her inside the yard did she notice the scraggly lawn and the peeling white paint around the windows.

"You don't have to go in with me," Andrea said.

The driver grinned up at her, showing gold-capped teeth. "Ambassador say make sure you get home okay."

Unaccountably, Andrea felt her heart thumping loudly in her chest at Philip's interest in her safety. Walking the rest of the way to the house's door, she couldn't stop thinking about him. He might be the enemy, but there was a certain vitality and charisma about him that struck a vibrant chord within her. As soon as he opened his mouth to speak, his rich voice and confident manner made her forget he was out to stop her.

Aggravated, she shrugged her shoulders, as if that could dismiss her errant thoughts. Besides being the enemy, Philip Dorough was rich and very powerful. He could have any woman he wanted. He'd never be interested in her. Somehow the thought made her a little sad.

Ahead of Andrea, the driver had reached the porch. As he crossed to the door, he handed her a sealed envelope. "Missus O'Neal not here. When I took her home from embassy, she gave me this for you."

Andrea ripped open the envelope. Inside was a key. No note of welcome. No instructions. Nothing to tell her when Jan would be home. Andrea stuck the key in the top lock, one of the five lined up in a row down the side door. Apparently, the locksmiths in Ganthaku didn't know how to change a lock without replacing the whole assembly.

When the bolt clicked, Andrea twisted the knob to be sure the door was really open. Then she smiled at the driver, waiting patiently behind her.

"What is your name?"

"Mohan," he replied. "I drive ambassador's car."

"You had a long wait for me tonight," she said. "Thank you, Mohan."

After he'd started off the porch, she went inside the house and closed the door, locking it behind her. Then she switched on the lights and took a quick look around.

The high-ceilinged living room was furnished with comfortable Western-style sofas and chairs, the parquet floor covered with colorful woolen Tibetan area rugs. Though the place was clean, the walls needed painting and the woodwork was scratched. Chipped tiles in the kitchen needed replacing.

The house smelled of cigar smoke. Andrea wrinkled her nose, wondering if someone else stayed here besides Janice O'Neal.

Upstairs the mystery was cleared up in one of the three bedrooms. It was obviously Andrea's, since her luggage was neatly stacked at the foot of the double bed. In one of the dresser drawers, she discovered men's underwear, overlooked when it's owner had removed the rest of his things.

So Mrs. O'Neal had a boyfriend.

That'll help, Andrea thought, pulling a nightgown out of her suitcase. The busier he kept the ambassador's secretary, the less interested she'd be in what Andrea was up to.

WHEN ANDREA awakened the next morning, the tantalizing smell of freshly brewed coffee told her Jan was back.

She glanced at her travel alarm. Eight-fifteen. She'd already slept more than ten hours. Stretching, she pushed the blanket back and swung her legs over the edge of the bed. After slipping into a cotton robe, she burst into the living room without bothering to run a comb through her rumpled blond curls.

Jan O'Neal, dressed in a businesslike brown cotton suit that highlighted her chestnut hair, sat on one of the sofas, a newspaper in her hand. A cup of coffee rested on the low table in front of her. When she saw Andrea, she took off her glasses.

"You'd better get dressed." She peered at Andrea over the top of her newspaper, her tone matter-of-fact. "Since this is your first day, the ambassador is sending his car to pick us up. It'll be here in fifteen minutes."

Andrea crossed to the chair in front of the sofa and sat down. "It'll take me longer than fifteen minutes to get ready." Andrea kept her voice cheerful. Why hadn't Jan called her earlier? "You go ahead. I'll arrange for a taxi." She leaned back and crossed her legs.

"How do you expect to do that?" Jan sounded exasperated. "This is a foreign country, Andrea. You've got no idea how to call a cab."

"The housekeeper can help me use the phone." Andrea glanced toward the kitchen. The fresh coffee smell mingled with the tantalizing odor of bacon frying.

"That shows how much you know." Jan eyed her with the patronizing air of a woman explaining something obvious to a small child. "Around here, the cabs don't have radios. You have to go two blocks to Mazipat Street and flag one down."

"Then that's what I'll do." Refusing to get aggravated, Andrea settled farther back against the chair cushion. "You go on without me."

Jan shook her head. "The ambassador expects us both by nine o'clock."

Andrea sighed. "I wish someone had told me that last night." She glanced toward the kitchen again. "Or maybe you should have had the maid wake me up."

From the look on Jan's face, she hadn't missed Andrea's subtle accusations. "Well, just how long *will* it take you to get ready?"

Andrea had won a small victory, but she was careful not to show it. "At least forty-five minutes and another fifteen or twenty to eat that delicious breakfast I smell."

Jan shook her head. "You don't have time. If you're hungry, you can get a sweet roll at the office." She picked up a small brass bell and rang it. "But I might as well have something here, since I've got to wait for you."

A woman appeared through the kitchen door. Small and dark, she had coarse Oriental features. In her hands were two plates, each containing bacon, scrambled eggs and a big chunk of unleavened bread.

Jan frowned at the woman. "Chandra, please take the other plate back. Mrs. Mitchell won't have time for break—"

"Yes, I will," Andrea interrupted. She smiled at the maid. "I'd like some coffee, too, please, Chandra."

For an instant, the maid stood motionless beside the kitchen door. Rising quickly, Andrea went to her. She took one of the plates. "Thank you very much," she said in Tisaran.

The maid's face lit up. "Do you speak our language?" she asked in her native tongue.

Andrea understood perfectly. She'd spent a year studying the language at the Defense Language Institute before she was assigned to the Pentagon Intelligence Agency as a current intelligence analyst.

But she couldn't let on. Secretaries weren't given language training. "I only know a few words like 'please,' and 'thank you.' Will you teach me more?"

"Chandra is too busy to be giving language lessons." Jan's eyes narrowed, betraying her annoyance. "Especially now that there are two of us to take care of."

The maid kept her eyes downcast while she carried Jan's plate to her. Jan took it with a curt "thank you."

After the maid had gone, Andrea glanced at Jan. "I won't interfere with Chandra's work. Just a little coaching here and there. Eventually, maybe I'll even be able to figure out how to walk to the corner and flag down a cab."

Jan froze with her fork midway to her mouth. A bit of egg fell off it. Her smile was tight with strain.

"Very funny," she sniffed. "For your information, I'm

not the only one who thinks you need help getting adjusted to this country.''

A warning bell sounded in Andrea's mind. She took a big bite of the chewy bread to give herself time to think. After swallowing, she glanced at Jan again.

''So the ambassador thinks I need help, does he?'' What had Philip told his secretary?

Chapter Three

Jan hesitated, her face clouded with uneasiness. Andrea wondered if she'd reveal her boss's confidence.

Then she nodded smugly. "He said to keep an eye on you so you don't get into trouble."

"And give him an accounting of what I do, of course." Andrea was fuming inside, but she kept her voice congenial, as though it were the most natural thing in the world for one staff member to spy on another.

Jan stirred uneasily on the sofa. "He just wanted to be sure you didn't get into trouble." Her voice was unconvincing.

"I'm sure he meant well." Andrea wasn't sure of anything of the sort, but she knew better than to trash the ambassador to his loyal girl Friday.

The maid returned with Andrea's coffee, setting it on the table beside her chair. Andrea took a satisfying sip. "Would it help if I gave you a list of where I went and whom I saw?" she asked innocently.

Visibly disturbed, Jan studied Andrea's face.

"I'm serious." Andrea didn't smile. "If you—or he—see anything on the list that might cause trouble, you can tell me and I won't go there again."

Jan laughed, her tone shrill. "Get real, Andrea. Ambassador Dorough would never ask for a report like that."

The woman's nervousness convinced Andrea that was just what he *had* asked for. She nodded reassuringly, knowing she'd found out something important.

"I want to cooperate every way I can, Jan. If he wants to know what I'm doing, I'd be happy to tell you—or him." She smiled sweetly. "For the record, I've come to help out. I don't want to change anything or upset your routine."

"You've already upset my routine." A frown creased Jan's smooth forehead. "Thanks to you, we're going to be more than an hour late. And I'm the one who's going to catch hell for it."

Andrea took a deep breath and adjusted her smile. "Then I'd better get dressed or you'll really be in trouble." Without a backward look, she headed for her bedroom.

FOR HER FIRST DAY at the embassy, Andrea chose a calf-length silk skirt in bright sea-green and a shocking-pink short-sleeved blouse with droopy shoulders that made her look curvy instead of angular. She added a lightweight green cotton jacket and slipped into low-heeled bone pumps.

The car waited outside, Mohan at the wheel. Traffic was heavier than usual because it was so late, Jan informed Andrea, belligerence in her tone. The usual fifteen-minute ride to the embassy took three times as long. Every scooter, motorcycle, motorized rickshaw, truck and cow in Ganthaku seemed to crowd the dusty streets along their way. There were few cars other than nondescript taxis identifiable only by their black-and-white license plates.

By the time they reached the compound, it was close to eleven. Mohan let them off at the staff entrance where a line of Tisarans waited to get inside for U.S. visas. Circling the line, Jan went through a door off to one side. It led to a small examination room. A Tisaran woman sat behind one desk, a Tisaran security guard behind another. Next to the guard's desk stood a metal detector.

Andrea eyed the device with distaste. In spite of herself, the tight security she saw around the embassy made her jittery. If the embassy compound had to be so stringently protected from people who didn't like the United States, what would happen to her, a U.S. spy, if she were caught?

Upstairs, a heavyset woman was at Jan's desk in the wood-paneled anteroom when Andrea and Jan walked in. Glancing at them, she flicked a switch on the intercom. "They're here, Mr. Ambassador."

Immediately, the door to Philip's office opened. He stepped through the doorway, an impressive, self-confident presence. Though dressed in an immaculately tailored blue silk suit, he radiated ruggedness and power. His red tie, instead of looking gaudy, added a striking richness to his appearance.

Folding his arms, he leaned against the door frame. "Good afternoon, ladies." Obviously being sarcastic, he focused his intense gaze on Jan. "As you know, Janice, the office hours here are nine to five." He turned to Andrea. "I'll say no more about this since it's your first day. But from now on, I expect both of you to be at your desks, working, at nine a.m."

"It's my fault we're late, Mr. Ambassador." Jan spoke quickly, before Andrea could say anything. "I didn't get Andrea up on time."

Andrea's eyes widened. Was this the same woman who had deliberately tried to fluster her by letting her sleep in and then imposing a fifteen-minute deadline?

Indeed it was. Andrea found that out after Philip returned to his office. As though to get even for the morning's unpleasantness, Jan put Andrea to work redoing the files. The folders in eight four-drawer cabinets needed to be replaced and renamed, she said. When Andrea pointed out that some of the folders were new, Jan told her to replace them all, new or not.

Would Andrea be able to escape Jan's watchful eye long enough to send a message to Tom Nolting from the embassy's communications center? Not today, that was certain.

Had Philip put Jan up to this? If so, he didn't play fair.

But then, who expected a rich politician from California to play fair?

DURING THE NEXT couple of days, Jan O'Neal watched over Andrea from the time she got up in the morning until she went to bed at night. Andrea didn't want to arouse the older woman's suspicions so she made no attempt to visit the embassy's third-floor communications center where she could send Tom Nolting a message—or go into town by herself and phone him.

Whenever Jan left the office for longer than a few minutes, Philip would appear with urgent work that had to be done immediately. The first time, Andrea thought it was a coincidence. But when the same thing happened three days running, she was just as sure it wasn't.

Today Jan had gone to lunch with Sam Connelly, the Marine warrant officer she was dating. Andrea waited until they'd left the building before dialing one of the other secretaries to cover for her so she could go to the comm center.

She'd barely hung up the phone when Philip appeared in the open doorway to his office, just as he had the last three days. With his eyes slightly narrowed, his face had the same demanding look it had worn yesterday when he'd kept her tied up with busy work until Jan got back.

Well, he'd managed to keep Andrea away from the comm center until now. He wasn't going to keep her away today, during the one chance she'd have to send a Sparrow message to Nolting without making Jan suspicious. *Sparrow* was the special code word identifying Andrea's mission.

"Would you call someone to cover the front office, please?" His tone was abrupt. "Then come in with your notepad. I've got some priority messages that need to go out in the next couple of hours."

The rich timbre of his voice seemed to reach to the soles of Andrea's feet. He was wearing a brown silk suit that highlighted his straight dark hair. As usual, he oozed authority. A weird, shaky feeling coursed through her.

She took a deep breath to steady herself so her voice wouldn't tremble, and looked him straight in the eye. "I've already called Shirley to cover for me while I send a message of my own."

Forcing herself to smile, she walked around her desk. "I'll only be gone a few minutes. Then I'll be in with my notepad."

She picked up the message she'd typed when Jan was in Philip's office taking dictation—with the door open, of course, so both of them could watch every move Andrea made.

He came toward her, his hand extended. "May I see it please?"

Since there was nothing to be gained by refusing, she handed the message to him. In a couple of succinct sentences, it asked Nolting to order Philip not to restrict Andrea's investigation of the Ishwaranath Temple compound or anywhere else in Tisara.

He studied it, his face expressionless.

One minute passed. Then another. Why was he taking so long to read a couple of sentences?

She heard a sound behind her. Turning, she saw the secretary she'd called to stand by for her.

Philip glanced up from the page in his hand. "Thanks for coming, Shirley." With a triumphant smile, he handed the message back to Andrea.

So that was his game. He'd been stalling until the other woman arrived because he knew Andrea couldn't openly defy him in her presence without undermining her cover.

"We'll be in my office for the next hour or so," he said, as Shirley settled herself behind Andrea's desk. "Hold my calls, please."

When he started toward his office, Andrea had no choice but to follow. He waited for her beside the door, closing it behind her.

Reminding herself that she couldn't allow him to intimidate her, Andrea went directly to one of the brocaded sofas and sat down. With the door closed, there was no reason to pretend she was his secretary.

Philip joined her. "You forgot your notepad." A congenial smile played on his lips.

Andrea didn't smile back. "You won this battle." Her voice sounded shrill to her. "But you're not going to win the war." Her heart was thumping loudly at her open defiance of this powerful man. Why wasn't he helping her instead of doing everything in his power to stop her?

Because he's a career politician out to protect his own tail section, she thought grimly. *He's afraid I'll muddy the waters and some of the muck will wash off on him.*

"You know eventually I'm going to get through to Washington," she warned him. She heard her voice rising but made no attempt to lower it. "And Washington's going to order you not to interfere with my mission. So why not call off your watchdog—Mrs. O'Neal—and start cooperating?"

To Andrea's surprise, she saw amusement in Philip's eyes when she called Jan his watchdog.

"Because you're wrong." His rich baritone voice seemed strangely muted after the sharpness in her own. "Tisara has no interest in biological weapons. I'd stake my life on it." Sincerity flashed from his dark eyes.

Andrea's anger began to fade. "Then why not help me prove it?"

His jaw jutted forward. "I've already told you why. Your theory's shot full of holes. Nobody in his right mind would set up a biological research lab in a temple compound visited by thousands of people every day. It wouldn't make sense to expose them to deadly experimental diseases.''

Staring at him, Andrea saw the sheen of purpose in his eyes. He truly believed what he was saying. The sincerity she saw in his face didn't fit her picture of him as a grasping politician. Had she been wrong about him?

To cover her confusion, Andrea stood up and walked across the thick red Indian carpet to the picture window behind his desk. Snow-covered peaks less than fifty miles away melted into a hazy azure sky.

She sensed him come up behind her, but didn't turn around. He stood next to her, so close his broad shoulder almost touched hers. Uncharacteristically nervous, Andrea wanted to step away from him, but somehow she couldn't move.

''Thanks for being honest with me, Philip.'' She used his first name purposely, to remind herself they were equals, both selected to perform essential missions. What a shame that Philip considered his mission to be in direct opposition to hers.

He turned so he was facing her, the outside brightness framing his muscular body. ''I meant what I said about staying away from that temple compound. I'll give you my full support in anything else you want to do.'' His voice was low, hypnotic. ''But I can't risk another international incident like the one your predecessor caused. Until I get clarifying instructions from Washington, don't go near the place.''

She searched his face. Philip's forehead was etched with lines.

''You'll have to let me investigate the compound sooner or later.''

He hesitated, and his expression softened. In the few days since Andrea had arrived in Tisara, this was the first time he'd seemed unsure of himself. She took a quick breath, wondering what was coming.

"The longer you're here," he said, his voice gruffer than usual, "the more familiar you'll be with the Tisarans and their customs and the less likely to get into trouble with your investigation."

Andrea saw his brooding gaze shift to her lips and quickly back to her eyes again. She felt her face flushing. If she hadn't known better, she'd have guessed he was interested in her as a woman, that he feared for her personally. The thought sent unexpected little shivers racing up the backs of her nylon-clad legs and across her shoulders.

"And the longer you keep out of trouble with your snooping," he added, his expression hardening, "the better for this embassy and for the United States." He turned toward his massive wood desk. "Now, let's get some work done so we keep your cover intact."

Mentally, Andrea kicked herself for what she'd been thinking. There was nothing personal in his interest in her welfare. All he was worried about was keeping himself covered—and that meant keeping his staff out of trouble.

Watching him stride self-confidently to his leather executive chair, she felt a reluctant twinge of admiration. No matter what he thought of her personally, he was his own man, and he made no bones about it. Better to have an honest enemy than a dishonest friend, she thought grudgingly. At least a woman knew where she stood with Philip Dorough. Andrea had never been sure how her husband, Jeffry, felt about her. How unfortunate that the only thing she and Philip had in common was a steadfast desire to block each other's goals.

Settling herself in the chair beside his desk, Andrea began planning how to outwit him.

SHE'LL BE SNOOPING around inside that temple compound as soon as she gets out of Jan's sight, Philip thought. He handed Andrea a yellow, legal-size tablet and a pencil so she could take down the messages he intended to dictate.

How the hell am I going to protect her if she gets herself nailed? He hated the helpless feeling that coursed through him. Helplessness wasn't an emotion he tolerated, but he couldn't shrug it off.

Only by the most fortunate combination of circumstances had Philip been able to get the former attaché, Colonel Butler, and his family out of the country before the police locked him up in Slonpo Prison. Andrea, if she were caught, might be jailed indefinitely. And there'd be nothing Philip could do. The Tisarans weren't famous for their kind treatment of prisoners, particularly foreign prisoners. What they'd do to a woman was something Philip didn't want to think about.

He eyed Andrea, sitting beside his desk. Although she seemed relaxed, he could sense her alertness. Like Philip himself, she missed nothing.

She was wearing a dress with a long skirt and broad belt. Its bold splashy colors suited her tall, slender figure and made her look enticing as hell. With her curly blond hair and regal carriage, Andrea Mitchell was the most striking woman Philip had met in a long time.

Not beautiful or even pretty. *Striking.* That was the word for her.

Her complexion was flawless, her eyes a clear blue, her eyebrows a couple of shades darker than her close-to-platinum hair. If it weren't for her somewhat larger-than-normal nose, she'd be a real beauty.

Thank God, she isn't, he thought, remembering the jet-setting model he'd been dating when he received his ambassadorial appointment. It had been apparent to him that she had no intention of spending even a token amount of time in Tisara, a backward third-world country where the main excitement revolved around religious festivals. Andrea would never have felt that way.

Now why did a thought like that occur to him?

Aggravated with himself, Philip pulled a couple of papers out of his desk and began dictating the first of several messages. Andrea didn't take shorthand, so he spoke slowly, allowing his errant thoughts free rein.

Brilliant as well as striking, Andrea impressed Philip as someone who would know better than to volunteer for a hairbrained mission like this. Anybody with a shred of common sense would have turned it down.

Was there more behind her action than a search for a biological warfare laboratory that didn't exist? He paused in the middle of his dictation.

"What's the real reason you volunteered for this assignment?" he asked, watching her closely.

Her head jerked up.

Elated by her reaction, he went on. "The real reason, whatever it was, must be pretty important for you to risk your future—maybe your life—by going undercover like this."

Philip saw her wince, almost as though he'd struck her. The pained expression slid across her face and vanished.

But Philip had seen enough to know he'd been right. There *was* another reason she'd volunteered. He leaned toward her, curious to hear her response.

"You already know the real reason, Philip." She studied him with suspicion in her eyes. He noted that she'd straightened. Her hands clenched the tablet on her lap.

"I know, I know," he said, deliberately relaxing so she wouldn't feel pressured. "Through your analysis at the Pentagon, you uncovered evidence of Tisara's biological warfare activities and wanted to check out your conclusions yourself."

"You've got it." Her words were clipped. "I'm not trying to get the Medal of Honor or research a script for a movie, if that's what you're getting at. All I want to do is find out the truth."

"The truth about the temple?" he persisted.

"The truth about this country's black market sales of biological weapons."

From the rosy glow coloring her cheeks, Philip was even more certain she was hiding something. God, but she was a vital-looking woman. But he damned well better find out what she was up to before she got them both in serious trouble.

To allay her suspicions, he returned to his dictation, keeping her occupied until Jan came back from lunch.

After Andrea left his office, Philip went to the four-drawer safe that stood unobtrusively in a distant corner. Twisting the combination dial, he opened it and pulled out the top drawer. Inside were duplicate copies of the staff personnel files. He took out Andrea's.

Back at his desk, he skimmed through her file, hoping to find some personal reason she'd volunteered for this assignment. But the file contained only factual data. He found nothing revealing.

He read through the information again, more carefully this time. Andrea's maiden name was Greene. She'd grown up in Vallejo, about thirty miles north of San Francisco, where her father was a machinist in the naval shipyard. She'd graduated from the University of California, Berkeley, with a major in English and minors in history and art.

He studied her military career. She'd spent a year at the Defense Language Institute studying the Tisaran language before she was assigned to the Pentagon as an analyst. Since the file had been sanitized to go along with her cover story, the last entry said she'd resigned her commission in order to accept a position as secretary to the U.S. ambassador to Tisara.

He glanced at her family background again. She was a widow, of course. Who was her husband?

The file only said that he was Captain Jeffry Mitchell, a pilot killed in the line of duty thirteen months ago. They'd been married less than a year when he died. The file didn't detail what had happened to him.

How did an intelligence analyst stationed at the Pentagon meet a pilot flying out of Andrews Air Force Base twenty miles east of Washington, D.C.? Philip wondered.

Through friends, perhaps. Or more likely, through work. That seemed curious. How would work bring them together?

Probably because she'd given him an area intelligence briefing. That meant his duty involved flying to Tisara. One of the primary jobs of intelligence analysts was briefing military people whose duties took them to the area of the analyst's expertise.

Philip leaned back in his chair and drummed his fingers on his desk. *Thirteen months ago.* That was shortly before he himself had arrived in Tisara.

Hadn't there been an incident about that time involving some Air Force personnel killed in a climbing accident? They were on a routine flight to the Indian subcontinent and Southeast Asia when their aircraft had developed engine trouble. A U.S. Air Force maintenance team was flown in from Europe to fix it. Since the crippled plane's crew had to spend a couple of extra days in Ganthaku, they had decided to try trekking. They'd plunged into a crevasse on their first day out.

Philip recalled one odd thing about the incident. The bodies were never found. Everybody in the party had vanished, including the experienced Sherpa guides.

Philip went to the safe and withdrew another folder, leafing through it until he came to the names of the ten Americans who were killed. One of them was Captain Jeffry Mitchell.

So that's why Andrea's here, he thought, fighting his disappointment. She had made up the biological warfare story so she'd have an excuse to come to Tisara to investigate her husband's death. What better way than as a specially trained spy? Now her snooping might fracture relations between the United States and the tiny Himalayan kingdom.

Philip's disappointment turned to hot, suspicious anger. Had Andrea purposely misled key officials in the administration, maybe even the President?

But maybe she hadn't done it on purpose. In her desperate need to find out the truth about her husband's accident, had she somehow convinced herself that something was there in her intelligence reports, something that didn't exist?

Whether she'd purposely come up with her germ warfare theory or not, she'd had ulterior motives for taking this assignment. But what the hell was he going to do about it?

THAT AFTERNOON Andrea figured out how to escape Jan O'Neal's watchful eye.

Now that Andrea was over her jet lag and had caught up on her sleep, she'd sightsee that evening until Jan was worn out. When Jan gave up and went home to bed, Andrea could call her controller from a pay phone—if there was such a thing in Ganthaku.

To ensure success, Andrea invited Bill Stoakes, the young carrot-topped Marine corporal, to be their guide. In his early twenties, Stoakes could be counted on to keep them moving at a lively pace.

When Andrea told Jan the corporal was coming along, Jan said she'd invite Sam Connelly and they'd make a night of it. Although Warrant Officer Connelly, as security officer and commander of the Marine detachment, was Corporal Stoakes's boss, warrant officers were the only ones authorized by military custom to fraternize with both enlisted men and officers.

The two Marines arrived together. Both were dressed in freshly pressed sport shirts and slacks and smelled strongly of after-shave. Seeing them, Andrea felt a twinge of regret that she'd be spending her first social evening in Ganthaku with Bill Stoakes instead of Philip.

Wishful thinking again, she scolded herself, slipping a jacket-style white cotton sweater over the bright cotton dress she'd worn to work that morning.

Sam Connelly was short for a man, about Jan's height. Corporal Stoakes wasn't much taller than Connelly. Andrea towered over all three of them. How strange that Philip seemed so much taller when he was almost the same height as she.

After Jan had introduced Connelly, Andrea smiled at the two men. "Hope you guys don't mind showing the sights to a newcomer."

Corporal Stoakes grinned his broad, freckle-faced grin.

Sam Connelly winked at Andrea. "He'll be the envy of the barracks when his bunkmates find out about tonight."

Grizzled, broad-chested and fiftyish, Connelly exuded the special congeniality peculiar to warrant officers. Tonight he took the lead, suggesting they stop at a local bar called the Yeti for cocktails before dinner. When they got out of the taxi in front of the place, Corporal Stoakes beamed a flashlight across the cobbled sidewalk with its omnipresent piles of dirt and bricks.

Jan nodded toward a mound of cow dung, a lingering reminder of the humpbacked cattle that roamed freely through the city. "You've got to watch where you step around here," she said, wrinkling her nose.

Inside, the Yeti was nicer than Andrea had expected. From the outside, like most of Ganthaku, it had the look of antiquity—dusty, falling apart, paint-peeling antiquity. A mixture of brick and stone, it featured a huge copper fireplace at one end.

Andrea smiled to herself when the older couple ordered martinis, a mind-dulling drink if there ever was one. She limited herself to a single bourbon and water in a tall glass. Stoakes had a beer.

When Jan had a second martini, Andrea felt like clapping her hands. She could see Jan was getting tipsy. By the time they left the bar, the older woman walked as though she was already feeling the effects.

The Laigsi, the restaurant where they were headed, was located in a five-star hotel on the other side of town. As usual, their nondescript taxi looked and ran as though it had been brought into the country in pieces. After nearly an hour weaving through three-wheeled tempos, ancient buses, bicycles and waves of humanity, they finally arrived at their destination.

The Laigsi was a small but elaborate restaurant decorated to look like a room in an Indian palace. It had marble floors, crystal chandeliers and walls painted with decorated elephants and horses. The menu was Indian and Tisaran. When Jan O'Neal had two more martinis and wine with dinner, Andrea suspected her housemate would be going home early.

She wasn't wrong. As soon as they left the restaurant, Warrant Officer Connelly insisted on taking Jan home.

"It's still early," Stoakes said, after the other couple had left in a taxi. "What say we hit the casino in the Everest Hotel for a nightcap? It's just down the street."

Happily, Andrea agreed. This was the chance she'd been waiting for. "But only if we go Dutch again, Bill," she said. Under no circumstances did she want the young corporal to think of this evening as a date.

He started to protest, but Andrea waved aside his objection. "I'm a liberated woman."

He grinned at her. "Okay, liberated woman. Dutch it is." Pointing his flashlight toward the ground, he led the way down a narrow sidewalk.

Like the two other luxury hotels in Ganthaku, the Everest was set well away from the street. The hawkers and common people of Ganthaku did not venture up the long concrete driveway. Andrea saw no piles of dirt or cow dung on or near the access road.

A uniformed concierge guarded the hotel's front entrance. A few steps away, not connected to the lobby, was the door to the casino. Corporal Stoakes led Andrea inside.

Two Tisaran men sat in a boothlike structure at one side of the door. A third stood opposite them. All three smiled broadly when they saw Andrea and Stoakes.

"Would you like to buy some chips, sir?" one said. His English was perfect.

Stoakes grinned and shook his head. "Maybe later. Right now, we're headed for the bar."

The bar was a long wooden affair facing a parallel mirror. It looked like something out of a fifties movie except that most of the patrons were Oriental or Indian.

Andrea ordered a crème de menthe on the rocks. She waited until their drinks were delivered and paid for before excusing herself. With Corporal Stoakes safely settled, she felt free at last to make her telephone call.

The lobby next to the casino had marble floors, handsome dark wood-paneled walls and polished brass trim. After a quick stop in the ladies' room, Andrea headed for a bank of telephones near the registration desk.

With the help of the hotel's long distance operator, her collect call to Tom Nolting went through without a hitch. Using the simple code he'd given her, she described her problem to a duty officer who answered the phone. In the same code, the man assured her that the ambassador would be instructed not to restrict her movements anywhere in the country.

Then Andrea made a second call. It was to the local contact Nolting had given her, a man named Tulak who would guide her through the parts of the temple compound open to tourists. Identifying herself as Nadja, the name she'd been instructed to use, she described her appearance and arranged to meet the man Saturday afternoon—the day after tomorrow—near a small shrine to the Hindu deity Bhairava in old Ganthaku.

Returning to the bar, she found that Stoakes had started on his second beer. If he thought she'd been gone too long, he gave no sign of it.

MARINE CORPORAL William R. Stoakes considered himself one of the "few good men" the corps was always advertising for. He kept his nose clean, got along with the other men, didn't do drugs and was a loyal American.

Stoakes realized he was no whiz intellectually, but hell! So what? He knew his job and did it well. Tonight his job was keeping an eye on Mrs. Andrea Mitchell. He wasn't sure why Mr. Connelly wanted to know every move Andrea made. All that mattered was that Mr. Connelly was the boss. What Mr. Connelly wanted, Mr. Connelly got.

Keeping an eye on Andrea wasn't the most obnoxious task in the world, either. She had a way of walking that reminded Stoakes of England's Princess Diana. Too bad Andrea was so tall and didn't fix herself up more. Then maybe she wouldn't have to pay her own way to get a date.

When Andrea excused herself to go to the restroom, Stoakes finished his beer in a couple of quick swallows. Then he followed her. Though he couldn't hear what she said on the telephone, he *could* tell she made two calls.

Who to? he wondered. Obviously not someone she could call from the phone in Mrs. O's house or from her desk at the embassy.

Stoakes gulped as a new thought hit him. Was Andrea selling government secrets? Was that why Mr. Connelly, the embassy security officer, was so interested in what she was doing?

Chapter Four

On Friday afternoon, Philip was informed that the embassy had received a top-secret message for his eyes only. Marked with a Sparrow code word, the one protecting Andrea's mission, the message could be read only in the communications center.

So she'd gotten through to her controller. Aggravated, Philip headed upstairs.

When he entered the vaultlike room, the senior of the two men inside stood and handed him a sheet of paper. Quickly, Philip read the message. As expected, it instructed him not to restrict Andrea's movements.

Now, he thought, there was no way he'd be able to keep her away from the Ishwaranath Temple compound, short of exposing her ulterior motive for being in Tisara—investigating her husband's accident. He wasn't ready to do that yet, not until he'd looked into the matter more thoroughly. If she'd flavored her germ warfare analysis purposely, Andrea would probably be drummed out of the Air Force, maybe even sent to jail.

A sense of frustrated anger swept over him. Damn it all! If he told her what he suspected, would that stop her? No. She'd deny it. That's the kind of spunky woman she was.

He paused, the message in his hand. Before he could accuse Andrea of lying about a monstrous biological warfare plot, he needed to find out exactly what her analysis was based on.

Probably intercepted Tisaran messages, he thought. Intercepted messages were often ambiguous and difficult to interpret, even when the codes had been broken by the National Security Agency. *She put the information from a bunch of messages together and came up with an unwarranted conclusion she could use to her own advantage.*

Philip turned to the officer in charge. "Has my secretary's Category Three security clearance been approved yet?"

"Just a minute, I'll check." A wispy little man, the communications officer rummaged around in a file and came up with a card. "Yes, here it is, sir. She had a Cat Three clearance when she resigned her Air Force commission. It was renewed after she accepted this assignment." He whistled softly. "She's cleared for Sparrow, too. The only one on the staff besides you and me, Mr. Ambassador."

Philip cleared his throat. "I needed someone to help me with the damned Sparrow paperwork, so I requested the clearance for her. As a matter of fact, I could use her right now. Get her up here, would you please, Bart?"

"ARE YOU CERTAIN Andrea's cleared for the comm center?" Jan spoke into the telephone.

Andrea couldn't see the other woman's face, but heard the surprise in her voice.

"Yes. All right. I'll tell Andrea the ambassador's waiting."

Jan hung up the receiver and swung her chair around toward Andrea's desk. "The ambassador is up in the communications center. He wants you to help him get out some special messages."

She eyed Andrea suspiciously. "Why didn't you tell me you had a special security clearance?"

Andrea shrugged. "I thought you knew." Darn Philip anyhow. He should have known Jan would be upset if she found out Andrea had a higher security clearance than Jan herself.

"It's probably donkey work he wants done." Andrea tossed the remark off casually. "Did he say to bring my notepad?"

Jan shook her head. "No, but you'd better." Sounding somewhat mollified, she turned back toward her desk. She didn't look up when Andrea headed out the door.

On her way to the third floor, Andrea felt like singing. Her controller, Tom Nolting, had come through like a champ. That had to be what Philip wanted to talk to her about.

Don't be so smug, she warned herself. *Message or no message, he'll still do everything in his power to stop you.* But she was still smiling when she reached the communications center.

The armed Marine guard posted outside, a man about Bill Stoakes's age, greeted her with a suspicious expression. "No one's allowed inside without a Cat Three clearance, Andrea."

Holding up her shorthand pad, she shrugged. "Guess I've got whatever clearance is required, Henry." She pressed the gray button below the keypad. "The ambassador issued a royal summons."

The communications officer, Bart Stratham, opened the door. As usual, he was dressed in a flamboyant sport coat and tie that reminded Andrea of an off-duty jockey.

"Come on in." He had a raspy Popeye voice that didn't suit his small frame. "The old man's waiting for you in the briefing room." He nodded over his left shoulder.

Inside, she quickly glanced around the place, a room about half the size of Philip's office. Unlike the message center she'd known at the Pentagon, this one was relatively neat. Two uncluttered desks faced the door. Papers were neatly stacked in cubbyholes built along two walls. One of three ticker tape machines positioned in a corner chattered nervously as paper piled up beneath it.

Through an open door on the opposite side, Andrea saw Philip. He stood and came toward her, his eyes dark and unfathomable. His well-muscled body moved with easy grace.

The accusing look he threw her made her catch her breath. Now that the order had arrived, was Philip going to chew her out for calling Washington?

He closed the door behind them and led the way to a round table at the center of the room. "Sit down." He pulled out a chair for her before seating himself opposite her.

Positioning her notepad on the table, Andrea stared at him expectantly. She noted his set face, his clamped jaw and his narrowed eyes. They made her feel strangely disloyal.

"I'm sure you've guessed what the EYES ONLY message was about," he began.

She nodded. "I called Washington last night and asked my controller to tell you to lift your restrictions."

He raised a heavy eyebrow. "I didn't expect you to be so candid."

To keep herself from making nervous movements with her hands, Andrea picked up her pen. Resting her notepad in her lap where he couldn't see it, she began sketching his face. He had an aquiline nose, generous mouth and thick eyebrows over wide-set dark eyes. It was a compelling face, full of strength.

"Since last night was the first time Jan wasn't hovering nearby, I had a chance then. Why shouldn't I admit it?" Glancing from his face to her tablet, Andrea realized how attractive she found him. She flipped the cover over the sketch she'd made.

Philip leaned back and folded his arms. "The message wasn't why I called you up here."

Andrea felt her face flush with alarm and was powerless to stop it. What new obstacle would he throw her way?

"We need to talk bout this biological warfare theory of yours," he want on. "Before Colonel Butler was declared *persona non grata*, he briefed me on your conclusions. But he wasn't familiar with the reports you'd based them on. If everybody who's heard your analysis believes you, you must have some pretty strong evidence to back up your theory."

For a moment, Andrea was struck speechless. "I beg your pardon?" She couldn't believe what she'd heard.

He locked his hands behind his neck. "It's finally time for you to tell me why you think Tisara's involved in biological warfare. Convince me, the way you convinced all the Washington brass."

Andrea leaned toward him. This was the chance she'd been waiting for.

"First," she said, "there was the establishment of a new communications network originating at Ishwaranath. Though the messages were scrambled, the National Security Agency monitored the new net and tracked its contacts with substations in Tisara and Delhi."

"Maybe they were sending religious messages of some sort."

She shook her head. "When one of the codes was broken, the intercepts referred to pharmaceuticals and key individuals. At least one of the people named was a physician connected to biological warfare production in the Middle East."

Watching her, Philip twisted uneasily. Andrea seemed to belive one hundred percent in what she said. If not, she was the best actress in the world. And he was a poorer judge of character than he'd been given credit for. Had he been wrong about her reason for coming to Tisara?

No, he assured himself. There must be two reasons: to ferret out the truth about her biological warfare theory *and* to investigate her husband's accident.

Andrea continued to present her evidence. "Intelligence sources—informants in Ganthaku—reported rumors about a strange new drug. The CIA picked up speculation that the drug was connected with biological warfare."

As she talked, her nervousness disappeared, he noticed. Her voice, low and musical, carried the weight of truth. She was the most convincing briefer he'd heard.

Philip unlocked his hands from behind his head and rested them on the edge of the table. "So the Tisarans talked about a new drug in some of their messages. So what? There's no real connection between a new drug and biological warfare. Did the CIA informers come right out and accuse the Tisaran Government of germ warfare research?"

She nodded, fire in her eyes. "Their exact words." She paused a moment, then went on. "According to Colonel Butler's reports before he left Tisara, there was a gradual buildup of troops around Ganthaku. Guards were posted inside the Ishwaranath Temple compound, where they'd never been before. And at other places in the city, too. Additional units were stationed in the surrounding valley."

Philip had read Butler's reports but had downgraded their significance. A few hundred more soldiers stationed near the capital didn't seem important. Now, as he listened, he began to see a pattern.

"Finally," she said, wrapping up, "air traffic between Ganthaku and Delhi has increased significantly in the past year or so—the same time the new network began operations, and we started getting reports from local sources about biological weapons."

She didn't have to explain the significance of the increased air traffic. If Tisara were peddling the weapons to India, there would probably be an exchange of technicians and materials between the two countries.

But a couple of things didn't add up.

"It doesn't make sense for the Tisarans to work with biologicals at the Ishwaranath Temple compound since it's so close to their capital city," he pointed out. "There's too much chance of an accident. Thousands would die if the people were accidentally exposed."

She nodded. "The weapons are probably tested somewhere out in the boondocks."

When he started to interrupt, she raised a hand, and he let her go on.

"I know that means the weapons have to be moved from the lab to the test site. That's risky, but that's what I think they're doing. I want to check out the test site as soon as I—" She stopped abruptly.

Philip didn't let her get away with it. "You sound as though you know where the test site is. I thought the temple compound was the focus for this operation."

She caught her lower lip between her teeth and eyed him doubtfully. "Maybe it's better if you don't know everything."

"Now that the Secretary of State has ordered me not to interfere, I can't do much to stop you." He put some authority in his voice. "But if you convince me there's something to these conclusions of yours, I won't be so apt to get in your way."

He could see he'd added just enough sweetening to get her to keep on talking.

She studied him for a second, then went on. "Production is done at the temple, but the test site is probably somewhere else, maybe at the coordinates of one of those other communications stations."

"Has satellite photography picked up any circular pens for the test animals?" he asked. Spotting such pens was the best indicator of biological warfare research. Test animals were put into a series of circular pens, each farther out than its neighbor, to determine toxicity of the weapons at various distances from the exposure center.

"No," she answered. "And we haven't spotted any heavily fenced and guarded buildings, either." She paused. "And that's another good indicator of germ warfare."

Philip saw the intense look in her eyes.

"These people are up to something, Philip." Her face burned with a crusader's zeal. It was an expression he recognized because he used to feel that way himself when he got caught up in something he believed in. He hadn't felt that way for a long time.

She leaned toward him, her eyes pleading. "We've got to find out what these people are up to."

Now that he'd heard her reasoning, Philip was halfway convinced she was right. But he was even more sure that, as an amateur involved in espionage, she was in terrible danger. His awareness gave him a sick feeling in the pit of his stomach.

"I can't help but be worried about you." Impulsively, he reached across the table and caught her hands. Her fingers were slender and delicate. For a moment, his fingers tightened around hers.

Her widened eyes showed her surprise, but she didn't pull away.

"Do me a favor and put off your investigation for a couple of weeks." His voice was gruffer than he would have liked. "By then you'll know your way around and be less apt to get into trouble."

He saw her amazement at his words. Gently, she pulled her hands away. "Don't worry, Philip," she promised. "When I do my investigating, I'm not going to get caught." There was a determined glint in her eyes. "Nobody will get in trouble because of me, Mr. Ambassador. I'm not your Colonel Butler."

"No, you're not." Though Philip smiled at her, his thoughts were more anxious. *You're a young woman, twenty-eight years old, on her first espionage assignment, who's about to self-destruct.*

How he wanted to stop her.

THE SMALL SHRINE to the Hindu deity Bhairava was located on Lampizat Street in old Ganthaku. Andrea arrived for her prearranged meeting with Tulak shortly before three o'clock on Saturday, the time she'd agreed to meet him when she'd called him Thursday night.

Since she wouldn't recognize him, she loitered near the shrine, certain he'd have no trouble spotting her. She had to be the tallest woman in the vicinity. She was wearing an outfit designed not to attract attention: a long dark cotton skirt, matching shirt and flat-heeled sandals. In the cab she'd thrust her blond curls under a black knit cap, and donned a capacious gray shawl. Dark glasses hid her blue eyes.

It wasn't the most perfect disguise, but the best she could manage with Jan watching her every move. Getting past Jan's watchful eye hadn't been easy. As soon as she saw Andrea's dark clothes, she'd insisted on coming along "to show you the sights," as she put it. Andrea's firm refusal had undoubtedly aroused the older woman's suspicion, but it couldn't be helped.

Let Jan think what she wanted. Andrea was positive her housemate had no idea Andrea was a trained spy on a top-secret mission for the U.S. Government.

A trained spy. The thought gave Andrea a tense, quivery feeling in the pit of her stomach. She wasn't kidding herself. There was no way she could pass as a Tisaran. But hopefully, she looked enough like a European tourist that she wouldn't be recognized as an employee of the U.S. Embassy.

Anxiously, she fingered the tiny camera in the pocket of her skirt. Built into a functioning ballpoint pen, the camera also contained a chemical compound similar to Mace. After working the device in training, she felt comfortable with it. She hoped to heaven she would never have to use it, but knowing she had it gave her courage.

She glanced at her watch. It was a quarter past three. Where was Tulak? As a paid informer, not a trusted operative, he might not be reliable. If he didn't show up, should she go to the temple on her own?

A wave of apprehension swept over her at the idea. *You'll never complete this mission if the mere notion of going there alone throws you into a panic.* Just the same, wandering around on the temple grounds by herself might not be the smartest thing to do. Philip was right about getting to know the territory before she ventured too far afield.

When Tulak hadn't arrived by three-thirty, Andrea called it quits for the day. Feeling disappointed, she threaded her way to the cobblestone street through the horde of ragtag passersby.

Amid a disorderly jumble of pedicabs and bikes, she spotted an ancient Renault with a black-and-white license plate marking it as a taxi. She waved at it. The vehicle pulled up in front of her and the driver leaned out his window. He was young, barely out of his teens.

"Madame Nadja?" he said, using her code name.

Andrea tensed. "Tulak?" He must have been watching for her to make a move.

"No, Tulak waits near Mandali Torana in Ishwaranath Village."

Mandali Torana or Gate was the entrance to that part of the temple compound open to tourists.

The driver reached across the back of his seat and opened the rear door. "I will take you to him."

After a moment's hesitation, Andrea got in.

Twenty minutes later, the Renault stopped at a corner crowded with people and cows. The dirt piles were even higher and the buildings shabbier than in Ganthaku. A steady stream of humanity flowed down the hill toward the river.

Andrea got out of the car and glanced around.

Coming toward her was a middle-aged man whose red turban identified him as an Indian Sikh. His mahogany skin framed intriguing eyes an unusual shade of light blue. His thick mustache was flecked with gray.

"Madam Nadja?" His voice was flat, nasal, toneless; his expression unreadable. "I am Tulak. I will be pleased to guide you through Ishwaranath."

He wore a long red-and-black-checked shirt bunched in front at the waist, and a shawl-like upper garment. On his feet were dirty thick-soled running shoes with no socks. They should have looked out of place, but didn't somehow. He walked with a quiet dignity that inspired Andrea's trust.

Andrea went to meet him, her heart thumping madly. The Ishwaranath Temple complex was only a short block away. What would she find there?

A BODY BURNED slowly on the stone platform at the river's edge. From the cobbled bridge where Andrea stood, she could see the remains of a corpse wrapped in orange, could smell the wood smoke circling from the stacked logs beneath it. The odor was powerful, acrid. It was more than wood smoke, she realized suddenly. It was the smell of burning human flesh. The insight frightened her. Never had death loomed so near.

"This is very holy place," Tulak informed her, his speech an interesting mix of broken English with a British accent. "The Bagmati is sacred river flowing to the Ganges. People come to that house to die." He gestured toward a rectangular building next to a long flight of stone steps. The stairs led up from the river to the off-limits part of the compound.

Next to Andrea, a middle-aged couple armed with cameras busily snapped pictures. They laughed and talked, speaking a European language Andrea took to be German.

Their light conversation sounded out of place, like laughter at a funeral.

Below, a white-robed man, his head shaved, performed the final rites on another body on a second cremation ghat. Andrea knew the name of the ceremony—*sraddha*. The white-robed man was a son sending the soul of a dead parent on its final journey. But somehow, the ritual that had seemed so fascinating in her research became disquieting when she could smell the burning flesh, could see the fire smoldering beneath the body. She moved away from the bridge's edge.

"Would you like to go down there?" Tulak asked, misinterpreting her action. "Is permitted."

Andrea didn't let her aversion show. "No. Let's watch from the other side."

They crossed the bridge to the far side of the river, where from a stone terrace more tourists snapped pictures of the never-ending spectacle on the opposite bank.

From here, Andrea could see the corrugated tin roofs of the buildings clustered around the three gilded roofs of the Temple of Ishwara. Two armed guards stood at the top of the long stairway to the temple and its courtyard. Getting inside wouldn't be easy. But she'd worry about that later, when she'd finished her reconnaissance of the grounds.

After walking the length of the terrace, Andrea could see it was used primarily as a viewpoint for the other side of the river.

Next to the terrace, a wide, long stairway led to the top of the hill. As Andrea climbed upward, rhesus monkeys ran alongside, their voices shrill, their small palms outstretched, mimicking the crippled beggars who lined the stairs. One man, his hands wrapped in bloody bandages, appeared to be a leper. Swallowing hard and fighting her revulsion, she handed him a rupee. Never in her wildest nightmares had she thought she'd ever be this close to someone with leprosy.

Turning away, she saw a circle of holy men sprawled on the ground on a higher terrace. Almost naked and dusty with sand, they gazed at her with dull, empty eyes.

On the other side of the stairway was another terrace area, this one dotted with small stone buildings. Andrea let Tulak guide her through the crowded temple grounds. She wasn't sure just what she was looking for, so she moved slowly through the labyrinthine stone corridors and steep stairways winding between a hodgepodge of temples and buildings.

By the time she'd spent an hour in the compound, she began to question her theory that the research labs might be located here. She saw no evidence. And, as Philip had said, it would be foolhardy to expose these hordes to biological weapons. No, the research and production facilities must be located near the test site. That way, the product could be tested without transporting it a long distance.

So what was the role of the temple? The communications network must originate here. Was this the organizational hub, with the work being done somewhere else?

Many of the buildings they passed weren't open to the public. Some had barred windows, but there were no armed guards around them. If the buildings had contained production or research facilities for biological weapons, they'd be guarded.

The sixth century temple they entered was full of wall paintings and carvings—some obscene by Western standards—and statues of Siva, his consort in her various incarnations, and Nandi, the bull he used as a mount. But Andrea saw nothing suspicious.

Finally, Tulak took her to the temple garden, in a remote corner of the compound. The area was surrounded by a five-foot-high brick wall. Unlike the rest of the structures in the compound, the wall wasn't crumbling. It looked new, as though built during the past year. Strangely, there was an armed guard stationed at its entry.

Andrea's pulse quickened. Why was there a wall around a garden? Why was it guarded by an armed soldier?

"Need baksheesh to go inside," Tulak said in his baritone voice.

"Baksheesh?" she said.

"A tip to the soldier to go inside," he replied slowly, to make sure she understood. Andrea had been careful not to let him know she spoke Tisaran. Since he wasn't a trusted operative, the less he knew about her, the better.

"You mean if I give him some rupees, he'll let us inside?" Andrea could hardly believe her good fortune.

"Soldier very poor," Tulak replied.

"Find out how much he wants." She waited while her guide negotiated with the guard.

"One thousand rupees." Tulak assumed a helpless, palms-out stance. "Best I could do."

Andrea did a quick mental calculation. One thousand rupees was about twenty dollars at the current exchange rate. That was probably more than the man made in a month, but to Andrea it was a bargain. She gave Tulak a handful of bills from her shoulder bag.

He took them to the guard who motioned for Andrea to follow.

When Tulak hung back, Andrea gave him a startled glance. "Aren't you coming, too?"

He grinned, the first time she'd seen him smile. "Not unless more baksheesh. One more person, one thousand more rupees."

"Then wait here for me." Burning with anticipation, she followed the guard through the gate.

The first thing Andrea noticed in the walled enclosure was the strong smell—a pervasive odor mingling a sickly sweet strawlike smell with the pungent aroma of manure.

After all, this *is* a garden, she reminded herself, examining the neatly tended rows the guard led her through. Instead of the vegetables she'd expected, the plants were exotic-looking, with orchidlike orange flowers dangling from spiky stalks.

Half-hidden behind some trees stood a ramshackle greenhouse, its clear plastic walls split with large cracks. Andrea pointed at the place and nodded her head to let the guard know she wanted to go in.

Inside, the small enclosure bulged with the same strange plants she'd seen outside. They were everywhere—on tables, on the muddy ground, hanging from baskets hooked to ceiling supports. The humid atmosphere and strong smell were nauseating. Pulling a cotton handkerchief from her shoulder bag, Andrea breathed through it, but that only made her feel suffocated.

She tapped the guard on the shoulder. "I've seen enough in the greenhouse."

Though he probably spoke no English, Andrea could tell he understood her. He glanced at her handkerchief and grinned, wiping the perspiration from his forehead. About twenty, Corporal Stoakes's age, he was wearing the khaki shirt and trousers of the Tisaran army.

He started past her toward the door where they'd entered. Andrea could see the sweat stain on the back of his shirt.

She tapped him on the shoulder again. "No," she said, nodding in the opposite direction. "I want to see the garden on the other side."

Without waiting for his response, she swung around and headed toward a wooden door at the far end of the greenhouse. Through the clear plastic on one side, she could see the door led to a flat-roofed building adjoining the greenhouse.

Behind her, Andrea heard the guard shuffling along, his boots packing down the moist dirt. Her own sandals were sopping wet. She could feel the gritty water between her toes and under her arches and heels, but tried to ignore the sensation. The humidity and overpowering smell were all she could handle.

She reached the door and tried the knob. It wouldn't turn.

She swung around toward the guard. "Please open the door," she said, smiling.

He gave it a shove. When it didn't move, he shrugged and grinned sheepishly.

"Don't you have a key?" Andrea searched in her bag until she came up with the key to Jan O'Neal's house. She waved it in the guard's face.

He shrugged even more sheepishly.

Irritated, Andrea bent down and stuck the tip of her key inside the lock on the knob. The lock was so simple she could have broken in in about two seconds.

But not with an armed guard watching me.

As she wiggled her key in the lock, Andrea noticed some figures scratched on the door's bare-wood surface. She drew closer for a better look. In the distinctive square writing of the Tisaran language, she read a name: *DASS VERMA.* Andrea forgot her nausea. Her heart thudded like a trip-hammer.

Dass Verma was a name she recognized. She'd seen it on intercepted messages from the temple network, the network that sent the messages she'd based much of her germ warfare analysis on. She believed Verma to be a key leader in the plot, along with a Middle Eastern physician who specialized in biological warfare. Was this little building behind the ramshackle greenhouse their headquarters?

Andrea couldn't wait to tell Philip what she'd found. Would she finally see an approving look in his brown eyes? No, she told herself firmly. She couldn't tell Philip anything. Not yet, anyhow. Not until she was sure he was on her side.

She felt a heavy hand on her shoulder. Without looking around or straightening, she shrugged impatiently. The young guard needed a lesson in courtesy. He shouldn't be touching her.

Her shoulder was squeezed in a painful grip.

"Sorry, madam." The voice was male, gravelly with a strong accent. "We don't allow tourists to peek through our keyholes."

Andrea stiffened. It wasn't the guard. Though she was still bending over, she could see the pants legs of the man behind her. The fabric was the same color as the guard's uniform.

A Tisaran military officer! He'd caught her spying in an off-limits area. What in God's name would happen to her now?

Chapter Five

Andrea's knees felt so weak she was afraid she'd topple to the muddy ground. For one horrible instant, she feared she was either going to faint or get sick. Without looking up, she took a long, deep breath, the way she'd been taught in training.

"Take your hand off me," she began loudly, as she straightened.

Obligingly, the hand was removed from her shoulder.

When she swung around to face her captor, she made sure her face wore an insulted expression, the kind of expression a tourist would have at being treated roughly by local authorities.

Standing before her was a huge man in a Tisaran army colonel's uniform. His skin was swarthy, his eyebrows thick and inky black, as was his luxuriant mustache. But his most disturbing feature was his eyes. They were different colors: One brown, one blue.

With a shock, Andrea recognized this man from her biographic files at the Pentagon. He was the Tisaran chief of intelligence, the most powerful man in the Tisaran military. Andrea felt her knees weaken again and the blood drain from her face.

"I am Colonel Ratna Khadka," he announced. "Please come with me, Miss..." His tone was irascibly patient.

"Mitchell," Andrea responded. Looking past Khadka, she took in the horrified look on the young guard's face. Beside him stood a captain, his weapon drawn. The guard's skin was ashen, his eyes wide with terror.

"Don't blame him." Andrea nodded toward the guard. "He was only trying to be friendly."

Khadka grunted. "Soldiers who disobey orders must be disciplined." He turned to the captain behind him and barked an order in Tisaran. "Take the dog to Slonpo and shoot him."

Shoot him! Bile rose in Andrea's throat. She couldn't believe she'd heard right. Was the amiable young guard to be killed for letting her inside what appeared to be a harmless garden? Her legs felt like rubber. She swallowed hard.

"He was only being friendly," she repeated, keeping her expression bland so the colonel wouldn't know she'd understood his order.

"We will take that under consideration." Khadka's smile was not reassuring. "Come with me, please, Miss Mitchell." He turned and started toward the door at the far end of the greenhouse.

"WHAT'S THE CHARGE against me, Colonel Khadka?"

Andrea had already told him she was a new employee at the U.S. Embassy. Surprisingly, he'd let her call the duty officer. After she'd explained her predicament to him, her wrenching fear began to subside.

Colonel Khadka's well-furnished office contrasted strangely with the rundown army base where it was located. Andrea was sitting on a massive overstuffed sofa with gold dragons embroidered on the upholstery. The sofa faced a massive desk with two equally massive chairs on either side.

From her Pentagon files, Andrea knew Khadka, who was six and a half feet tall and weighed nearly three hundred pounds, had had the furniture specially made for him. Lord, what she'd give to be back in her comfortable executive chair in the Pentagon basement, reading about the colonel's furniture instead of sitting on it.

The man behind the desk stared at her, his bicolored eyes lethally calm. "There is no charge against you, Miss Mitchell."

She stiffened. "Then why am I here?" Was he going to hold her as a spy with no charge? Gathering her wits together, she forced herself to act the part she was playing.

"I was only sight-seeing in your beautiful temple," she went on defensively. "If I got into an area where I wasn't supposed to be, I'm sorry. I thought the guide was there to show visitors around the garden."

"You were in a place that is closed to tourists." His expression was cold, unreadable. "In addition, your ambassador has declared Ishwaranath off-limits to embassy personnel. Were you not aware of his order?"

Dumbly Andrea shook her head. "I just got here a couple days ago. If somebody told me to stay away from the place, I don't remember."

The lie was necessary, but she felt like squirming under Khadka's cold scrutiny. To her annoyance, she began to perspire. With an effort, she stared him straight in the eye, trying to look honest.

In a patronizing way, he cocked his shaggy head to one side. "Perhaps you should listen more carefully when you're given instructions." He spoke with cool authority. "Don't you agree, Miss Mitchell?"

Deliberately, Andrea let her gaze fall to her hands, clenched tightly in her lap. "From now on, I'll listen to every word," she promised.

Just let me out of here and I'll promise anything, she thought grimly. Why didn't someone from the embassy get here to rescue her?

As though in answer to her thoughts, there was a soft knock on the elaborately carved door to Khadka's office. He bellowed "Enter" in Tisaran.

A corporal strode into the room, pausing at one side of the massive desk. "Warrant Officer Connelly is here to pick up the prisoner, Colonel." He didn't look at Andrea.

Andrea kept her face expressionless. But an involuntary shudder raced through her as she heard the corporal call her a prisoner in Tisaran. She wasn't out of the woods yet.

"Tell him she'll be ready in a few minutes." Khadka waited until the enlisted man left the room, then turned back to Andrea, a thin smile on his lips. His teeth were dark near the gums, a sure sign he chewed addictive betel nut leaves.

"Your security officer has come for you, Miss Mitchell."

So Colonel Khadka knew Mr. Connelly was the embassy's chief of security. What else did he know about embassy personnel? That four months ago Andrea had been the primary military intelligence analyst for Tisara? Or worse, that she was still in the Air Force, working undercover?

No, that couldn't be. Otherwise, Khadka wouldn't be releasing her. According to his biographic report, he was a ruthless man with no reluctance to eliminate someone who got in his way. She'd have to be a lot more careful from here on out. If he caught her again . . .

The big man across from her stood up. "Miss Mitchell, I am being easy on you because you are new in our country and because I want Tisara to maintain good relations with the United States."

Andrea leaped to her feet and followed him to the door.

Khadka paused with his hand on the knob. "From now on, I suggest you listen to the advice of your ambassador."

He opened the door.

Mr. Connelly's grizzled face looked as welcome as sunshine on a foggy San Francisco day. In spite of his frown, Andrea felt like hugging him.

"Thanks for coming," she told him quietly.

"Don't thank me." His words were abrupt, disapproving. "I was only following orders." Andrea could tell he thought she was a stupid fool to get herself—and the embassy—in trouble.

Connelly, in uniform to show he was on official business, turned to Khadka. "We're sorry about this, Colonel. The ambassador will be sending a formal apology along with something—" he cleared his throat "—shall we say *tangible* to demonstrate U.S. appreciation for your generous act in releasing Mrs. Mitchell so quickly."

Khadka bowed slightly. "Please thank your ambassador for me, Mr. Connelly. I will expect his letter."

Connelly didn't speak until they were inside the embassy car. "Take us to the residence, Mohan," he said.

Andrea caught her breath. "The ambassador wants to see me at his house? But it's Saturday."

Connelly threw her a sympathetic look. "He's mad as hell, Andrea. Quite frankly, I wouldn't want to be in your shoes right now for the Congressional Medal of Honor."

THE AMBASSADOR'S HOUSE, officially called "the residence," was located on the embassy compound. Although much smaller than the embassy, the house had the same square institutional look.

Inside that house, Philip waited. Andrea felt an unexpected shiver of anticipation at the thought. She was actually looking forward to seeing him, she realized, surprised at herself.

Let him rant and rave all he wanted. There was nothing he could do to stop her. Now that he'd gotten explicit orders from the State Department, he couldn't send her home. And maybe, just maybe, when he was through chewing her out, she could tell him what she'd found. Then he could help her figure out why the name Dass Verma was scratched on that dilapidated greenhouse door.

Squaring her shoulders, Andrea followed Connelly up the circular walk to the house's brick entry. Connelly struck the knocker against the door. A Tisaran man answered. He was dressed in a uniform of sorts: a white shirt and black baggy pants with a wide red sash tied neatly at his waist.

He grinned at Andrea. "Ambassador will see you in reception room."

Reception room. The words had an ominous business-like ring.

Connelly threw her a half salute. "Good luck, Andrea."

"Thanks, Sam." Breathing deeply, Andrea followed the servant into the house.

The foyer floor and walls were lined with the same shade of red brick she saw all over Ganthaku. A ponderous brass chandelier hung from a high ceiling. Ahead, a curving wood stairway led to the upper floors. To the right were tall double doors. The servant threw them open to reveal a space the size of a small ballroom.

Andrea's heart sank. Philip wasn't here to meet her.

"Ambassador say to wait." The servant nodded toward a chair near the door and then left the room, closing the door behind himself.

Pausing, Andrea glanced around. A crimson Indian carpet covered the floor. It was surrounded by at least sixty high-backed chairs with elegant red brocade seats and backs. She crossed the room and sat down.

Outside, it was starting to get dark. The room's three crystal chandeliers had already been turned on.

To calm her shaky nerves, Andrea took her sketch pad out of her handbag and began drawing the exotic-looking flowers she'd seen in the temple garden. Had there been several varieties? Thinking back, she recalled differences in the shading of the colors and in the shapes of the blossoms.

Five minutes passed quickly. Andrea didn't let herself get so wrapped up in her drawing that she forgot to watch for Philip. There was another door, smaller, at the back of the room. When she saw it open, she thrust the sketch pad back in her purse.

He came toward her with the springy athletic step she'd come to know so well in the past few days. Acutely conscious of his powerful, well-muscled body, she couldn't seem to stop staring at him. Though his cream-colored T-shirt and tan sweater-jacket made him look oddly collegiate, he had a fierce critical look that was distinctly unboyish. He planted himself in front of her and folded his arms across his chest.

"I thought you weren't going to get caught." His voice was cold and lashing.

Andrea crossed her legs demurely. "Nobody suspects anything. I don't think there was any harm done."

"No harm done?" His glare burned through her. *"No harm done?* Don't you realize your name's on that bas—on Colonel Khadka's record now? If this damned investigation of yours gets you caught again, he'll throw away the key." Philip's gaze grew fiercer. "And there's not a thing I'll be able to do."

Andrea detected a huskiness in his voice. "You worry too much, Philip," she said calmly. "I won't get caught again."

He dropped onto the chair next to hers, twisting so he was half facing her. "Somebody's got to worry about you. You sure as hell aren't worrying about yourself."

"Don't you believe it," she said, unnerved by the sudden change in his attitude. He actually seemed concerned about her—not as an employee or someone who could get the embassy in trouble, but as a person.

She caught herself up short. Why did she keep getting this unrealistic feeling?

"If you're truly concerned about your safety," he said, "Why not do as I ask?" He leaned toward her, and Andrea was sharply conscious of his fresh-scrubbed smell. "Put your investigation on hold until you're more familiar with the country."

"I can't do that." Her response came easily in spite of her conflicting emotions. "I've been ordered to find something out as quickly as possible."

His dark eyebrows drew together. "So what important information did you uncover on today's excursion?" His expression bordered on mockery. Clearly, he thought she'd risked her life for nothing.

Andrea hesitated. Philip Dorough was the only person outside of Washington, D.C., who shared her secret. He was the only one she could talk to. What luxury it would be to tell him what she'd learned and get his reaction. But would he use the information to throw more obstacles in her way? Or would he understand its significance and try to help?

She'd trust him this one time, she decided quickly. If he disappointed her, he'd be an outsider from now on.

She lowered her voice. "Is this room secure?"

He gave her a sidelong glance. "Yes, that's why I had you meet me here. Sam Connelly went over it early this afternoon for bugs with his degaussing team. He didn't have time to do the rest of the house."

"So that's what I interrupted. No wonder he was so abrupt on the way over here."

"He was abrupt because he thought you disobeyed my direct order," Philip declared with unwelcome frankness. "The Marines consider disobeying a direct order an offense worthy of a court-martial."

"I know."

Philip stood and pushed his hands deep in his pockets, shifting restlessly from one foot to the other. "I've been sitting too long today. Walk up and down the room with me and tell me what you found out."

WATCHING ANDREA rise fluidly from her chair, Philip had to admit he admired the way she handled herself under fire. That bastard Khadka had let her go quickly, so she must have fooled him. Furthermore, during the past few minutes, she'd reacted to Philip's own accusations with dignity and composure.

He also admired the simple dark outfit she was wearing. Without pretending to be anything she wasn't, she'd dressed in a manner designed not to attract attention.

Even in the loose-fitting skirt and shirt, Philip could discern the flare of her hips and gentle swell of her breasts. Though Andrea couldn't be considered beautiful, she had a dazzling aliveness that brightened everything around her.

He glanced at her face and found her intense blue eyes level with his, in spite of her low-heeled sandals. Philip liked tall women and appreciated the way she matched his step, stride for stride.

A couple of tables occupied the center of the room just ahead of them. Off to one side was an ebony grand piano. He made his way toward it. "Don't tell me you stumbled on a functioning germ warfare lab?" He was only half kidding. After the briefing she'd given him in the communications center yesterday, he was ready to believe such a lab did indeed exist.

"No, but remember those messages I told you about?" She lowered her voice, obviously reluctant to talk about the intercepts in an area not cleared for communications intelligence.

He nodded encouragingly.

"There were names on some of them," she went on, her voice almost a whisper. "One of the names was that Middle Eastern physician I told you about who specializes in germ warfare. Another was Dass Verma." She paused.

Glancing at her again, Philip saw the excitement in her eyes. "You heard the name in the temple?"

"I *saw* it," she corrected. "It was scratched in Tisaran on a door at the back of an old greenhouse."

"I remember the greenhouse from my tour with Interior Minister Nakarmi." Philip tried to recall his impressions. "It stunk to high heaven."

"Then you went inside?" Her voice sounded breathless.

"Not clear through to the back," he admitted. "It wasn't the most inviting place in the world. When Nakarmi said storerooms were behind the greenhouse, I believed him."

As they reached the ebony piano, she stopped walking and faced him. "I'm betting the headquarters or the labs or both are there."

Philip frowned. If Andrea was right, the Tisaran interior minister had made a fool of him. The notion was unpleasant because he considered Ganesh Nakarmi a friend.

"Was the door locked?" he asked.

"Yes, but not securely." She began walking again, and he fell into step beside her. "I could have broken in in two seconds, but that doesn't mean anything. The door from the greenhouse might have hidden another, much more secure barrier."

More worried by the minute, Philip headed toward the ballroom exit. "I'm going to call Nakarmi and ask if he's heard of this Verma fellow."

Andrea touched his arm to stop him. It was a gentle nudge, one he should have hardly felt. Instead, he found himself intensely aware of the pressure.

"Since the name's from an intercepted message," she said, "won't we be risking a security violation if you mention Dass Verma to the interior minister?"

"That's a good question." Philip studied her through narrowed eyes. In the light from the chandelier above them, he saw a shadow of alarm cross her face.

"You saw Verma's name in the temple garden. I'll say I heard he did some work there, and I need somebody similar for the embassy."

She glanced at him with amused wonder. "You wouldn't really call the interior minister for advice on a gardener?"

Philip grimaced in good humor. "The U.S. ambassador can call almost anybody he damn well pleases. It's one of the perks of the job." He paused. "Besides, Nakarmi and I are friends. I'm teaching his boys to play basketball."

He headed for the door out of the grand ballroom. "We'll call him from my office."

A few minutes later, seated on a corner of his desk, with Andrea on a leather couch opposite him, Philip dialed the number of the Tisaran minister of interior. As he'd predicted, Ganesh Nakarmi was more than pleased to help.

"No, Philip, I've never heard of this man Verma," he said in his well-modulated tenor voice. "But the priest who oversees the garden may know him if he's one of the temple gardeners."

"Could you arrange for me to talk to the priest?" Glancing at Andrea, Philip saw her enthusiastic nod.

Nakarmi fell silent. Several moments passed before he spoke again. "The devotees are sometimes difficult to reach. It may take awhile to make such an arrangement. He may be reluctant to come to your embassy."

Philip drummed his fingers impatiently on the desk. "I'd like to get this matter taken care of as soon as I can, Ganesh."

Nakarmi made a clicking sound with his tongue. "You Americans are always so impatient."

Another silence. Philip caught Andrea's eye and shrugged. Perhaps the temple priests were more difficult to reach than he'd thought. "There's no reason for the priest to come to the embassy," Philip conceded finally. "My secretary can meet him somewhere on the temple grounds, if that would be easier for him."

Across from him, Philip saw Andrea's eyes widen. He didn't like the idea of sending her back to the temple garden, but saw no alternative. He couldn't go himself, not without arousing Nakarmi's suspicion. The U.S. ambassador would hardly risk assassination or kidnapping to locate a gardener for the embassy grounds.

Nakarmi chuckled. "Is that the same woman our esteemed Colonel Khadka caught there this afternoon?"

"I'm afraid so." Philip stared sternly at Andrea. "She's new and wasn't aware of my restriction."

"It would not be wise for her to return to the temple, even under my auspices," Nakarmi warned. "The colonel is increasingly suspicious of you Americans. He fears that you will desecrate our holy places."

Like hell he does, Philip thought. *Andrea's right. Somebody's hiding something in that temple. If not Khadka, it's somebody he takes orders from.*

"What do you suggest, my friend?" Philip asked.

Nakarmi was silent for a long moment. "I'll try to arrange a meeting between the temple gardener and your secretary outside the compound, but you must be patient. Some of the priests do not live in the city."

"I understand," Philip said, understanding only too well the advantage of being hard to locate. "I'd appreciate any help you can give."

The interior minister said he'd do what he could, and Philip hung up the phone with the frustrated feeling that very little had been accomplished.

Watching from the sofa, Andrea saw a shadow of annoyance cross his face. "Did I hear what I thought I heard?" she asked lightly, hoping to change his mood. "Is Mr. Nakarmi going to arrange a meeting for me with the temple gardener, right on the grounds?"

"Unfortunately, no." Philip repeated what his friend had told him.

Andrea listened with rising dismay. "It may be days before Mr. Nakarmi can make the arrangements."

"If we're lucky." Philip's frown matched his cynical comment. "The Tisarans aren't famous for their speed in such matters."

He rose from his place on the corner of his desk and came toward her. Again Andrea was struck by the agile way he moved, full of grace and virility.

"Maybe I can make the arrangements myself," she began slowly. "My source may know who the gardener is."

He stopped in front of her, a startled look on his face. "You can't be planning to sneak back onto the temple grounds." He stared at her in utter disbelief.

She shook her head, annoyed he'd think her so foolish. "Of course not. But my source may be able to find the gardener and lure him outside. Around here a little baksheesh seems to go a long way."

"I assume this source you mention is the one who was with you on the grounds this afternoon." His eyebrows drew downward in a frown. "Was he taken into custody, too?"

Philip dropped to the sofa beside her. Andrea caught his subtle male scent, musky and intoxicating. Suddenly, his cozy office seemed a lot smaller. She felt the urge to inch away, but found herself leaning toward him instead.

He was leaning toward her, too. Andrea felt a disturbing surge of excitement. She tried to deny the tingling in the pit of her stomach. A hot ache grew in her throat. If she didn't move soon, she was afraid she'd do or say something foolish.

"Shouldn't we go back into the ballroom if we're going to talk about my source?" Her voice sounded tremulous to her. "I can't say anything about him unless there's no chance of being overheard."

Philip's broad shoulders were tense. The smoldering flame she saw in his eyes startled her.

"The ballroom?" He was watching her intently but made no move to get up.

The air was taut with tension. Andrea licked her suddenly dry lips.

She hesitated. For a moment, the world stood still. Then she pushed herself to a standing position.

He was beside her in an instant. "Since the ballroom's been degaussed, of course we'll go there to talk about your source."

Swiveling quickly, he started toward the door. Andrea followed, already wishing she hadn't been so security-conscious. What would have happened if they'd remained on the sofa? Now she'd never know.

In the ballroom they stood close together near the ebony grand piano.

"No, thank God. They didn't arrest Tulak." She forced herself to remember the vivid scene outside the temple garden, picturing the moose of a colonel; the little captain with his weapon drawn; the frightened young guard who knew he was going to be shot; the curious onlookers thronging about them until they passed through a special gate closed to the general public.

There had been no sign of Tulak.

"Wasn't he with you in the garden?" Philip sounded suspicious. There was no sign of the previous sensuous look in his eyes. They were coolly alert, questioning.

Andrea shook her head. "I had to give the guard one thousand rupees per person for baksheesh. It seemed a waste of money to pay for Tulak when he could easily wait outside."

Obviously exasperated, Philip took a deep breath. "Did it occur to you that you might have been set up?"

She shook her head again. "Not possible. If Tulak had set me up, Colonel Khadka would never have let me go so easily this afternoon. Tulak knows I'm working for Washington."

Through the shuttered windows, Andrea could hear blaring auto horns and the distant ringing of bells.

"I hope you're right, Andrea." Doubt crept into Philip's expression. "But doesn't it seem odd that Khadka arrived within fifteen or twenty minutes of the time you entered the garden? It takes longer than that to drive through the city."

Andrea shifted uncomfortably from one foot to the other. "It must have been a coincidence." She was unwilling to condemn Tulak, but in her mind she could hear her instructors repeating: *There are no coincidences in our line of work, ladies and gentlemen. When something looks like a coincidence, get ready to duck.* "I'm sure somebody noticed the guard post was empty," she went on stubbornly. "The colonel just happened to be in the temple area and followed up on the report." She concentrated on the scene in her mind. "If it had been a setup, Khadka probably would have sent someone else to pick me up and have me brought to him."

Philip hesitated, measuring her for a moment. Then he nodded in agreement. "I can't believe he would have let you go if he thought you were spying. Still—" she heard a faint huskiness in his voice, as though some emotion had touched him "—be careful in your dealings with this man Tulak."

"He knows nothing about me," she said, grateful she'd been tight-lipped with the informer.

"Good." Philip glanced at his watch. "I wish I could ask you to stay for supper, but, unfortunately, I'm expected at the palace." His dark eyes searched her face, as though reaching into her thoughts. "Don't do anything rash. If we move slowly, take things step-by-step, we'll find out the truth, and we won't risk our lives doing it." His voice was rough with anxiety.

"Don't worry. I won't do anything until we hear from Mr. Nakarmi." A glow of satisfaction washed over her. Philip was on her side. He'd made that abundantly clear when he said "we" would find out the truth. No longer would he throw obstacles in her path, interfering with her mission.

Not until she was in the car on the way to Jan's house did Andrea realize that—in some way she couldn't quite figure out—Philip had nevertheless managed to plant the biggest barrier of all in her way. By assuring him that she'd wait for Mr. Nakarmi's call, she'd effectively promised to call a halt to her investigation.

Chapter Six

Sunday morning dawned hazy and cool, with subtropical sunlight, the way most mornings arrived in Ganthaku before the the monsoons. Sometime during the night Jan had arrived home. Her door, open last night when Andrea went to bed, was now closed. Moving quietly so as not to disturb her, Andrea fixed herself coffee, cold cereal and a plate of bananas, papayas and mangoes—luscious fruits grown only miles from the city.

What was she going to do with this day? she asked herself, feeling a little blue. Between Colonel Khadka's threatening warning and her promise to Philip, she felt unable to continue her investigation.

The phone rang while she was finishing her coffee. She grabbed it before the second ring and almost fell off the couch when she heard Philip's voice. An unexpected warmth surged through her.

"This is Ambassador Dorough," he said formally. "I'm sorry to spoil your Sunday, Andrea. But I'm going to need you this afternoon at the embassy."

From his businesslike tone Andrea knew he was guarding against possible eavesdroppers. In a twinkling, her whole outlook changed. A spurt of pure energy raced through her.

"Is one o'clock all right?" Her breath quickened.

"Fine." He paused. "And Andrea?"

She waited, her pulse leaping.

"Since this isn't a regular workday, you can wear some-thing—er—*comfortable* to the office."

Andrea's heart gave a mighty jump. Philip's emphasis on "comfortable" was a clue that something out of the ordinary was going to happen.

Mr. Nakarmi's arranged for me to talk to the temple gar-dener. She knew it as surely as she knew her own name. Triumphant elation washed over her. She'd won after all. Philip had made the necessary arrangements. He was going to help her find out the truth.

After a quick shower, she dressed in another of her un-obtrusive outfits: a loose-fitting blue denim dress, belted at the waist, with elbow-length sleeves. Remembering yester-day's ruined sandals, she pulled on a comfortable pair of hiking boots. Like her pen camera, the heels of the boots were armed with a chemical compound similar to Mace.

Unwilling to face Jan's question about the day, Andrea didn't stay in the house. With her camera slung over her shoulder and her sketch pad in her bag, she set out for Dur-bar Square, the heart of Ganthaku's old city. Not far from the square, the long-haired dreamers of the sixties—lured by the availability of mind-altering drugs and the Shangri-la atmosphere—had hung out in crude cafés that smelled of charcoal smoke and dust and exotic herbs.

Andrea ate lunch in such a place. Called the Sunny Gar-den Restaurant, its patrons were urged to Enjoy Food in a Healthy Atmosphere, according to the sign in front. Look-ing at the rough-hewn chair opposite her on the dirt floor, Andrea thought of Philip. What a shame an ambassador couldn't enjoy quaint local places like this unless accom-panied by armed bodyguards.

On an impulse, she pulled out the picture she'd drawn of the flowers in the temple garden and showed them to the waiter. A stoic Tisaran youth who hadn't smiled since Andrea had sat down, he studied the sketch for a moment, then handed it back to her.

"Very good picture," he told her seriously.

"What is it?" She put the sketch pad back in her bag. "What kind of flower?"

He shrugged. "Mussenda is name. Grows wild but only in Ganthaku Valley. Very good plant."

Andrea's ears perked up. "Mussenda is a good plant? Why?"

The boy ran his fingers through his shiny black hair. "Mussenda good for head."

She eyed him quizzically. Maybe the plant had medicinal properties. "You mean it's for pains?"

He shook his head vigorously and ruffled his hair again. "No, madam. *Head.*"

Puzzled, she watched him. "Do you mean hair?"

At last he smiled. "Yes. Good for hair."

Andrea pictured a bunch of Tisarans standing around, crushing the orange flowers into their hair. Obviously an old wives' tale, the story provided welcome comic relief. When she'd finished eating, she left an extra-large tip.

Outside the restaurant, she hailed a three-wheeled tempo for the ride to the embassy. Philip was waiting for her in his office. Andrea took in his tan knee-length shorts with matching shirt and socks. His legs were as brown and firm as tree trunks. A pair of binoculars was slung around her neck.

"My, my, my," she said, letting her gaze rove from his hiking boots to his straight dark hair. "Looks like we're off on safari this afternoon." A faint ripple of anticipation touched her spine, along with the familiar leaping of her pulse at his blatant masculinity.

He broke into a leisurely smile. "Not exactly, but at least we'll be seeing some of the countryside. Ganesh—Mr. Nakarmi—says our gardener-friend sometimes holds forth with a small community of peasants who work a terraced hillside twenty or thirty miles from here. Ganesh thinks that's where he is this weekend.''

Anxiety spurted through Andrea. ''Is it safe for you to go out in the boonies like that, Philip? These days, U.S. ambassadors are fair game for every nut on earth.''

He gave her a reassuring nod. ''We'll be okay. The biggest danger is in driving along a prearranged route. Since nobody knows where we're headed today except Ganesh, we should be all right.'' He paused. ''Plus, we'll use Mohan to drive my Cherokee. He's a trained antiterrorist driver.''

Downstairs, Philip's black Jeep Grand Cherokee waited in the embassy's circular driveway. Mohan leaped out and opened the back door for them with the same alacrity he demonstrated in the embassy car.

During the next hour and a half, Andrea jolted along on the most hazardous ride she'd ever taken. Shortly after leaving Shinjo, a town about ten miles from Ganthaku, the road narrowed to little more than one lane, and they began climbing. In some places, there were sheer drops of forty or fifty feet to the terrace below.

Near villages, people on foot dotted the road, making little attempt to get out of the way when Mohan blared the horn. Oncoming vehicles clung to the far side of the road like fat flies hanging on to the outside of a jam jar. When two elephants lumbered by single file, their mahouts perched high on the animals' gargantuan shoulders, Andrea felt as though she were living a fairy tale.

For one five-to-six-mile stretch, the road was being repaired. Dozens of men and women squatted alongside the road, using crude hammers to pound big pieces of stone into gravel.

Philip shook his head. ''With the proper equipment, one man could do that job in a couple of hours.''

Andrea nodded. ''Sounds like something our economic officer should look into.''

Suddenly, the lofty peaks surrounding them loomed directly ahead. In the distance, Andrea saw a column of white smoke spiraling toward the heavens. She turned away from the window toward Philip. "What's that smoke?"

He shrugged. "Maybe it's from a tea house for trekkers."

Andrea leaned forward, her heart in her throat. "Do the trekkers come this way to start climbing Laigsi?" Perhaps Jeffry had driven along this mountain road to begin his climb of the majestic peak.

Philip nodded. "The trail up the south face begins where this road ends."

Had Jeffry started up the south face? Andrea couldn't remember, wasn't even sure she'd been told. Since his climbing party had disappeared without a trace, perhaps no one knew what part of the mountain they'd assaulted.

Philip raised his binoculars. "The smoke's not in the mountains. It's by the river, near that cluster of huts." Slowly turning the binoculars, he surveyed the hillside sloping away beneath them.

"There's a wide spot about half a mile up the road," he said to Mohan. "Pull over as far as you can and park. We'll walk downhill from there to the buildings."

Andrea studied the terraced hillside they were approaching. Instead of the animal pens and circular test areas she'd expected to see—the indicators that would mean biological warfare research was going on—there were only fields of orange flowers. The entire terraced area below them, a space of about seven to ten acres, was covered with the same kind of vegetation.

A warning bell sounded in her brain. She turned back toward Philip. "Those plants look like the ones I saw in the temple garden."

He surveyed the hill falling away beneath them. "Let's take a close-up look."

As soon as she got out of the car, Andrea recognized the familiar sickly-sweet yet pungent aroma she'd smelled in the greenhouse. These plants appeared somewhat less vigorous than the others, but they looked like the same species.

Philip spoke to Mohan. "When you interpret for me, don't tell the villagers I'm the U.S. ambassador. Just someone from the American embassy who's looking for the temple gardener."

Mohan nodded his understanding.

They started across the first terrace single file with Philip in front and Andrea behind him. A well-worn path led to a large cluster of thatch-roofed buildings a mile or so below them near the river.

"Recognize the smell?" Andrea asked to Philip's back.

He stopped and turned toward her. "It does seem vaguely familiar."

"When you were in the temple greenhouse," she prompted. "Remember you said the place stunk to high heaven?"

"Damned if you're not right. Out here in the open, the smell's not quite so obnoxious, but it's sure the same."

"These plants are healthier-looking than the ones in the greenhouse, but essentially the same plant." Her voice had risen with excitement.

Andrea stopped walking and pulled her sketch pad from her bag. "Look at these flowers. Don't they seem the same to you?"

Behind them Mohan halted, too.

Philip whistled softly. "Did you draw these? They're very professional."

Her cheeks flushed with pride at his compliment. "I would have been an artist if I could have supported myself that way," she admitted, aggravated at herself for being embarrassed.

He studied the drawing. "The flowers are the same. No doubt about it. I've never seen anything like them before."

"They're called mussenda," Andrea offered. "I asked a waiter what they were when I had lunch today."

Looking past Philip, she saw someone coming through the bushes on the terrace below them. "We have company," she observed softly.

It was a portly middle-aged man swathed in a long white garment that was tied and bunched at the groin. A white turban covered his head. His feet were bare. His hands were steepled in a prayerlike gesture.

"May I be of assistance?" he asked in Tisaran. His tone was cool, impersonal, his eyes sharp and assessing.

"I'm sorry, we...do not speak...Tisaran." Philip's words were halting. He beckoned to Mohan. "Ask him if he's the temple gardener."

When the priest replied in the affirmative, Philip stuck out his hand. "We're from the U.S. Embassy," he said, waiting for Mohan to translate.

The round little man did not take Philip's hand. Instead, he bowed slightly at the waist over his steepled fingers.

"Who is the woman?" The priest directed his question to Mohan.

"She is only a secretary, holy one."

"Is she the consort of the man?"

Mohan grinned. "Not yet, but soon."

Understanding every word, Andrea concentrated on keeping her face expressionless. If she blushed, she'd give herself away. But the two men continued talking about her without glancing in her direction.

"She arrived only six days ago," Mohan went on, "and already he spends more time with her than anybody else."

"What's he saying?" Philip asked.

"He asks questions about you," the driver replied.

Not about Philip, Andrea thought, disturbed. *About me.* Why was the fat little priest so curious about her? Had he found out somehow that she'd been caught trespassing in his garden?

"As him if he knows a gardener named Dass Verma," Philip directed. "Tell him we're looking for someone to take care of a special garden we're planning for the embassy grounds."

When Mohan complied, the priest responded instantly—too instantly, Andrea thought. "I know of no Dass Verma." He waited, seemingly patient, but a vein twitched in his jaw, betraying his nervousness.

Philip bent down and plucked a stalk of orange flowers. He smiled at the priest. "They're very pretty. What are they?"

The priest's eyes narrowed. "Mussenda."

Philip handed the stalk to Andrea. "How are they used?"

"Decorations," the priest replied through Mohan. "They are sacred plants for religious ceremonies."

That would explain their cultivation in the temple garden, Andrea thought. But if the plants were sacred, why hadn't the waiter said so? Why had he made a joke about them being good for your hair?

She lifted the stalk to her nose and breathed deeply. The odor was sickly-sweet, like honeysuckle. Mingled with it was the pungent aroma of manure. Grabbing a hankie from her bag, she sneezed.

The priest stepped forward and took the flower from her. "This is a powerful plant."

"It would seem so," the driver replied.

"Ask him if he'll take us to meet some of the people who live down there." Andrea nodded toward the huts by the river. "And see their houses."

After Mohan had translated, the priest shook his head vigorously. "Dhara Village does not welcome white visitors with their cameras and bad manners."

Mohan turned to them and shrugged. "He says it is not possible."

On the way back to the city, Andrea asked Mohan if he'd ever seen mussenda plants used in a religious ceremony.

The driver shook his head.

Andrea exchanged a glance with Philip. He didn't believe the priest's story any more than she did.

"How about using them for your hair?" She felt foolish asking, especially after Philip shot her a quizzical glance.

"Supposed to be good for hair." Mohan ran his hand through his thick black hair. "I never try. My hair okay."

"Just how is the plant used to treat hair?" Andrea persisted. Was the waiter's story more than an old wives' tale?

Mohan shrugged. "Chewed. Like betel nut."

The fruit of the betel nut palm, mixed with leaves and lime, was addictive when chewed. The mixture left a dark red stain on teeth and gums. Maybe the mussenda flowers had a similar narcotic effect.

Before she could ask more questions, the sound of a pulsing motor rose over the dull roar of the Jeep's engine. Andrea leaned across the back of the front seat so she could peer out the windshield. A moment later, a helicopter hove into view overhead.

"Pull over," Philip ordered. Lifting his binoculars, he watched while the small craft beat its way to the huts near the river.

Andrea could hardly believe her eyes, the helicopter seemed so out of place over the remote hillside. "Do many come through here?" she asked.

Mohan turned toward her. "Probably trekkers," he said conversationally. "Or tourists looking at Laigsi."

"Then there *is* a lot of chopper traffic along this corridor?" Andrea heard her voice rising.

Philip threw her a warning glance. It meant she was sounding too much like an Air Force intelligence officer.

"As Mohan said," he pointed out, "this is the tourist route to the mountain."

During the ride back to Ganthaku, Andrea said no more about the helicopter. Or about the orchidlike orange flowers. Or about the nagging suspicion that she'd been wrong to suspect the Tisarans of biological warfare. So far, except for the name Dass Verma, she'd seen no evidence of any such thing.

If she could only find out Verma's identity, maybe that would lead her to the truth.

THE NEXT MORNING, on a hunch, Andrea stopped to talk to the embassy gardener on her way into the office. He was trimming the rhododendrons around the staff entrance.

After she'd made a few complimentary remarks about his work, she asked if he'd heard of a gardener named Dass Verma.

He gave her a searching look, as though he hadn't heard her right. A wizened man with the face of an elf, he looked at least sixty.

"I do not understand." His face wore the apologetic grin of an uneducated native struggling to comprehend a second tongue.

What a relief it would be to speak to him in his own language, Andrea thought. But that was impossible. For her own safety, no one but Philip could know she spoke Tisaran fluently.

She tried again, slower this time. "Mr. Dass Verma is a gardener. Do you know him?"

The little man broke into a broad grin.

Hallelujah, Andrea thought.

"Dass Verma not gardener, madam." He coughed, a moist wracking cough that twisted his small body.

"Not a gardener?" Andrea stepped closer. "Then who is he?"

His coughing stopped. "Dass Verma not man. Dass Verma is fertilizer."

"Fertilizer!" She repeated the word so loudly that two staff members heading for the door glanced in her direction. She lowered her voice. "Are you sure?"

He nodded. "Yes, madam. Very expensive fertilizer. Use only for special plants."

Andrea stood there dumbfounded. *Fertilizer.* How could that be? The name had appeared numerous times in messages that also mentioned the code name for the Middle East physician who specialized in biological warfare. Lord, but she wished she had the intercepts in front of her.

Then she remembered something that made her blood run cold. The messages hadn't been completely deciphered. In some, only the names were recognizable. Others were garbled. With a nasty sinking feeling, Andrea recalled that she'd filled in the blank spaces to come up with a translation that suited her biological warfare theory. According to her theory, Dass Verma was a key player in the plot. If she was wrong about him, then maybe her whole germ warfare theory was wrong. Lord in heaven! What had she done?

Andrea thanked the gardener and started toward her office, her mind searching frantically for answers. Could Dass Verma, the name of a fertilizer, be the code name for the plot leader? Did the door with *Dass Verma* scratched on it lead to his headquarters as she'd thought? Or did it lead to a storeroom filled with bags of fertilizer?

Andrea had to know more. The first person she thought of asking was Tulak. The man was an informer, paid to tell Andrea what was going on in Tisara. Perhaps he'd heard a rumor—anything that would give her a clue as to who or what Dass Verma really was.

During her lunch hour, she made arrangements to meet Tulak that night outside a local hole-in-the-wall coffee shop. Andrea didn't tell Philip what she planned. Once she'd talked to Tulak, she would decide what action needed to be taken—including her possible confession to Washington, as well as to Philip, that her biological warfare theory was wrong.

That evening, after taking a circuitous route past the shop, Andrea spotted Tulak, smoking a cigarette near the entrance. As before, he was wearing a red turban, a dark skirt bunched at the groin and a red-checked shawl. Instead of running shoes, his bare feet were thrust into loose-fitting sandals.

Pulling on a black wool cap to hide her platinum-blond hair, Andrea got out of the cab a block away. Tulak headed toward her.

"Madam Nadja desires a guided tour?" he asked in his flat, toneless voice with its odd mix of broken English and British accent.

She nodded. "Yes. A walking tour of this part of the old city." It was the response they'd agreed on.

For the benefit of anyone watching, they haggled a moment over the price. Then, carefully, Andrea counted out the agreed-upon number of rupees. Tulak thrust them into a fold of his capacious skirt.

Briskly, he led the way through the masses of people in the old city, pointing out the various shrines and markets. The city was named after a type of brick-and-plaster shrine called *Granthakut* that Andrea saw everywhere. While they walked, Andrea asked Tulak about the mysterious name Dass Verma.

He eyes her curiously. "Is fertilizer." Like the embassy gardener, he seemed totally confident of his response. "If madam desires, Tulak will find out about it for you. What is in it, where it is made, and so forth and so forth."

"Yes, please do." Maybe the information would come in handy. "And you've heard no rumors that Dass Verma might be a name for something or somebody else?"

"What rumors has madam heard?" The question came so quickly that Andrea was thrown off guard for an instant. How much could she safely reveal to this man?

Nothing, she decided quickly. And why was he questioning her? With vivid clarity she remembered Philip's warning not to trust him.

"That's what I'm asking you," she returned shortly.

He bowed slightly. "Sorry, madam. I did not mean to be—how you say?—impertinent. But I have heard nothing unusual about this fertilizer except that it is used in Ishwaraneth Temple."

He coughed, the same wracking cough of the embassy gardener.

Did all the natives have tuberculosis? Andrea wondered.

When the spasm had passed, Tulak apologized again. "I thought perhaps if you had heard rumors, I might ask questions, find out if the rumors are true." He smiled so confidently Andrea wondered why she'd doubted him.

She shook her head. "No, if you get me a list of ingredients and the name of the manufacturer, that will be all the information I need."

Then Andrea asked about the trekking party that had vanished last year. Perhaps Tulak could add to her sketchy knowledge about Jeffry's accident.

"I read about the trekkers who disappeared in the papers at home," she explained. "I wondered how a thing like that could happen."

He shrugged. "Thing like that happen all the time."

Andrea's eyes widened with disbelief. "You mean whole trekking parties regularly disappear without a trace?"

"The Americans did not disappear, madam. They fell into a deep crevasse." His voice was patient, as though explaining an obvious fact to a backward child. His forehead was unfurrowed, his expression guileless.

Was she missing something? "Aren't bodies usually recovered when climbers fall into a crevasse?"

"Not from a deep, dangerous crevasse." He grinned congenially.

"But surely if a group of people falls, some of the bodies are visible." A twinge of annoyance coursed through her. Either she wasn't asking the right questions or he was deliberately avoiding a straight answer.

"Not from Laigsi's deep crevasse."

Andrea studied his lined mahogany face. "You mean the Americans fell into a certain crevasse on Laigsi Peak?"

He nodded. "Now madam understands. The crevasse curves so the bottom is not visible. Ice fell and buried the bodies soon after the accident. Too dangerous to go down, get them out."

Andrea regarded him thoughtfully. According to the Air Force investigators, no one knew exactly where the group had disappeared. Tulak had to be guessing when he named a specific crevasse.

"How do you know where they fell?" she persisted. "Nobody saw them, and nobody's been able to find the bodies."

He shook his head matter-of-factly. "A holy man saw them fall. He was watching through binoculars."

"A sadhu with binoculars?" Andrea didn't try to hide her skepticism. During her short time in Tisara, Andrea had seen a number of holy men—some almost naked and covered with white sand, others in a colorful assortment of odd costumes. None carried binoculars.

"Where did you hear about the sadhu?" she asked.

"It is my business to hear things." He lifted a bushy eyebrow flecked with gray. "The sadhu feared he would be detained in Ganthaku as a witness, so told very few people about the accident." He flicked his earlobe with his finger. "But Tulak hears all. Information worth plenty dollars, yes?"

He was obviously trying to impress her with his omniscience, but Andrea was oblivious to his bragging. In her excitement, she reached for his arm, but stopped short of touching him. When he stepped back, she dropped her hand to her side.

"This holy man. What's his name?" She could feel her heart pounding. "Where can I find him?"

Tulak shrugged. "Who knows where he is, Madam Nadja? He is a sadhu, a wandering holy man."

A wandering sadhu who, of course, would never be heard from again. Was he real, this wandering holy man? Or a creative attempt by Tulak to earn more money from the rich Americans?

"The crevasse on Laigsi Peak," Andrea persisted. "Is it on the south face?" Could it be true? On the day Jeffry disappeared, did he pass by the place where she'd gone only yesterday—past the terraces filled with exotic orange flowers?

"Perhaps you know the crevasse?" Tulak paused, waiting for her to respond.

Suddenly, Andrea realized he was baiting her, trying to determine how much she knew before giving an answer. He'd done the same thing before, when she'd asked about rumors that Dass Verma might be a name for something other than fertilizer.

Was he informing for someone else? she wondered. Telling them what Madam Nadja asked about?

She kept her face impassive. "I know nothing about Laigsi other than that the south face is the one closest to Ganthaku."

They threaded their way through a knot of people gathered around a simple pagoda-shaped shrine. Waving off the hawkers, Tulak didn't answer until they'd reached the edge of the crowd.

"Madam correct," he said. "Americans fall into deep crevasse on south face." Playing his role as guide, Tulak gestured toward a temple to Krishna. On a pedestal in front of the temple squatted the god's companion, Garuda.

"Whom did the sadhu tell?" Andrea hardly dared to hope Tulak was right. Perhaps she could question these people herself and confirm his story.

He threw her a helpless glance. "The information comes to me like a leaf on the wind. The man who tells me finds out from someone else and so on and so on."

"Then your information isn't reliable and isn't worth anything." Andrea hoped to goad him into revealing where he'd gotten the information. "It will be worth many dollars to find out who the holy man told about the accident."

His expression turned conspiratorial. "The sadhu spent the night with farmers near Laigsi. Maybe they are ones he told."

Andrea's blood pounded in her temples, her initial skepticism evaporating. Someone had seen the accident and told others about it. Did that mean Jeffry was really dead?

"You mean the sadhu spent the night with the people who live in Dhara Village?"

Her guide eyed her shrewdly. "Yes. If madam talks to the villagers in Dhara, please to not mention Tulak."

She frowned, annoyed he'd think she'd reveal him as an informer. "Of course not." But his simple request convinced her all the more his story was true.

Chapter Seven

Philip heard the phone ring through a haze of sweat and straining muscles. Lifting maximum weight on his tricep press machine, he dripped with perspiration.

There was a knock at the door.

Philip frowned. He didn't like to be disturbed during his exercise sessions, not until he'd showered and dressed afterward.

"Come in," he called out.

The door opened. It was his butler, Tanka. "Mrs. Mitchell on phone, Mr. Ambassador."

Philip's aggravation changed to alarm. *Andrea?* What trouble had she gotten herself into now?

"I tell her to call back," Tanka said, obviously fearing Philip's reaction to this breach of orders. "But she say you want to talk to her right away."

"That's right, I do." Philip grabbed a towel and rubbed the sweat from his face and shoulders. Then he put a short terry robe over his exercise trunks and headed down the hall toward his bedroom. It was the only upstairs room that had a phone.

"Ambassador Dorough." He spoke into the receiver in a businesslike way, in case anyone was listening.

"This is Andrea Mitchell." She was equally businesslike.

Philip detected no panic in her musical voice and breathed a silent sigh of relief. "Yes, Andrea."

"I'm sorry to bother you at home, Mr. Ambassador." There was an undercurrent of excitement in her voice. "But I need to discuss something with you right away."

"Could it wait until—" Philip stopped abruptly. To his annoyance, he realized that he didn't want to pass up a chance to see her again, even though he'd just spent the day with her in the office. He glanced at his watch. It was a little after seven. "On second thought, have you had dinner?"

She paused a moment before answering. He sensed her surprise.

"No," she replied slowly. "I—er—had some errands to run after work."

"Then we'll talk about your problem over dinner at the residence. I normally eat at eight. Where are you calling from?" He knew it wasn't from Jan's house. Andrea would never arouse Jan's curiosity with a call to him.

"The Everest Hotel, but there's no reason for me to interfere with your dinner." A note of embarrassment crept into her voice.

"Believe me, it's no bother." He'd never spoken more truly. Philip hadn't been looking forward to dinner alone in the house's big dining room. The night had turned much brighter at the prospect of Andrea's company.

"My cook usually prepares enough food for the staff and me and an extra ten hungry men," he explained.

Her gentle laugh rippled along the telephone line. "In that case, I'll catch a taxi and be there in twenty minutes or so."

"Good. I'll see you then."

After he'd hung up, Philip pressed the intercom button to notify Tanka that there'd be a guest for dinner. He hurried to his bedroom to shower and dress in brown trousers and a yellow sport shirt with long sleeves rolled up past the elbow. He normally didn't receive guests unless he was wearing a coat and tie, but Andrea was different—more like a friend than a guest. Had he known her only a week?

When she arrived, he was waiting for her in the cozy bar that adjoined the grand ballroom. Tanka showed her in, closing the door when he left.

Studying her face, Philip felt a familiar warmth course through him. Her hair curled appealingly around her oval face. Her cheeks, ruddied from the night air, shouted her vitality. Tonight, the lashes surrounding her intense blue eyes seemed longer and darker than ever.

She's not pretty, or beautiful, he thought. *She's something more than beautiful.*

His gaze dropped to the peasantlike skirt and blouse she was wearing. Like the clothing she'd worn yesterday, her ensemble was designed not to attract attention. But its very shapelessness made him even more conscious of the slender curves underneath.

"I see you've been out sleuthing again." He rose as she walked toward him.

"Is it that obvious?" Her gaze dropped to her formless dark skirt. "Yes, I suppose it is." Her eyes sparkled with barely repressed excitement. "You'll never guess what I've found out."

He caught one of her hands and drew her with him to a high-backed stool at the intimate little bar that curved out, U-shaped, from one wall. On the surrounding walls were primitive paintings by the descendents of Tisara's original inhabitants. The room's thick Tibetan carpeting, along with the beveled mirrors behind the bar, gave the place a luxurious feeling.

"Before you tell me your news, let me fix you a drink." He nodded toward the highball he'd made for himself only minutes before she'd arrived. "As you can see, I didn't wait."

Andrea hesitated. She needed a clear head for tonight's discussion. Just being in the same room with Philip was intoxication enough. Her gaze slid from his face to his chest. Wisps of dark hair curled against the V of his open shirt.

Quickly, she lifted her eyes. "A Perrier will be fine."

He poured two drinks instead of one.

"Perrier sounds good to me, too." He sat down next to her. "Now, tell me what you've found out."

She took a sip from her glass. "You're not going to believe this. I could hardly believe it myself."

Andrea was keenly aware of his total concentration on what she was saying. "Dass Verma is the name of a fertilizer." She burst her bombshell with the air of street preacher announcing the end of the world.

"A fertilizer?" He gave her a sidelong glance of utter disbelief. "Who the hell told you that?"

Even though his reaction was what she'd expected, Andrea couldn't help smiling. "Both the embassy gardener and Tulak, my source here in Tisara. I don't think there's any doubt about it."

"A fertilizer," he repeated softly. "So that's what we were smelling yesterday. Dass Verma Fertilizer." He eyed her quizzically. "So what does that do to your biological warfare theory?"

She studied the glass on the bar in front of her. "I'm not sure," she admitted, unwilling to meet his steadfast gaze. "It's possible that the ringleader uses the fertilizer as a code name."

"But not likely."

Andrea heard the probing doubt in his voice and glanced up. His eyes were sharp and assessing.

"You saw the name of a fertilizer scratched on a greenhouse door," he declared. "What could be more logical?"

She lowered her voice. "I also saw it on intercepted messages that named a biological warfare expert. There's got to be a connection."

"Maybe the messages had nothing to do with biological warfare." He stared at her pointedly. "Maybe the expert is here doing something else. You put two and two together and came up with ten instead of four. You've got to admit that so far you've found no evidence to support your germ warfare theory."

Andrea shifted uneasily on her stool. "Maybe it's not biological warfare, but something underhanded *is* going on here. I'm sure of it."

He leaned toward her and took her hands in his. Andrea wanted to draw away, but couldn't. She looked down at her lap, afraid of what she might see in his eyes.

"Maybe you're reading something into this entire affair that really isn't there." He put his hand under her chin and made her look directly at him.

Andrea saw compassion in his gaze but something else, too, something troubling. She tensed.

"Please don't take this the wrong way." His tone was mild. "Did you, perhaps, have a personal reason for coming up with your germ warfare theory?"

She jerked her hands out of his. "What are you saying, Philip? That I made the whole thing up because I'm some kind of psycho who wants attention? Or maybe so I could make major on the next promotion list?"

"Nothing like that." He sighed deeply. "Sometimes we humans unknowingly flavor information to suit ourselves. If you had a personal reason for wanting to come to this country, perhaps you read much more into those intercepts than was really there."

What was he getting at?

Suddenly, Andrea knew. She felt the blood rush to her face. "You're obviously talking about my husband's accident." She paused as the full implication of his words struck her. "And you're accusing me of making up, or *flavoring* my analysis, as you put it, so that I could come over here and investigate his disappearance."

His eyebrows drew together. "Am I so far off the mark? Would you have volunteered for this assignment if your husband hadn't disappeared here without a trace?"

Andrea didn't trust herself to answer. There was too much truth in what he was saying for her to give him a yes. But a no could be construed as an admission that her analysis was nothing but a lie.

She swallowed hard, lifted her chin and boldly met his gaze. "My husband didn't disappear without a trace," she asserted, dodging the question. "My source said a sadhu saw my husband's party fall into a deep crevasse on the south face of Laigsi."

Philip's luminous brown eyes widened in astonishment.

Having seized the offensive, Andrea hurried on. "What I'd like you to explain is if Tulak, a paid informer, knew about the holy man, why didn't the Air Force investigators find out? Why didn't you? Your predecessor must have briefed you on the investigation. It happened only weeks before you got here." Pausing, she shot him an accusing glance. "And if you knew, why wasn't I told? Was there some kind of cover-up going on? Something somebody didn't want me to know about?"

She heard Philip's quick intake of breath.

"There was no cover-up, believe me, Andrea." A muscle twitched in his jaw, betraying his tenseness.

"Then how do you explain what Tulak told me?"

"What, exactly, did he tell you?"

"That a wandering holy man saw the party fall, and told villagers he stayed with that night. Incidentally, they were the people in Dhara Village, where we were yesterday." She paused to collect her thoughts. "The villagers went to the crevasse, but couldn't spot the bodies because of the curvature of the ice. And the place was too dangerous to try to get down to the victims." A shudder went through her as she repeated the story.

Philip's jaw was clenched, his eyes slightly narrowed. "Your source is either wrong or lying. Nobody saw those people fall. If they had, the investigative team would have known."

There was a knock at the door and a servant entered. He bowed slightly. "Dinner is served in the dining room, Mr. Ambassador."

Philip's irritation at the interruption was evident. But his expression smoothed as he turned toward the waiting servant.

"I think we'll have dinner in here instead of the dining room, Tanka." He glanced at Andrea. "Is that okay with you?"

"Fine," she said shortly. The way she felt now, she'd be lucky to get down a bite of food no matter where it was served.

They didn't speak while Tanka put place settings before them and brought the meal's first course, a spicy chicken soup. Andrea took a couple of swallows and put down her spoon.

Philip raised a bushy eyebrow. "My cook will get his feelings hurt if you don't eat more than that."

"I'm not very hungry." She threw him an accusing glance. "How is it possible that Tulak would know about the sadhu and not have told your investigators?"

"They weren't *my* investigators," he corrected. "They were assigned by the Air Force, not by the State Department."

He swallowed another spoonful of soup, then put his spoon down. "As for Tulak helping the investigators, I doubt they talked to him. He's a source for you spooks in the spy business. An investigating team would never be given his name."

Picking up her spoon, Andrea took another swallow of soup. What he said made sense. Sources' identities were closely held. "Even if you're right, it seems as though someone on the team would have heard something."

"Not necessarily," Philip returned. "The villagers probably said nothing to Tisaran government officials working with the investigating team. The locals don't trust them."

Andrea sighed. "I know. Too many government and military people have their hands in the peasants' pockets."

Watching her intently, Philip's eyes narrowed. "We'll find out about the sadhu," he promised. "I'll send Mohan to the village tomorrow to ask around. If there are stories about a holy man who saw the accident, he'll dig them out."

Tanka served the main course, a Tibetan goulash made with roast pork and noodles. Andrea's stomach did a flip-flop at her first bite. What was wrong with her tonight? Was she queasy because she was, at last, going to find out the truth about Jeffry's accident? Or was it because she hadn't been completely honest with Philip about her reasons for coming to Tisara?

Through narrowed eyes, Philip watched Andrea put down her fork and take a small sip of her Perrier. She'd barely touched her dinner.

He swung his stool around, half facing her. "Do you feel okay? You've been here a week now, so you're overdue for the Revenge of the Yeti." he smiled at her questioningly. "That's embassy slang for a nasty stomach disorder that puts most newcomers in bed for a couple of days."

A small smile touched her lips. "I wish it were that simple."

He searched her face, trying to discern her meaning. "If you're upset about your husband's accident, there was no cover-up, believe me."

"That's not it." Andrea's words were clipped. "What's bothering me is that you think I shaded my analysis to suit my own ends." She turned toward him and crossed her legs. Though they were draped in a heavy cloth skirt, her position made him uncomfortably aware of her nearness.

"I didn't say you did it purposely." He kept his voice low and his tone apologetic. "Sometimes when we want something badly, our judgment gets clouded, and we see things that aren't there."

"That didn't happen." She spoke with quiet but desperate firmness.

He sensed uncertainty in her voice—and pain. His heart went out to her over the anguish she'd feel if she had unwittingly misled everyone from the President on down.

He cleared his throat. "The important thing is that you analyzed and reported the facts as you saw them."

She was silent, her face clouded with doubt. Philip seized the moment to get her talking about her husband. "You were the Pentagon's Tisaran desk analyst before you met Captain Jeffry Mitchell?"

Her nod confirmed what Philip had already surmised.

"And it was just a coincidence that he was killed in an accident here in Tisara, where you're the expert?"

Her troubled expression told Philip he was hitting some sore spots. He didn't like to bring back painful memories. But this was the only way to find out if he'd been right about her reasons for volunteering to come here.

"No, it wasn't a coincidence," she replied. "We met when I briefed him. Pentagon intelligence analysts brief military people who are assigned to our areas of expertise. Jeffry flew a scheduled run from Washington to Delhi, Ganthaku and Bangkok. I briefed him and so did the Indian and Southeast Asian experts."

That, too, confirmed what Philip had suspected.

"Had you been married long?" Philip knew he was treading on tender ground, but he had to ask the question. Suddenly, he wanted to know all about her marriage and how she'd felt about it.

"Less than a year."

She turned away, but not before Philip glimpsed the tears glistening in her eyes. He had an uncontrollable urge to comfort her. Standing, he pulled her to her feet and gathered her into his arms. Gently, he rocked her back and forth.

"I shouldn't be crying after all this time." Her voice, next to his ear, sounded choked. The warmth of her breath on his cheek stoked the fire already burning inside him.

He smoothed her pale blond hair. How silky it felt beneath his palm. "I know, I know. Air Force captains don't cry." Philip was surprised at how husky his own voice sounded.

"At least not in front of ambassadors." She sniffled, and he reached into his pocket for a handkerchief. Taking it from him, she dabbed at her eyes and nose. Then she pulled away.

Philip was conscious of where her warm flesh had pressed against him. He couldn't let her go. Quickly, he swung her back into the circle of his arms.

A flash of confused awareness crossed her face. Then she locked herself in his embrace, her trembling arms clinging to his neck. Philip's mouth covered hers with savage intensity, demanding a response.

Andrea tasted his lips, felt them moving over hers. The kiss was urgent and exploratory. The touch of his mouth, the pressure of his body against her, awakened passions she thought she'd never feel again. She was shocked at her own eager response. Jeffry had never kissed her like this.

Jeffry.

In God's name, what was she doing? Until she uncovered the truth about Jeffry's disappearance, she was a married woman.

Arching her body, she pushed herself free of Philip's embrace. "We can't do this, Philip. It isn't right." Her voice sounded thin and reedy to her, as though she were gasping for breath.

He stepped forward, but didn't touch her. "Why not?" He sounded as breathless as she.

"Because I'm still married."

She heard his quick intake of breath.

"You've got to be kidding." He was staring at her as though she'd suddenly gone mad.

"I feel Jeffry's alive somewhere." Her voice trembled so badly, she wasn't certain Philip could understand her, but her eyes met his steadily. "That he's being held prisoner in some awful place."

His eyebrows shot up in surprise. "Whatever gave you that notion?"

"I'd always suspected he was alive. When the investigation team could turn up no evidence of the accident, I was pretty well convinced."

She let him take her arm and lead her back to the bar. They sat down facing each other.

"But you weren't positive?"

"No. Philip, I had to find out for my peace of mind. I couldn't let him rot in some prison if there was something I could do." Andrea said the words hesitantly, hoping desperately that he'd understand.

"You volunteered for this assignment so you could come to Tisara and conduct your own special investigation." Philip's voice was tender, almost a murmur. "That's the real reason you came."

"But I didn't make up my germ warfare analysis to get over here," she insisted defensively. "The notion of replacing Colonel Butler with an undercover attaché didn't even occur to anybody until after he was declared *persona non grata*." Andrea paused. "And that was two months after I wrote my first bio warfare item." She was unable to keep the note of triumph from her voice.

He offered her a conciliatory smile. "As I recall, the good colonel was following up on one of your inquiries when he was caught."

"Then you don't think I flavored my analysis?" She watched him closely to catch any negative reaction.

"Not intentionally. Absolutely not."

She felt a surge of relief.

"And you have my utmost respect for what you're doing for Jeffry Mitchell," Philip went on. "Sweet Mother in heaven, any man would be lucky to have such a wife."

Andrea was surprised at how pleased she was by his words. When she heard them, a thousand pounds rolled off her back. Glancing at her plate of cold goulash, she felt the stirring of her normally healthy appetite.

She looked at Philip and smiled. "Do you suppose Tanka could heat up my dinner?"

Philip gave her a smile that set her pulse racing.

"If we ask him nicely, I'll bet he'll give us hot food on clean plates."

There was a buzzer behind the bar to call the residence steward. As Philip went to push it, his stomach tightened. Andrea would never be truly free until she found out what had happened to her husband. Philip promised himself that she *would* find out, and soon. *He* would see to that.

AFTER THEY'D each eaten two helpings of goulash, Tanka served the last course, *sikarni,* a whipped yogurt dessert. Taking her first bite, Andrea found it spicy but with a subtle sweetness.

"Let's not dismiss your germ warfare theory just yet," Philip said thoughtfully. "The briefing you gave me Friday was pretty convincing."

"The more I investigate, the more I think I was off on the wrong foot. Finding out Dass Verma was a fertilizer—well, that was the last straw."

Resting one elbow on the bar, Philip leaned toward her.

A shiver of awareness rippled through her, but she told herself to ignore it.

"Maybe you weren't as far off as you think." He paused, his jaw tense.

Andrea couldn't tear her eyes from his face.

"Dass Verma may be the name of a fertilizer," he went on, "but it could also be the name of a man, as you thought."

"I know." With an effort, she forced herself to concentrate on what he'd said. "That's what threw me off. I thought the references in the intercepts were to a person."

The lines of concentration deepened along his eyebrows. "Maybe you were right when you said it was a code name for an individual. What better cover than the name of a product?"

"Especially if the product is used around the area where the individual has his headquarters." Andrea felt her cheeks flush with excitement. If Philip agreed with her assessment, maybe she hadn't been so far off after all.

"What can we do to find out?" she asked.

He thought for a moment. "Learn more about that fertilizer—who makes it, what's in it, what kinds of vegetation it's used for."

Andrea chuckled, remembering the waiter's preposterous tale.

"Hey, what's so funny?" Philip asked, enjoying the way her eyes lit up when she laughed.

She shrugged, feeling foolish. "It's such a silly story, I hate to repeat it."

He nodded encouragingly. "If we're going to get to the bottom of this, we have to share information, even if we think it's silly."

"All right, then." Andrea concentrated on the warmth in his brown eyes. "The waiter who told me the name of the flowers the fertilizer's used on said they were 'good for hair.' That's the same expression Mohan used last Sunday."

Philip's eyebrows lifted. "So that's why you asked him about using the plants for hair."

She nodded. "Since the leaves are mashed and chewed like betel nut, I figured they might have a similar narcotic effect."

Philip shook his head. "I don't think so. But maybe the plant's used as a hair restorer." He whistled softly. "Do you know what a product like that would be worth if it's effective?"

She examined his face, excited by his reaction. When he was enthusiastic, he radiated vitality.

"Billions, Andrea, billions. Ninety percent of the bald men in the Western world would give a year's pay to get a healthy head of hair." He leaned toward her, his voice animated. "That clinches it. Tomorrow, I'll get the embassy economic people working on a detailed report about that fertilizer."

Andrea tried to throttle the current of awareness racing through her. "I've already asked Tulak to run down some basic information. Mainly who manufactures it and what it's made of. The information's probably written right on the sack."

"Call him on the way home and tell him you want the report tomorrow night," Philip said, "along with anything interesting he can find out about the stuff. We'll compare notes and see if a paid informer comes up with the same information embassy staffers do."

"That's a good way to test Tulak." Andrea finished her yogurt and took a last sip of her coffee. "I think he embellishes the truth to make what he says sound more impressive."

Philip nodded grimly. "That's a sure way to get more dollars from Uncle Sam." He reached out and took her hands. Andrea let herself enjoy the feel of his flesh touching hers. Instinctively, she knew he would never overstep the boundaries she'd set. So what was the harm in letting him hold her hands for a few brief moments?

"I'll call you into my office tomorrow afternoon, and we'll decide where to go from there."

A faintly eager look flashed in his eyes, and Andrea wondered what he was thinking. Gently, he pulled her to her feet. "By then we should have Mohan's report, too, so we'll know what the sadhu told those villagers."

At the residence door, he didn't try to kiss her good-night. Andrea got into the waiting car with the feel of his hands still burning hers, his musky male smell still fresh in her nostrils.

TELLING MOHAN to wait in the car, Andrea hurried inside the now-familiar lobby of the Everest Hotel. She dialed Tulak's number and asked for him. There was a long silence. In the background, Andrea heard an odd snuffling sound, as though someone was weeping.

"Hello?" she repeated. "This is Madam Nadja calling for Tulak. It's urgent that I talk to him and arrange a meeting."

"Tulak not here." The woman's voice was strangely muffled.

Andrea shifted impatiently from one foot to the other. He'd always been there when she'd called him before.

"When should I call back? Or can you take a message? I need some information by tomorrow night."

"Tulak gone forever," the woman replied.

Andrea couldn't believe her ears. "What do you mean by 'forever'? Has he left the country?"

"No. Tulak dead."

"Dead?" A tiny frisson of fear raced down Andrea's spine. "He can't be. I just saw him a few hours ago." Her breath seemed to have solidified in her throat. Had someone found out Tulak was a paid informer for the U.S. Government? Is that why he was dead? And if so, did whoever killed him know about Andrea?

"Was terrible accident." The words were so blurred, Andrea could barely make them out. "Don't call again, Madam Nadja."

She hung up before Andrea could ask the questions trembling on the tip of her tongue. The woman had said there was an accident. What kind? Was it really an accident? Maybe another source could give her some answers.

Nolting had told her the informers did not know one another and were unaware of one anothers' existences. Identifying herself by a different name from the one she'd used with Tulak, Andrea arranged to meet her other source at noon tomorrow at a jewelry shop in the Thamal District. She'd ask him to find out details about Tulak's accident.

Next, she called the emergency number Nolting had given her in Washington, D.C. The overseas lines were tied up for nearly an hour, but finally she got through. Using her agreed-upon code number and identifying Tulak only as her first contact, she reported his death and asked that his real name and occupation be sent to her tomorrow.

Trembling under the strain, Andrea lifted her hand to dial Philip at the residence. She dropped her hand and put down the receiver before she dialed the first number. Using this insecure telephone was like broadcasting her news to the world. Even though she'd used only code names and numbers in the other two calls, the mere fact that she was now calling the residence would tell an eavesdropper she was connected to the U.S. Embassy. Her talk with Philip would have to wait until tomorrow morning.

For a long moment, she stood motionless before the telephone, her breath coming in shallow, quick gasps. She remembered Tulak's erect posture, the confident way he'd guided her through the temple compound's labyrinthine stone corridors. Had he died because he was helping her?

Chapter Eight

On Tuesday, Philip was out of the office when Andrea got there a few minutes before nine. Jan, who hadn't waited at the house for her this morning, was already at her desk when Andrea walked in.

"The ambassador is in a special meeting with Interior Minister Nakarmi," Jan announced smugly, flaunting her superior knowledge. "He won't be in until later."

Andrea spent the next couple of hours on the edge of her chair, nervously awaiting his return. Not being able to tell him the shocking news about Tulak left her with an odd empty feeling.

A Sparrow message from Tom Nolting came in at about ten-thirty. In response to her call last night, it contained Tulak's real name and occupation: taxi driver. Andrea's flesh quivered when she read the last paragraph:

NO MATTER HOW ACCIDENTAL TULAK'S DEATH SEEMS, IT WAS PROBABLY NO ACCIDENT. ASSUME HE WAS KILLED TO KEEP HIM FROM REVEALING SOMETHING. ALSO ASSUME WHOEVER KILLED HIM KNOWS WHO YOU ARE AND THAT TULAK WAS PROVIDING INFORMATION FOR YOU.

Andrea memorized Tulak's real name and then thrust the message into the shredder.

At noon, she met her second source, as arranged, inside the jewelry store. A paunchy young Tisaran in a Nehru jacket and form-fitting pants, he was as unlike Tulak as salt from pepper. Whereas Tulak had pretended to be a guide, this man played the role of jewelry salesclerk. At least Andrea thought he was playing a role, until she observed how the other clerks deferred to him. He appeared to be the store's real owner, or perhaps the son of the owner.

"Our shop has fine star sapphires from Bangkok," he informed her, playing his part. "Like this one on my left pinkie. And diamonds from the African mines. And topaz from China. All at bargain prices. If madam is interested..."

"Yes, very." Andrea let him seat her on a tall stool at a glass-topped counter filled with glittering precious stones.

"Would madam like a beverage?" He opened the wooden door on a cabinet behind him to reveal assorted liquors and soft drinks. Beside the cabinet was a small refrigerator.

"A diet cola would be nice."

Obligingly, he opened a can and splashed its contents over ice cubes in a lead crystal glass. Then, rolling up the cuffs of his jacket, he sat down behind the glass counter.

"Now we get down to business," he declared, smiling.

While showing Andrea some of the most beautiful gems she'd ever seen, the young clerk answered her questions about Tulak's accident. He'd already heard about it.

"Very tragic." He shook his head. "The taxi driver failed to make a curve on Lazimpat Road. His car dropped about fifty feet to the terrace below."

"Did he have a passenger?" Andrea tried on one of the topaz rings he showed her, a beautifully cut square stone.

"No passengers and no witnesses to the accident." The clerk lifted an eyebrow. "Strange, is it not, that in an area occupied by so many people, no one was at the scene."

"Strange indeed," Andrea murmured.

After leaving instructions for the clerk to find out all he could about the man she knew as Tulak, she arranged to meet him at the jewelry store next week. He would need at least that long, he insisted, to get her the information she wanted.

She went back to the Sunny Garden Restaurant for lunch and asked for the same waiter she'd had before. This time he greeted her with a welcoming smile.

A big tip makes friends quickly, she thought, remembering the young man's stoic expression last Sunday.

While he was taking her order, she pulled her sketch pad out of her bag and again showed him the pictures she'd drawn of the temple flowers.

"When I was here last Sunday, you said mussenda was good for hair," she reminded him. "How is it good?"

He smiled with understanding. "Makes hair grow."

So Philip was right. The plant called mussenda had hair restoration properties—at least that's what the people around here thought. She beamed at the waiter. "How does it work? Do you chew the flowers, like betel nut?"

He giggled. "No, madam. We *eat* flower. Make some people very sick, but also make hair grow."

A sense of impending disaster swept over Andrea. Is this what her horrendous germ warfare plot boiled down to? A Tisaran attempt to develop a hair restoration product that made hair grow without causing illness? Is that why the plants were being cultivated on the remote terrace? Why experiments were being conducted on them in the greenhouse at Ishwaranath? If so, she'd steered official Washington in the wrong direction. When that happened, somebody always paid.

Two hours later, in Philip's office, Andrea told him what the waiter had said. She figured she'd start with the flowers and brief him on Tulak's death afterward.

He leaned across his desk toward her. "There's something about all this with the fertilizer and those nasty-smelling plants that doesn't add up."

For appearance' sake, Andrea had her notebook open, her pencil in hand.

"That fat little priest we met Sunday was supposed to be in charge of the temple garden," he went on, "but he said he'd never heard of Dass Verma. Given what we now know—that it's a known fertilizer—he had to be lying."

"You're right." Andrea's gaze was riveted on his face. "Why would he lie about such a simple thing?"

"Maybe it's not as simple as we think. He might have answered quickly, hoping to hide something." Philip picked up a sheet of paper on his desk and handed it to her. She didn't miss the way his fingers caressed hers when they touched. "With his usual efficiency, my economic officer has come up with the report I asked him for last night on Dass Verma Fertilizer."

Apparently, Philip had called the economic officer at home last night after Andrea left. Impressed that he'd become so involved in her operation, she scanned the page quickly. The fertilizer's main ingredient was elephant dung.

"Note that it's made by a pharmaceutical company in Delhi," Philip pointed out. "The company makes a complete line of drugs, from cosmetic items like the hair restorer to lifesaving medicines."

He paused. "It's the perfect cover for a germ warfare operation." His voice held a rasp of excitement.

Andrea couldn't help smiling fondly at him. "You're the most perverse man I've ever met. First, you did everything you could to torpedo my analysis. And now that I've about convinced myself I was wrong, you're ready to hop on board."

The warmth of his laugh sent shivers down her spine. "Your briefing was too persuasive to dismiss out of hand."

Andrea handed the fertilizer report back to him.

He laid it on his desk. "It'll be interesting to see what your man Tulak comes up with. Were you able to reach him last night?"

She hesitated and looked down at her hands. They were clenched tightly in her lap. She glanced up to find Philip staring at her, his dark eyes expectant.

"He was killed in an automobile accident." She struggled to keep the shakiness out of her voice. "Not too long after he left me."

"My God!" he muttered, his face strained. "Somebody found out he was an informer."

"That's what my controller thinks."

"You've already notified him?" The worry lines on Philip's face deepened.

She nodded.

"Good. Then he must realize it's important to get you out of here ASAP. Whoever killed Tulak probably knows he was spying for you."

"That's what Nolting thinks." Andrea quoted the Sparrow message she'd received that morning.

"He didn't order you home?" Philip sounded incredulous. His heavy eyebrows drew together in an agonized expression.

"No. He didn't give me the option." She leaned toward him, exhaling with agitation. "Why should he? My job here isn't finished."

"The hell with your job." Philip stood and faced her. With his arms folded across his chest, he was the picture of the protective male. "Andrea, you've got to leave Tisara."

She didn't rise when he did. "I'll leave when I've done what I came to do." Carefully, she hid her fear at Tulak's death by maintaining her even, conciliatory tone. "Now sit down and think up a good reason for me to take a trip to Delhi."

"Delhi!" Surprisingly, Philip did as she asked, and sat back down behind his desk. "Why Delhi?"

"Because the pharmaceutical company that makes Dass Verma Fertilizer is there. I'll need to leave in the next couple of days." She watched him closely.

His lips drew together in a firm line. "There's no way I'll authorize a trip for you to Delhi."

She sighed softly. "We've been over this before. If you make things difficult for me, the trip will just end up taking a few days longer. But eventually, I'll get there."

"Damn it all, Andrea. A trip like that's too dangerous."

Suppressing a smile, she eyed his frustrated expression. "With every day that passes, things are getting worse."

"If you go, I'm going, too." He looked as though he expected her to argue with him.

An argument was the furthest thing from Andrea's mind. The thought of spending two or three days alone with Philip alarmed her only because it seemed so alluring.

She flashed him a warm smile. "Good. Coming with you as your secretary is the best cover I could have."

The squawk box buzzed as she rose to go.

"You had a four-o'clock appointment to see Mohan in your office," Jan's voice said. "But I've just checked, and he's not back yet from that errand you sent him on this morning."

Andrea saw the same fear in Philip's eyes that she was feeling. The young chauffeur had gone to the terrace to question the villagers about the wandering holy man, the sadhu who allegedly saw a climbing accident through binoculars. Tulak had told Andrea the story only hours before he died.

Her heart sank. *Friendly, likable Mohan.* Had he, like Jeffry, disappeared without a trace? Or, like Tulak, had he met with a deadly accident on the road from Ganthaku?

Philip saw the color drain from Andrea's face at the mention of Mohan's absence.

"Let's not overreact," he cautioned. "Mohan was driving an old rattletrap of a car. Maybe it broke down."

She didn't look reassured. "Can't we send somebody out to look for him? He might be in some kind of trouble."

Rising from behind his desk, Philip paced back and forth in front of the big picture window, his arms folded across his chest. "If he's not back in half an hour, I'll have one of the other drivers look for him in my Jeep." He glanced at his watch. "Unfortunately, it'll be dark soon. Between the curves and the pedestrian traffic, the road's not safe to drive at night."

Andrea got up to go. "You'll tell me if you hear anything?"

"Yes." He kept his voice confident, his gaze steady. "I'm sure there's no reason for alarm."

"I hope you're right, but I'm starting to think something odd's going on in Dhara Village. First, an entire trekking party disappears. Then the temple gardener, who lives in the village, lies about a dumb thing like fertilizer." She paused a moment. "When you and I get back from Delhi, I'm going to give the place a good once-over."

He measured her with an indulgent smile. "Do you honestly think those villagers will welcome a secretary from the U.S. Embassy into their homes? Especially if you're right, and they're up to something illegal?"

"Of course they will," Andrea assured him. The glow of her answering smile warmed him. "The Tisarans are famous for their hospitality."

In spite of her confidence, Philip didn't like the idea. He tried not to sound patronizing. "Let me know what you come up with so Mohan can go to the village with you. Or maybe I'll go myself."

Her smile vanished as soon as he mentioned Mohan. "Oh, Philip. Do you think something's happened to him?"

Philip smiled, more reassuringly than he felt. "He'll turn up."

She started toward the door.

"Tell Jan to come in with her book," Philip added, as Andrea left his office.

A moment later, his secretary came in and seated herself in the chair beside his desk. He didn't beat around the bush. "Make arrangements for an official visit to Delhi for Andrea and me as soon as possible—day after tomorrow if that's convenient. We'll stay a couple of days and are particularly interested in..."

He was watching Jan intently as he spoke. When she glanced at him, obviously startled, he stopped in midsentence.

"Do you have a question, Jan?"

A blush rose from her throat. "Maybe I'm out of line in saying this, Mr. Ambassador, but *I've* gone with you on your other trips."

He nodded, anxious to put Jan's suspicions to rest. "Exactly. Since you've accompanied me on the others, this is a good trip for Andrea's indoctrination."

"Yes, sir," she replied, a little curtly, Philip thought.

His squawk box buzzed. He pressed a button. "Yes, Andrea."

"Mohan's back." Philip heard the relief in her voice. "He's in the garage. Do you want him in your office?"

Philip noticed the interested expression on Jan's face. "No," he answered, unwilling to give his secretary the impression that Mohan had been on a mission of great importance.

"He'll be driving me home in an hour or so. We can talk then." He turned the intercom off.

When he began dictating details about his coming trip to Delhi, Philip sensed Jan was acutely interested in every word he said.

JAN O'NEAL SMELLED trouble. When she got back to her desk, she sat in front of her typewriter, thinking.

Ever since Andrea Mitchell had arrived in Tisara, there'd been suspicious goings-on. From the start, Jan had suspected Andrea was different somehow. Just how different became apparent the night Marine Corporal Billy Stoakes watched her make two phone calls from the Everest Hotel.

Why hadn't she made the calls from the office? Or from the house? She must have worried about being overheard, or having the calls appear on an official register.

When Billy suggested Andrea might be involved in something underhanded, though, Jan had pooh-poohed the notion. She remembered what she'd told Sam Connelly. "They were personal calls she doesn't want anyone to know about, Sam. You can't accuse a person of treason for making a couple of phone calls."

A few days later, Andrea had actually been arrested by the Tisaran authorities for trespassing in the temple compound. Jan could hardly believe it. What reason would Andrea have to disobey a direct order if she wasn't spying for someone and selling the information?

Then there were the mysterious excursions into town all by herself in dark, shapeless outfits. Andrea Mitchell was up to something, no doubt about it.

And now, a final and potentially more dangerous ingredient had been added. The ambassador had developed a yen for her. Jan told herself she should have seen that coming when he didn't send Andrea packing after the temple fiasco.

Now that Andrea and the ambassador had worked together for more than a week, the attraction was obvious. Jan had been around the block enough times to recognize only too well the sensuous looks they tried so hard to hide, the way they put their heads together and talked in low tones so nobody else could hear.

Now the ambassador was taking Andrea to Delhi with him when Jan should have been the one to go. On the trip,

Andrea might be able to glean even more secrets from him, secrets she'd sell to an unknown someone.

Pillow talk. Wasn't that what the movies called it? Wasn't that how women traditionally got secrets from gullible men?

Well, Jan wasn't going to let her boss get bamboozled.

She rose from her desk. "Keep an eye on things," she told Andrea in an authoritative tone. "I'll be gone for a half hour or so."

Her high heels clicking on the hardwood floor, she headed for the office of Hugh Boggs, the embassy's political officer. Only a few staffers knew Boggs was also the CIA station chief. Jan didn't want to cause trouble, but something needed to be done and quickly. Hugh Boggs was the man for the job.

When she reached his office, Hugh ushered her inside and shut the door. He eyed her expectantly.

"Now, what can the political officer do for you, lovely lady?" he asked, in his usual jocular manner.

A lanky fair-haired man who always looked slightly hung over, Hugh Boggs had a cynical laugh that intimidated Jan. If there was one thing she couldn't tolerate, it was being laughed at. But the ambassador's projected trip to Delhi with Andrea erased her hesitation. Cautiously, she began her tale of suspected espionage.

To her great relief, Hugh didn't laugh at her suspicions. He didn't even smile. When she got up to leave, he patted her arm reassuringly.

"You were right to come to me about this," he assured her, walking with her to the door. "If we have a problem with Mrs. Mitchell, I'll get to the root of it."

Boggs waited until Jan had left the office and then penned a message to his counterpart in Delhi.

Ambassador Dorough and secretary Andrea Mitchell arrive your station day after tomorrow. Request detailed follow-up report on their schedule.

He sent the message Limited Distribution through a back-door channel used by the CIA station chiefs for private messages. On the way back to his office from the communications center, Boggs smiled quietly to himself.

If Andrea Mitchell was playing footsie with somebody who wanted to buy U.S. secrets, the CIA would find out the details. For the next few weeks, an operative would watch her wherever she went. The next time she met her buyer, Hugh Boggs would spring the trap.

ANDREA DECIDED to risk calling Philip about Mohan from the house. Had the chauffeur found out anything about the sadhu who had supposedly witnessed Jeffry's accident?

She spent the early part of the evening fidgeting while Jan showered and changed clothes for her date with Sam Connelly. For some reason, Jan was unusually pleasant tonight. When she was finally ready, she and Sam spent more than an hour chatting with Andrea over highballs in the living room.

Much as Andrea wanted to shoo them away, she forced herself to play the congenial housemate. At last they left.

Andrea waited another ten minutes. Then, holding her breath, she dialed the residence. When Philip's resonant voice came on the line, she let her breath out slowly and sank back against the sofa cushions.

"This is Andrea, Mr. Ambassador. Should I come in early tomorrow to type up that report you received this afternoon?" She made sure she conveyed the no-nonsense tone of a secretary calling about the next morning's business. Would Philip understand she was referring to what Mohan had told him?

He didn't miss a beat. "No, but thanks for calling, Andrea. You won't have to come in. The man's report was negative."

Andrea's heart sank. So Mohan hadn't found out anything significant. "I'm sorry to hear that, sir."

"I was, too. Very sorry." Across the miles that separated them, Andrea heard the regret in his voice.

"Apparently, there was a big funeral celebration at the site," he went on. "It occupied everybody's attention. We may be able to get a more positive report at a later date."

Andrea longed to say something personal that would let him know she missed him and would like to be with him tonight. Of course, she didn't. "Then, if you don't need me early, I'll see you tomorrow morning at the regular time."

"Fine." His voice sounded gruffer than usual. Was he feeling lonely, too? "Thanks again for calling, Andrea."

After she hung up the phone, Andrea thought about Philip—the way his dark hair glistened under the sparkling chandeliers in his office, his masterful take-charge aura. Much later, after she'd finished a generous helping of the casserole Chandra had left in the oven, Andrea concentrated on what Philip had told her.

The villagers had been occupied because of a big funeral celebration. That's why Mohan hadn't been able to find out more about the wandering holy man.

A big funeral celebration. In her mind Andrea pictured the spiral of white smoke she'd seen rising over the river last Sunday. Had it been from a cremation fire like the ones at Ishwaranath? Now, only two days later, Mohan reported the villagers were celebrating another funeral. That seemed unusual for a small village. How many funerals did they hold in a week? In a month?

There was a way to find out. From experience, Andrea knew that pictures taken by reconnaisance satellites were so accurate that the makes of individual automobiles could be determined by a skilled imagery analyst—the tech-age name for a photo interpreter. Smoke would be easier to spot than any object on the ground.

The next morning, she sent a Sparrow message to Washington requesting an analysis of satellite photography over that area for the past six months. She specifically asked for sightings of smoke near the river and of animals that might be used in germ warfare testing.

Andrea was astounded when she received a reply only hours later. Her controller, Tom Nolting, must have put ten analysts to work to get the information to her so soon. Since she couldn't take the message out of the comm center, she memorized it and hurried to tell Philip. He was in his office with the door ajar.

Ignoring Jan's curious glance, Andrea buzzed him on the intercom from her desk. "Mr. Ambassador, I've just read a report you should know about."

"Come on in, Andrea." His voice rang with welcome.

Across from her, Jan lifted an eyebrow and smiled.

An unwelcome flush colored Andrea's cheeks. Much as she wanted to deny it, she *was* looking forward to talking with Philip in his office. Was her anticipation so obvious that Jan O'Neal could spot it clear across the room?

Philip stood up when Andrea entered his office. Her appreciative eye traveled from his craggy face to his brown business suit and yellow tie.

Moving from behind his desk, he closed the door and led her to the brocaded couch.

"So what's this about a new report?" he began, sitting down next to her.

It seemed the most natural thing in the world to have him so near she could smell his fresh clean scent, to feel his thigh barely touching hers.

"Last night you said something about a funeral celebration." Without thinking, she moved a tiny bit closer.

He leaned toward her, his eyes warm. "When I talked to Mohan last night, he said he thought the funeral was the main reason the villagers wouldn't say much to him."

"If there was a religious function, I'm sure a priest was there," Andrea observed thoughtfully. "If the priest was our friendly temple gardener, he must have recognized Mohan. Maybe that's why the villagers wouldn't talk."

"The priest was there all right." Philip's eyes narrowed. "Mohan saw him." He turned to face her and slid his arm along the back of the couch behind her.

Intensely aware of his movements, Andrea felt a warm melting glow. She cleared her throat. "Getting back to the funeral celebration—" She heard her voice tremble and took a deep breath. "We saw smoke when we went over there last Sunday. Last night I wondered how many cremations these villagers have every week or month." She paused dramatically.

His smile warmed her heart. "Don't tell me Washington provided the answer?"

She nodded. "In a way. I asked Nolting to find out how often spirals of white smoke appeared near the river in pictures taken by reconnaissance satellites. During the time period of his report, the satellite passed over the area ten times a week at various hours of the day and night. Smoke like I described was spotted on the photography twenty-seven percent of the time."

He stared at her with an incredulous expression. "That small settlement can't possibly have that many deaths. There must be some other explanation for the smoke."

"Smoke was visible in almost every frame," she admitted. "But the low-lying smoke from the village was visibly different from the spiral of white smoke along the river. The analysts thought the low-lying stuff was probably cooking or heating smoke."

Andrea narrowed her eyes. "Another interesting thing."

Philip watched her intently.

"The low-lying cooking or heating smoke was concentrated over the huts at the eastern side of the settlement. The buildings on the western side had very little."

Taking his arm from the cushion behind Andrea, Philip leaned toward her. "Then people aren't living in those buildings." His eyes blazed. "Something else is going on there."

Andrea heard the excitement in his voice.

"Maybe that's where they're developing the hair restorer," she suggested.

He shook his head. "I don't think so. The more we investigate, the more I think you were right. They're doing research there, but it's for germ warfare, not hair restoration." He threw her a quizzical look. "As for your spiral of white smoke, maybe that's how they get rid of the test animals."

She stared at him wide-eyed. "There aren't any test animals."

"Maybe they keep them hidden away somewhere."

"Where a satellite camera couldn't see them?" She didn't hide her skepticism.

He thought for a minute. "In caves maybe. Or maybe they've got an aerosol dissemination test chamber underground." He frowned. "The test animals might be tethered inside the chamber or penned up in some of those buildings. The outside testing might be done at night—or maybe during the monsoon, when cloud cover would block satellite photography."

Andrea shook her head. "It won't wash. The last rites are sacred religious ceremonies. These people would never cremate animals the same way they do humans."

"They're dirt-poor. They'll do what they must to survive." He paused. "Besides, the animal cremations would be nothing but a cover. They wouldn't be actual funerals, just a way to get rid of the infected animals' carcasses."

Andrea shook her head again, more strongly. "In a poor country like this, the infected animals would never be burned. Their carcasses would be put to some useful purpose."

Before Philip could respond, his intercom buzzed. He strode to his desk.

"Delhi's on the line, Mr. Ambassador." It was Jan's voice.

Andrea stood up. Philip paused, hand on the phone.

His eyes met hers and his smile flashed briefly, dazzling against his tanned skin. "Mohan will pick you up at seven o'clock tomorrow morning."

He lifted the receiver. "Ambassador Dorough."

Unexpectedly, Andrea's knees turned weak. Trying to ignore the strange reaction, she somehow made it to the door.

This rich, powerful man is off-limits, she reminded herself again. *Don't be a fool and fall in love with him.*

Chapter Nine

The next morning passed in a blur of excitement. From the moment Philip picked Andrea up in his car at seven, she knew this day was going to be one-of-a-kind. She'd expected to meet him at the airport and was astounded to find him in the back seat when Mohan arrived with the car. From that minute, she was all too aware of his commanding presence beside her.

He'd taken care of all their arrangements, she quickly discovered. From baggage transfers, to their first-class seats on the Air India 727, to their adjoining rooms at Delhi's five-star Taj Mahal Hotel, everything bore his stamp of approval.

During the flight, he seemed more relaxed than Andrea had seen him—almost as though he were off on a holiday. Seated next to him on the aircraft, Andrea felt their closeness like a drug, dulling her self-protective instincts.

"So how does a rich kid from Santa Barbara make good in the rough-and-tumble world of American politics?" she asked lightly, hoping to entice him into a conversation about himself.

He gave her an indulgent smile. "He picks a candidate he believes in and works like hell to get said candidate elected."

Andrea leaned toward him to hear better over the roar of the engines. The touch of his shoulder sent a warming shiver through her. She told herself to ignore it.

"Maybe I shouldn't ask this," she began slowly. "But when the candidate's elected, do you expect special favors?"

His face went grim. "You mean like this ambassadorial appointment?"

Andrea was already sorry she'd asked the question. But unwilling to back down, she forged ahead. "Yes, I suppose this appointment would be a good example."

His eyes caught and held hers. "No, I didn't expect this appointment. I almost didn't take it. If I hadn't thought I could accomplish something positive in this part of the world, I would have turned it down."

Philip wasn't sounding at all like the scheming politician she'd pictured when she'd read his bio in Tom Nolting's office.

"Have you done what you set out to do here?" she asked softly.

He nodded. "I usually get what I go after." The melancholy frown that crossed his face didn't match his words.

Suddenly, Andrea realized why he looked so downcast. She sighed. "I've screwed things up for you by coming here, haven't I?"

His eyebrows rose with surprise. "Why do you say that?"

"Because I've threatened your plans for Tisara with my snooping."

He seized her hand and held it between both of his. "So far nothing has threatened my plans for U.S. support for Tisara—certainly not you. I'm sorry if I was frowning."

She caught her breath. "Why *were* you frowning?"

He sighed, deep within himself. "Because, for the past few years, nothing seems to satisfy me the way it used to. These days, everything I achieve seems unimportant."

Andrea put her other hand on top of his and squeezed. Hard. She was startled by the tender look on his face when he felt her touch. During the rest of the flight, they talked about his boyhood days in private schools, his summers at the family compound at Lake Tahoe.

But, in the back of her mind, Andrea couldn't stop thinking about Philip's dilemma. He'd lost the sense of pleasure most people feel in attaining their material goals. Did that make him a cynic or a saint?

THE EMBASSY'S economic officer, Scott White, met Andrea and Philip at Delhi's crowded airport. Thanks to Philip's diplomatic position—and the correlative danger of a terrorist attack in the airport's public areas, where every seat and almost every inch of floor space were occupied—they were taken to a hot back room for processing.

There, the economic officer guided them through the confusing tangle of Indian bureaucracy, where official after official, with infinite devotion to duty, painstakingly examined every page of their passports. Andrea didn't let their officiousness bother her. The day was too full of promise to spend any part of it fretting.

Finally, after the required forms were filled out, they exited through a side door to the waiting embassy limousine. Parked behind was a smaller black vehicle, the engine running.

Andrea swallowed hard, recognizing the smaller car's purpose. It was a chase vehicle designed to protect them if the limo were attacked. Familiar as she was with the necessary security precautions, the chase car reminded her of the constant threat to Philip's life because he was a U.S. ambassador.

They stopped to freshen up before going on to the embassy. Like the luxury hotels in Ganthaku, the Delhi Taj Mahal was set apart from the ragged multitudes that thronged the city. A long driveway led to the white all-marble lobby. Eyeing the uniformed policeman across from the registration desk, Andrea wondered if he ever had occasion to use the rifle slung over his shoulder.

After she and Philip had registered, they were shown to their rooms. Since she'd worn a calf-length print skirt and matching shirt suitable for work, Andrea didn't need to change. She rinsed her face and repaired her makeup in the big marble bathroom. When she was finished, she knocked on the adjoining door to Philip's room.

"It's open," he called.

Entering, she glanced around but didn't see him. The room was the mirror image of hers, with a king-size bed, dark Oriental-looking furniture and woodwork, thick carpeting and framed prints of palace paintings on the walls.

Philip appeared in the bathroom door, and Andrea's heart gave an unexpected lurch. Stripped to the waist, he'd obviously been shaving. His cheeks were still damp, and she could smell the cream he'd used.

"I'll be ready as soon as I put on my shirt," he said.

Fascinated, her gaze dropped to the crisp mat of hair covering his muscular chest. She lifted her eyes almost instantly, but not before she'd seen the way his body tapered V-like from his shoulders to his waist, the way his chest hair disappeared below his belt.

To her annoyance, Andrea felt her face redden. "I'm sorry. I didn't mean to barge in." She remained motionless, rooted to the floor.

"If I hadn't wanted you to come in, I wouldn't have told you to." He looked her over seductively, his eyes and mouth crinkling at the corners.

For a moment, Andrea felt as if she were floating. She couldn't seem to tear her gaze from his face. Then, aggravated with both herself and him, she whirled around.

"Knock when you're ready," she told him over her shoulder as she fled to her own room. Safely seated on her bed, Andrea felt overheated, out of control somehow.

Why had she agreed to this adjoining room? she wondered. If one glimpse of his bare chest did this to her, how in the world was she going to keep her distance?

AFTER LUNCH with Ambassador Zimmerman, Philip and Andrea left for their scheduled visit to the Prana Pharmaceuticals Company in one of the embassy limousines. Following them were a chase car and a blue Jeep-like police vehicle with a canvas top.

Economic Officer White sat on a jump seat facing them.

"'Prana' means 'breath of life,'" he informed them as the air-conditioned vehicle started down Shanti Path, the broad tree-lined street in front of the embassy. "It's an appropriate name for a company that makes medicine, don't you think?"

An energetic young man with a protruding belly and light brown curly hair, White directed his question to Philip, but Andrea answered. "Prana Pharmaceuticals also makes fertilizer."

Ignoring Andrea's comment, White kept his gaze on Philip's face. "We wondered why you picked that particular company for a visit, Mr. Ambassador." Ever since meeting Andrea and Philip at the airport, he'd focused wholly on Philip.

Maybe he thinks secretaries aren't worth his attention, Andrea thought. She was pleased her cover was working so well, but found White's behavior irritating.

"As Mrs. Mitchell just said," Philip answered, his eyes sharp and assessing, "Prana Pharmaceuticals makes both fertilizer and drugs. It's the only company that does in this part of the world."

Andrea cast Philip an approving glance. His evasive answer would throw White off the track regarding the real purpose for their visit.

They continued down Shanti Path around a couple of traffic circles. Through the window, Andrea could see raggedly dressed men stretched out on the patchy lawns in the circles' centers. An occasional cow wandered among the prostrate forms. A mile or so away loomed the taller buildings of downtown New Delhi. Compared to those in Ganthaku, the twelve-to-fifteen-story structures seemed like skyscrapers.

After more turns, they crossed a bridge over the railroad tracks and headed south on Mathura Marg, a four-lane asphalt highway with dirt frontage roads running parallel on either side. Dust-laden trees hid the buildings beyond.

"Isn't the factory in town?" Andrea asked.

"Just ahead," White answered. "Before we get to the road to Agra."

They turned onto the red dirt frontage road on the left. Through the trees, Andrea saw a complex of four flat-roofed two-story buildings. They were surrounded by an eight-foot-high iron fence with barbed wire around the top. The contrast between the modern-looking plant and the dusty world bordering it was startling.

Outside, the debris-strewn dirt road teemed with humanity. Inside, the area was an immaculate expanse of concrete. The workers Andrea saw moving between the buildings were garbed in white technicians' smocks.

A uniformed guard stood in a small kiosk at the gate. The limousine pulled up next to it.

"Are all pharmaceutical companies fenced like this and guarded?" Andrea asked.

"Some are, some aren't," the economic officer responded, moving his gaze from Philip's face to Andrea's and then back to Philip's. "I suppose it depends partly on the neighborhood and partly on the type of medicines made."

Andrea thanked White and waited for the driver to circle the car and open the door.

Getting out of the air-conditioned limousine was like stepping into a furnace. Though it was only mid-March, the temperature must have been close to ninety degrees. The sun seemed so bright it hurt Andrea's eyes in spite of her dark glasses and the wide-billed golf cap she was wearing.

In the air was an indefinable smell of something burning combined with exhaust fumes, hot dust and spices. And all around her there was noise—of honking horns, of people talking, of birds screeching from the rooftops.

After White said a few words to the guard, he waved them through. Their guide was waiting for them. A skinny little man with horn-rimmed glasses too big for his face, he led the three of them into the nearest building. Inside, they passed a series of administrative offices to a stairway. It led to a second-floor walkway around a huge work area.

From the balcony Andrea could see hundreds of workers, some busily tending distillation vats, some hunched over microscopes, some operating machines. All were dressed in similar-looking white smocks. At points throughout the plant, six-foot-high dividers separated the various functions.

Their guide, who spoke English with a trace of a British accent, described some of the functions in an oily, patronizing voice. Since he was using words like *acetylation* and *halogenation* that Andrea didn't understand, she didn't try to follow the numerous processes. Rather, she concentrated on the look and feel of the place.

The temperature was comfortable. The workers seemed to be going about their tasks with unhurried dedication. Every now and then, she caught a whiff of a pungent odor she recognized: Dass Verma Fertilizer.

Their guide pointed to one of the vats. "A steam distillation process is used to extract the volatile oils such as cod liver and castor." After he'd explained the process, he pointed to another area. "Whereas, insulin—being produced there—requires mincing of the pancreas and the immediate addition of acidified alcohol."

When he said *pancreas,* Andrea's antennae went up. "I thought there was a new process for insulin that didn't require animal organs."

He smiled at her as though she were a child. "That process is still experimental. We make our insulin with absolutely fresh pig or sheep organs."

"Are the animals slaughtered here?" The thought brought back her uneasiness. Maybe the animals were being used for research and then killed. But for what kind of research?

The guide's eyes narrowed, and he pressed his lips together. "Our religion frowns on taking animal life."

He hadn't answered her question. When Andrea met his gaze, he looked away from her, toward Philip. She tensed, knowing the guide was hiding something.

Philip focused on the guide. "Does your religion frown on taking animal life if it means saving human life?" He came closer, until he was standing directly in front of the Indian. "Besides, what difference does it make where the animals are slaughtered? If you're getting fresh organs from them, they're obviously killed somewhere."

The guide hesitated and then appeared to reconsider. "They're killed in a building in the rear. That fact isn't made public, Mr. Ambassador. We'd appreciate your discretion."

"Of course," Philip assured him.

Andrea felt a stab of suspicion. "Will we get a chance to see that building? I'd like to take a look at your laboratory facilities."

Their guide rolled his eyes helplessly. "Oh, my, no. Nobody goes into the rear building but authorized staff with special badges."

He hasn't denied there's a lab in that building, she thought with a quiver of dread. *What else is Prana hiding there?*

She caught Philip's eye and saw the same awareness she was feeling.

"Is your research facility inside?" Philip's voice was matter-of-fact.

The guide shot him a startled glance through his thick glasses.

"I'm interested in how your research facility operates," Philip went on, without waiting for an answer. "How can we get inside today?"

Raising his hands in a gesture of impossibility, the guide took a step backward. "I'm so sorry, Mr. Ambassador. As I just told Mrs. Mitchell, it cannot be done, not even for you."

Philip turned to Economic Officer White. "Who can grant me authority to go inside that building?"

"It may take awhile," White advised slowly, "but the Bureau of Internal Affairs can arrange it, I'm sure." He raised an eyebrow. "It'll mean another trip to Delhi."

Andrea, who was watching Philip's face, saw his eyes light up and wondered if he was thinking of bringing her along. For a brief instant, excitement overcame her uneasiness.

"Get going on it, would you, White," Philip said.

"As soon as I get back to the office," the economic officer promised, nodding.

ANDREA'S UNEASINESS returned as the guide led the way to the stairs down to the first level and then through the center aisle of the vast plant. Something was very wrong here. She could see it in the furtive way the workers looked at her, stealing a glance and then averting their eyes. If something sinister was going on in the research lab, they probably had an idea of what it was—even those workers who weren't permitted access.

Stepping outside, Andrea was acutely conscious of the blazing afternoon heat. Reflected off the concrete walks and driveways surrounding the buildings, it rose in dry, dusty waves.

The compound's buildings were laid out in a diamond pattern, with the first building on-line with the last, and the two middle structures on either side. To Andrea's right was a building similar to the one they'd left, its windows and doors closed. To their left was one about the same size, but its garage-style doors were wide open. The odor of Dass Verma Fertilizer permeated the air.

"How did your company decide on that name for the fertilizer?" she asked the guide, as they entered the building. Dark and dismally hot, it was the most hellish workplace Andrea had ever seen. The acrid smell suffocated her. The workers, loosely clad in baggy pants and ragged soiled shirt, had faces streaked with sweat and the silt that seemed to be everywhere.

"Dass Verma was the name of the company's founder," the guide returned.

"Why didn't he name the company after himself instead of the fertilizer?" The smell was overwhelming. Andrea felt around in her bag for a handkerchief to hold to her nose.

Grinning, the guide watched her. "The company *was* named after him. Last year, Prana bought it, and moved it here."

Last year, Andrea thought in dismay. Why had so many odd things happened during the past year? Jeffry's disappearance. The initial interception of the illicit broadcasting terminal. Smoke appearing near the Bagmati River at Dhara Village. Increased small airplane traffic between Delhi and Ganthaku. The troop buildup around Ganthaku.

And the wall around the temple garden had looked new, she remembered, as though built recently.

Andrea searched for a common thread but could find none. Still, every bone in her body told her something sinister was going on. If not black-market sales of biological warfare weapons, then something equally evil. Did this malodorous fertilizer have anything to do with it?

The guide started walking. "Everything is done here." He waved his hand at the throng of laborers. Like bees around a hive, workers were everywhere—mixing the foul-smelling ingredients, tending pots filled with yellow liquid, shoveling the dried product into plastic sacks. "We manufacture. We package. We ship. Prana Pharmaceuticals is the world's only maker of Dass Verma Fertilizer. Certain flowering plants require it to grow properly."

"Like mussenda?" Andrea daubed at her eyes with her handkerchief. The acrid smell of the fertilizer was incredible. Next to her, both Philip and White had their noses and mouths covered with their pocket handkerchiefs.

The guide eyed her quizzically for a moment. "So you have knowledge of Tisara's beautiful mussenda plants?"

She nodded. "Yes, and I was told this fertilizer is the only one used on them."

"Can we move along?" Philip walked past her toward the open door at the building's far end.

"Let us go back the way we came," the guide suggested. "It's shorter."

Philip shook his head. "No, I'd like to see the whole place."

Silently, Andrea applauded his decision. By going ahead, they'd exit near the research building. The guide had probably been trying to steer them away from it.

Philip's stride lengthened, and Andrea found herself breathing heavily into her handkerchief as she hurried to keep up. Her shirt was dripping with perspiration. Her bare toes, in her open sandals, felt clogged with dirt. In spite of the handkerchief she held in front of her face, there were tiny particles of fertilizer in her nose and throat. A silty layer of the stuff lay on her exposed skin, on her clothes and hair. She'd never felt more gritty and uncomfortable in her life.

She stepped outside, took a deep breath of air and immediately felt better. Hot as it was, nothing could compare to the conditions inside. She wondered how the workers could function in such a place. Removing her handkerchief from her nose, she thrust it into her shirtfront.

Their Indian guide hurried to join them. "Have you seen enough of the fertilizer manufacturing phase of our business, Mr. Ambassador?"

Though the guide wasn't smiling, Andrea sensed that he'd enjoyed their discomfort.

Philip nodded. "I've seen enough for now. Maybe when I come back, I'll take a closer look."

Moving to Philip's side, Andrea studied the last structure in the compound, the one they weren't allowed to visit. Obviously, it was air-conditioned, since the doors and windows were closed. Although it appeared similar to the other two air-conditioned buildings, there was something different about it.

She surveyed the one adjoining the fertilizer plant and realized what the difference was. The end building had bigger bars on its windows. They appeared sturdier than those on the others.

"That building looks like a jail," she told Philip, inclining her head toward it.

Before he could answer, the guide piped up. "The reinforced bars are to keep people out, not in." His reply was as glib as a used car salesman's. "An area inside that building is used to store narcotics."

Obviously interested, Philip turned toward him. "You keep animals in the same place with narcotics?"

The guide squinted at Philip through his big lenses. "It's a large building, Mr. Ambassador. The animals and the narcotics are not together. Not by any means."

Philip grunted as though unconvinced. He began walking and Andrea fell into step beside him.

When they turned the corner to pass between the two middle buildings, the dull roar of sound around them—the traffic noise from the highway, the raucous screeching of the birds, the purring of the air conditioners—turned strangely silent. For a brief instant, they passed through a place— possibly caused by the convergence of the buildings—where sound stood still. In that brief instant, Andrea heard a muffled cry of anguish so poignant she stopped dead in her tracks.

"What was that?" Holding her breath, she turned her head, listening for the cry to come again.

Behind them, the guide and White also stopped walking.

"I didn't hear anything," White said.

"I did," Philip responded. "It sounded like someone calling for help."

"Perhaps it was a pig squealing, Mr. Ambassador," the guide suggested. "I happen to know there are pigs inside right now."

They waited a long minute, listening. Nothing.

Philip didn't look convinced, but he swung around and resumed his steady pace toward the front of the compound. As they moved beyond the center buildings, routine noise enveloped Andrea. She didn't hear the strange cry again.

THEIR INDIAN GUIDE accompanied them to the compound gate. Standing in the tiny pool of shade provided by the guard's kiosk, Andrea surveyed the area around her. Maybe she'd been spooked by the odd sound she'd heard, but the commonplace scene didn't look right to her.

Always trust your instincts, her instructors had said at the school. Then they'd backed up their warning with repetitive training designed to sharpen the students' instincts. Right now, Andrea's instincts told her something was wrong.

Do the passersby on the dirt road look uneasy or suspicious? No, she thought after glancing around. Most of the pedestrians were poorly dressed, carrying bundles or baskets on their heads. But none looked threatening.

Cars, trucks and buses inched along the crowded four lane highway that paralleled the dirt frontage road. Exhaust smoke filled the air. In the closest lane, a tour bus inched its way along Mathura Marg, one of the main roads leading out of the city.

Is the Delhi police vehicle in position? Yes. She spotted it a couple of car lengths back. But the two officers were leaning against the vehicle smoking and talking. *They're not watching the embassy cars,* she observed warily. But that wasn't what was raising the hackles on the back of her neck.

About one hundred yards beyond the police car was another vehicle that looked official, but she couldn't see inside. Nearly two blocks away, it was hardly a threat. She doubted its occupants could see her and Philip—or the limousine and chase car—clearly.

When Philip started toward the waiting limousine, she put a restraining hand on his arm. Startled, his gaze met hers.

"Not yet," she warned softly.

Not noticing the exchange, Economic Officer White headed for the limousine.

"Wait," Andrea called after him, her voice urgent.

Either he didn't hear or chose to ignore her.

Nervously, Andrea scrutinized the limousine and then the chase car parked a short distance behind.

The windows on both vehicles were tightly closed with the engines running. But the rear door of the limousine was slightly ajar. *As though someone were waiting inside.*

That's what was wrong!

"Mr. White." Andrea yelled as loudly as she could. "Come back." He didn't turn.

Philip was looking at her as though she'd gone mad. "What's the matter?"

"Somebody's commandeered the embassy vehicles," Andrea declared tersely. "They're after us." She yanked on his arm. "We've got to get out of here."

He stared at her, complete surprise on his face.

Glancing wildly around the crowded highway, she spotted the tour bus she'd seen before. It was directly across the dirt road from them, inching along the main thoroughfare.

"That tour bus," she gasped. "With the police nearby, nobody will dare try anything once we're aboard it." Yanking his hand, she started across the dirt road.

White had reached the limousine now. The rear door opened and a man reached out and grabbed the economic officer under the arms, yanking him headfirst into the vehicle. The door slammed, and the limousine veered away from the curb, its horn blaring.

Andrea's head raced like an out-of-control engine. What was happening to White? Where were they taking him? Then all thoughts of White vanished. The limousine was coming straight at them.

Chapter Ten

Instantly, Philip realized what was happening. *Terrorists. After a U.S. ambassador.* He gripped Andrea's hand and dived to one side.

Without warning, a crowd of surly young men appeared between them and the tour bus. Only a few yards distant, the embassy limousine bore down on them from the other direction.

Fear and anger knotted Philip's stomach. He tried to jerk his hand from Andrea's, but she held on tightly.

"It's me they want," he shouted. "Let go, and run like hell."

The shabbily dressed crowd closed in. The limousine screeched to a stop. A heavyset man jumped out and ran toward them. He lifted a revolver.

Philip felt a mighty wrath building inside him. If they wanted him alive, they'd have a terrible fight on their hands.

But they weren't going to get Andrea, too.

He jerked his hand free. "Run!" he shouted again.

When he glanced at her, he saw grim determination etched on her face.

"Cover your nose and mouth," she cried, yanking her handkerchief out of her shirtfront.

Dumbly, he felt in his pocket for the cloth he'd used in the fertilizer plant.

A shiny silver object appeared in her hand. She waved it back and forth like a magic wand. He heard a hissing sound, and the air was charged with something that burned his eyeballs.

The mob surged backward, moaning. The man with the weapon doubled over. Philip's eyes and nose watered.

"Come on!" Andrea sprinted toward the tour bus. Seconds later he caught up with her. They reached the bus. Philip pounded on the glass doors.

"Let us in!" he shouted. "They're trying to kill us."

Inside the bus, he saw some movement. He pounded harder.

The bus's doors slid open. A man reached down to grab their hands. "Hurry," he urged. The doors closed behind them and the big vehicle moved sedately away, leaving the horror outside behind.

Philip stood motionless in the aisle, a gamut of emotions surging through him. "What happened back there?" he asked Andrea. "You moved so fast I couldn't keep up."

She lifted the silver pen in her hand. "It sprays a tear gas chemical like Mace, only more potent. Every lady should carry one."

In spite of her teasing words, her voice was trembling. Philip could see she was shaking all over. Tenderly, he drew her into his arms and held her close, while smoothing her silky curls with his hand.

"We're here for each other," he whispered. "It's all over and everything's all right."

She clung to him. "It's not all over, Philip." She pulled back and looked him in the face again. "That man was going to kill us." Her voice still trembled, but not as much. "He's probably still after us."

Looking into her eyes, Philip saw her fear. "Not *us*. *Me*. He wants me, not you." He hugged her tightly. "You saved my life, Andrea. Thank you."

"Thank my training." She spoke softly. "Everything happened so fast, I reacted automatically."

Holding her by the shoulders, he stepped backward. "You're one hell of a useful lady to have around." He stroked her back with his hand.

Her mouth curved into a doubtful little smile. "I am as long as I've got my handy-dandy little pen." She still sounded breathy.

A man cleared his throat.

Suddenly, Philip was aware that they were standing in front of the bus with curious eyes watching them. He surveyed the interior. An Indian man, probably the tour director, was sitting on the front seat by himself. Behind him were a dozen or so people, mostly elderly, who looked European or American. The driver and an assistant, in a large space behind a glass partition, were Indian. A small shrine near the windshield was decorated with marigolds.

Philip held out his hand to the tour director. "I'm Philip Dorough. I want you to know how much we appreciate this Mr.—"

"I'm Ashok, Mr. Dorough." He took Philip's hand and shook it vigorously. "But don't thank me." A distinguished-looking man about Philip's age, he spoke with a Hindi accent. "These nice people urged me to open the doors."

Philip turned to the passengers. Every eye was on him. He put his arm around Andrea's waist and drew her to his side.

"We thank you all very much. If you hadn't helped us, we might have been hurt by that mob."

He turned back to Ashok. "Do you mind if we stay with you until you get to your hotel? We can catch a taxi there."

Ashok beamed at Philip. "Since it's all right with my group, you can stay with us as long as you like. But we're not going to the hotel. We're on our way to Agra to spend the night near the Taj Mahal. Should be there in time for dinner."

Philip frowned. "Then I guess you'll have to let us out here in Delhi, near a hotel where we can get a taxi."

He felt Andrea nudge his arm. Her initial shock seemed to have passed.

"Let's take a quick look around before we decide where to get off." She pulled away and started toward the back of the bus, still holding his hand.

Ashok's eyes widened. "Is somebody after you and your wife?"

Philip didn't deny Andrea was his wife. He wasn't quite sure why. "God only knows." He smiled reassuringly. "Don't worry. We're not involved in anything criminal."

At the back of the bus, Andrea and Philip sat down close to each other, grateful they'd survived and were together. Feeling Andrea's warmth along his side, Philip breathed a silent prayer of thanksgiving.

She twisted around to look out the back window. Watching her face, he saw her frown. He faced the window, but saw nothing unusual in the rapidly thinning traffic behind the bus.

"See that official-looking black car about a block behind?" she asked.

He spotted the vehicle among a jumble of scooters, trucks and black-and-orange taxis. "Is it the chase car coming after us?"

Her frown deepened. "I don't think so. I'm almost positive the chase car was commandeered by the same people who took the limousine."

"So why is that black Ambassador behind us different from the other thousand cars on this road?" The Ambassador was a car manufactured in India.

"It was parked a couple of blocks from Prana Pharmaceuticals while we were inside." She bit her lower lip thoughtfully. "Maybe the embassy sent another chase car without telling you?"

He shook his head. "Zimmerman wouldn't do that."

"Then we're in trouble."

He heard the tension in her voice, saw the fear in her eyes.

She caught his hand. "We'll probably be kidnapped—or gunned down—as soon as we set foot outside this bus."

WHEN THEY REACHED the outskirts of Delhi and the road narrowed to two lanes, Andrea was positive the black Ambassador was following them. Traffic thinned to almost nothing, and the vehicles in their vicinity—mostly brightly painted trucks—were easy to see from the rear window. The few times she lost sight of the Ambassador, it reappeared a short time later, trailing them like a satellite attached to the bus by an invisible thread.

"We can't put everyone on the bus in danger," Philip warned for at least the fifth time since they'd boarded. "Protecting them has got to be our first consideration."

Andrea inclined her head in compliance. "But let's decide what we're going to do before we say anything."

He nodded. "Right. We sure as hell can't simply get off at Agra and expose all these people to target practice by the ba . . . by whoever's tailing us."

Andrea smiled at his small slip. *Bastard* was too nice a word for whoever was following them. Lord, but she wished she knew who it was.

Always assume the worst, she told herself, quoting one of her instructors. "Maybe the safest thing we can do is get off with these people at their hotel." Concentrating, she caught her lower lip in her teeth.

Philip's face took on an accusing expression. "Safest for us maybe. But how about them?"

"Whoever's in that Ambassador probably thinks we'll stay with the group," Andrea explained. "They're quite a way behind and might miss us if we get off sooner. In order to find us, they might threaten the other passengers."

She was gratified when his expression softened. "Besides, they want us," she went on. "If we do what they expect, they'll have no reason to hurt anybody else."

Philip hugged her quickly. A warming glow went through her.

"I'm sorry," he apologized contritely. "I should have known you wouldn't suggest exposing anyone unnecessarily."

"Whoever's after us probably won't try anything as long as we're on this bus." She glanced out the window again and then back at his face. "The problem will come once we get to Agra."

She snuggled a tiny bit closer to him. His nearness brought a familiar ripple of warm awareness. It was wonderful to have him so close, but she couldn't let herself relax.

"The espionage school's solution would be for us to walk into the hotel with the group and then to take evasive action," she said. "By that, I mean to get away from whoever's after us. But in our case, I'm not sure that solution's right."

He searched her face with studied intensity. "So what *is* right?"

Andrea heard the urgency in his voice. She didn't hesitate. "Since you're a U.S. ambassador whose picture's been on TV and in the papers, it's going to be difficult—and dangerous—for us to get around Agra unnoticed. So we can't just disappear."

He nodded. "When I gave Ashok my name, I was afraid he might recognize it."

"I think we should level with the people on this bus," she declared firmly. "Tell them who we are and what's going on."

His craggy face was unreadable. Andrea couldn't tell if he agreed or not.

"Then what?" he asked.

"When we get to the hotel where this group is registered, we should lock ourselves in our rooms, call the embassy in Delhi and let them and the local authorities worry about getting us out of Agra safely."

Andrea saw Philip's tight expression relax and hurried on with her proposal. "This is a civilized country, after all. The police are everywhere, even in the hotel lobbies. I'll bet they'd be happy to escort us wherever we want to go."

He broke into a smile. "I'll talk to Ashok right now."

The narrow, bumpy road to Agra was lined with acacia trees. Outside the tinted windows of the bus, the setting sun cast purple shadows across the verdant fields beyond the trees. Inside, the vehicle's subdued overhead lights came on. The passengers settled back for the rest of the trip.

At Philip's invitation, Ashok followed him to the back. When the tour director was seated, Philip pulled out his passport and handed it to him.

"I'm the U.S. ambassador to Tisara," he said quietly. "The woman with me is Andrea Mitchell, my secretary."

Ashok's eyes widened. "You're an ambassador and this is your secretary?" His voice rang with disbelief. "I thought she was your wife." Leaning forward, he gave Andrea, who was on Philip's other side, a quick glance.

She shook her head. "No. I'm just his secretary on a business trip."

Recalling how Philip had held her when they'd first boarded the bus, she felt the blood race to her face. The tour director probably thought they were having an affair.

Beside her, Philip turned toward Ashok. "We don't want to involve the people in your group any more than necessary, so we didn't try to explain. But we've discussed our situation and feel they should be told."

Ashok nodded. "If you're an ambassador, I understand perfectly. Someone is trying to kidnap or kill you for political reasons."

Philip spent the next few minutes detailing some common-sense precautions the group members could take to protect themselves when they got off the bus at Agra.

Returning to his place in front, Ashok introduced Philip and Andrea over the bus's loudspeaker system and repeated Philip's brief instructions. As he talked, heads turned toward the back. Andrea caught some reassuring nods along with expressions of alarm. But when Ashok asked for comments, most of the group voiced support. After he'd answered a couple of questions, he returned to the back of the bus and made a "V" for victory sign.

"As you heard, our group is behind you one hundred percent, Mr. Ambassador," he announced. "If you want to give final orders when we reach Agra, let me know."

Andrea shook her head. "That's not a good idea. Standing at the front of the lighted bus, the ambassador would make a perfect target."

Ashok broke into an open smile. "That's an excellent secretary you've got there, Mr. Ambassador."

As the tour director returned to his seat, Philip took Andrea's hand. Gently, he slid his arm along the back of the seat behind her, watching her with a gaze as soft as a caress. Andrea had to fight her urge to move even closer.

Switching gears, she forced herself to concentrate on what had happened at Prana Pharmaceuticals—her shock at seeing the open limousine door and knowing instinctively what it meant. She trembled, reliving the moment.

Philip's hand dropped to her shoulder, and he pulled her closer. "What's the matter, Andrea?" His voice was a velvet murmur.

In the circle of his warmth, her memory of the frightening afternoon didn't seem quite so vivid.

"I've just thought of something scary," she began slowly. "Commandeering those embassy vehicles took planning. Do you suppose the terrorists were waiting for us at Prana?"

He didn't answer immediately. With a strange inner excitement, she guessed that his mind had been as far from Prana Pharmaceuticals as her own a moment earlier.

"I'm sure they were waiting for us." His voice lost its huskiness. "That mob assembled too quickly to have been a coincidence."

Andrea studied his face. "Then that means someone either at the embassy or at Prana is on the terrorist payroll." She felt his grip on her shoulder relaxing.

"Or somebody at the Bureau of Internal Affairs," he added. "Or the local police. They were notified, too."

Andrea gave a rueful smile. "Not much chance of finding out who it was then, is there?"

He eyed her thoughtfully. "The thing that bothered me most about Prana's setup, was that fourth building. Like you said, the damn thing looked like a jail. The company spokesman wasn't very convincing when he said the bars were to keep people out."

"No, he wasn't," she agreed. "Why were the bars on that building stronger? The windows on the other buildings were barred, also supposedly to keep people out."

Philip's brown eyes met her blue ones. "His explanation about the narcotics didn't sound right, either. There must be narcotics in the packaging and manufacturing facilities, too. Why didn't those buildings have the same kind of bars?"

The lines of concentration deepened along his eyebrows. "Then there was that sound. If that wasn't the most heart-wrenching cry I've ever heard . . . You know what I think?"

Andrea shook her head, waiting for him to continue.

He hesitated, as though his idea was too unthinkable to share, even with her. "I think that was a human cry we heard."

Andrea nodded. "That's what I thought, too."

He eyed her thoughtfully. "I think humans, not animals, are being used to test the biological weapons in Tisara."

Unable to control her shocked gasp, Andrea stared at Philip, too startled to say anything.

"The victims are being kept in that jail at Prana Pharmaceuticals, until they can be flown to Ganthaku."

Andrea's breath caught. "They'd have to be crazy to try something so dangerous. The diseases could wipe out whole populations."

"Some people would risk anything to get what they want," Philip declared grimly. "Look at Saddam in Iraq, at the Ayatollah, at Adolph Hitler." He paused for emphasis. "Using destitute Indians for test subjects would explain most of the odd happenings we've seen so far—increased small-plane traffic between Delhi and Ganthaku, the choppers in Tisara, the new communications net, even all the funeral celebrations near the river by Dhara Village."

Remembering the spiral of smoke, Andrea recoiled. The idea that research victims were being cremated to get rid of their bodies was almost too gruesome to contemplate.

"What about Dass Verma Fertilizer?" she asked pointedly. "I saw that mentioned in the intercepts. And what about the mussenda flowers growing on the hillside? Your theory doesn't take them into account."

He frowned. "There are a few things I can't explain."

"And how about the attack on us this afternoon?" she went on. "And the car that's following us now. Are they tied in somehow?"

Philip rubbed his forehead with his hand. "Now that you mention it, this afternoon's attack might very well be connected to the germ warfare plot." His eyes narrowed. "Maybe our visit to Prana Pharmaceuticals tipped somebody off that we were getting wise to them."

An especially severe bump in the narrow road lifted them both off the seat. The jostling threw them apart. Smiling, Philip drew her close again.

"We went to Prana to check out Dass Verma Fertilizer," Andrea reminded him. "If the attack was connected to our visiting the plant, then there has to be a connection to the fertilizer.''

A shadow of annoyance crossed his face. ''That fertilizer is the one thing that doesn't fit in. The fertilizer and those damned flowers.''

''If there's a connection, I'll find it when we get back to Ganthaku,'' Andrea promised, with a sense of conviction.

But she forced herself to ignore a very real possibility. If the occupants of the car behind them had their way, she and Philip would never leave Agra.

APPROACHING THE CITY, the country road became spotted with the single headlights of motor scooters and three-wheeled tempos, but few cars. Then the bus turned onto a street teeming with people. On each side of the road, Andrea saw crowded hovels with dirt floors, open in front, each lit by a single bare bulb. Squatting women cooked the evening meal over open fires outside. In the dirt margins lining the street there were table-high trays loaded with bananas, mangoes, oranges and papaya.

A fine thread of tension rippled through the bus now that they'd reached their destination. While the vehicle crept through crowded, narrow streets on its way to the Taj View Hotel, an eerie silence descended over the passengers.

At the front, Ashok took the microphone. ''Let's go over the instructions again.''

Andrea detected a shrill note of excitement in his voice that chilled her. Zero hour was fast approaching. Would she and Philip be gunned down the instant they left the bus's protective shelter?

''The driver will get as close as he can to the hotel entrance.'' Ashok spoke over the loudspeaker. ''Ambassador Dorough and Mrs. Mitchell will get out first. When they're inside, we'll file into the hotel as quickly as possible.''

Ashok paused. ''Remember, everyone, the terrorists are after Ambassador Dorough, not us. The ambassador believes we won't be in danger as long as we stay away from him. So don't go near the registration desk while he's there. You could be targets. I'll get your keys and have the clerk bring the registration forms to your rooms." Another pause. "Any questions?"

Someone raised a hand. Andrea heard a high-pitched woman's voice but couldn't make out her words.

Ashok listened, then lifted his microphone again. "The ambassador advises haste as a precaution, Mrs. Foley. Leave your parcels in the overhead bins instead of carrying them off. We'll bring them to your rooms along with your luggage." He glanced around. "Any more questions?

Silence settled over them like a heavy mist. Outside, Andrea heard blowing vehicle horns, their sharp sounds muted by the dull rumble of the bus's engine. Inside, no one spoke, or coughed, or moved.

"The hotel is just ahead," Ashok announced a few minutes later.

Philip examined Andrea's face. There were tension lines across her normally smooth forehead, but he saw no fear in her luminous blue eyes. Seizing one of her hands, he cradled it in his two larger ones.

"I wish I could leave you behind with the others," he said. "But we can't risk it. They might be after both of us."

"I'd never stay behind." Her voice rang with determination.

He stared at her, his mood suddenly buoyant in spite of their dire straits. "Do you realize what you just said?"

Her blue eyes gazed levelly into his. "Yes, I think so."

"Would you really risk your life for me?"

She smiled at him quizzically. "I already have."

"Nothing's going to happen to you because of me," he promised, torn with fear for what might occur in the next few minutes. "Leave some space between us when you follow me into the hotel. I don't want you getting shot when the one they probably want is me."

She didn't answer. From her strained smile, he suspected she'd do exactly as she pleased—just as she had from the time he'd first met her.

The bus slowed. It turned off the crumbling city street through an iron gate to an immaculate concrete driveway leading to the hotel's covered lobby entrance.

Philip pulled Andrea to her feet. "Let's wait in front with Ashok."

Under the worried gaze of the other passengers, they made their way forward. The wide driveway in front of the hotel's main entrance was relatively free of vehicles. Two tour buses were unloading passengers outside the covered area. A line of European-looking travelers filed across the driveway into the lobby.

After conferring with Ashok, the driver drove the bus under the covered area in front of the big glass doors and stopped there, blocking the driveway.

A concierge came toward them, smiled and waved toward a space farther down.

Ashok pulled a lever. The bus door slid open.

Glancing to his right and left, Philip saw the black Ambassador swing through the open gate and stop. He gave Andrea a meaningful glance and hit the ground running. The more distance he put between him and her, the safer she'd be. But he could hear her sandals slapping the concrete close behind him.

In an instant, he reached the glass doors. A doorman swung them open. He burst into the lobby. Andrea followed a second later and the doors closed behind them. Staring back toward the driveway, he saw the bus move ahead without discharging the other passengers.

Thank God! The others were safe! And so were he and Andrea. Philip drank in the sight of her with her blond hair flying wildly around her head.

"We made it so far," she declared, her face filled with relief. "I had my doubts when I saw the Ambassador pull in after us. But nobody got out."

Ignoring the curious glances in their direction, he started toward the registration desk in the opulent lobby.

Andrea fell into step beside him. "You know, now that I've seen that car up close, I'm getting an odd feeling about it."

"Odd?" He let his gaze roam over her face. Though she wasn't breathing heavily, her skin was flushed with excitement. She was so vital, so alive, that he had to touch her. He put his arm around her waist, drawing her closer as they walked.

"What do you mean, odd?" He spoke in a tone filled with warmth and concern.

They reached the desk and the uniformed clerk eyed them expectantly.

"I'll tell you after we register," Andrea answered.

Philip addressed the clerk. "I'm Philip Dorough, U.S. ambassador to Tisara. My secretary and I have arrived in Agra unexpectedly and need adjoining rooms for the night."

The clerk studied them with narrowed eyes. "We have no reservations for a U.S. ambassador."

Philip smiled congenially and handed him his passport. "You can check with the U.S. Embassy in Delhi if there's a problem."

The clerk beckoned to a man in a business suit, who turned out to be the manager. After some preliminary conversation about Philip's status, he smiled hospitably. No adjoining rooms were available. But the hotel reserved a three-bedroom suite with a spectacular view for important visitors. Would the ambassador like to see it?

"I'm sure it will be fine," Philip said.

The hotel manager surveyed the marble floor where they were standing. "Is the ambassador's luggage outside?"

Philip glanced toward the door. Everything seemed normal.

"We have no luggage." Philip handed the clerk a thin stack of rupees. "We'll pay for the suite in advance."

The clerk thanked him and beckoned for a porter to show them to their rooms.

Philip didn't want a porter listening to his conversation with Andrea. Impatiently, he took the key from the clerk. "We'll find the suite ourselves." He turned and started toward two elevators across the lobby. Each had elaborate brass scrollwork on its doors.

"Now what's so odd about the car?"

"I got a glimpse of the men inside," she replied. "They were Western-looking."

"So what?" Philip didn't like the anxious way she was breathing—in shallow, quick gasps. Whatever was on her mind was upsetting her. "Some of the world's best terrorists are Westerners."

"There's more," she went on. "There's the car itself. It has an official look. That's why I asked you in Delhi if another chase car might have been assigned to us."

They reached the elevators, but Philip didn't press the UP button. "Are you saying you think somebody from the embassy's in that car?"

It's not possible, he told himself. But he could feel a molten core of anger inside himself, spilling over, starting to catch fire.

"They're acting like a surveillance team, not like terrorists out to kill or kidnap a U.S. ambassador." There was a confident note in her tone. "Would the CIA be interested in our trip?"

"The CIA!" Philip spit out the words, his festering anger turning to rage. "You bet they'd be interested. Any time the ambassador does anything out of the ordinary, they're interested." He balled his fists in disgust. "After all we've been through, now we've got to worry about those clowns.

"Here." He handed her the key. "Wait for me in the suite." He wheeled toward the lobby entrance.

"Where are you going?"

He heard the frantic worry in her voice.

"I'm going to find out what those dirty, rotten bastards are up to." He started toward the registration desk.

Andrea trailed along after him, half running to keep up. "We're just guessing about the CIA. We don't know who's in that car."

He didn't slow down. "If we're right about this, I'm going to have Hugh Boggs for breakfast."

"Philip, you can't go out there."

She sounded so panicky Philip turned to look at her. She'd gone completely white. Slowing, he led her to one of the elegant couches in the big lobby.

"I'm not going alone," he explained, sitting down beside her. He gripped her hand and squeezed it. "A policeman must be on duty around here. I'll have him check the car."

She didn't look reassured. "If they're terrorists, they'll kill both of you."

"I won't go out with him. I'll wait until he sees who's inside the car." He examined her face. The stark terror he'd seen was gone. Her color was coming back.

She stood up. "Let's find that policeman."

Chapter Eleven

To Andrea, the policeman on duty at the Taj View Hotel looked more like a soldier. Dressed in an olive drab uniform, a rifle slung by his side, he spoke little English. The hotel manager told him that Philip wanted him to check out a black Ambassador sedan parked outside the lobby.

Philip and Andrea walked to the entrance with him. Andrea spotted the car in a small parking area for civilian vehicles facing the hotel. Between an Audi and a Mercedes, it was about twenty yards from the covered part of the driveway in front of the lobby. Since the parking area was to one side of the lighted entrance, the car was in shadow.

The policeman started toward it.

Andrea gripped Philip's arm, afraid he might follow. "Let's get back, out of sight."

Philip didn't move. "He'll be there in a second."

Fascinated, she watched the policeman bend over to peer in the car's window. Abruptly, he straightened and yelled something in Hindi. The concierge yelled back and started toward the car.

"What's wrong?" Philip shouted.

The concierge didn't stop. Philip lunged after him.

Andrea hesitated only a moment. Then she took off down the driveway after them. Her skirt swirled around her legs, her sandals flapped and her shoulder bag banged against her side, but she didn't slow.

Once clear of the covered entrance area, she jerked to a stop. Philip and the concierge had reached the Ambassador. Quickly, she looked up and down the driveway and along the concrete expanse next to the hotel. Civilian vehicles and another tour bus. Nothing suspicious.

Then she saw him—the same stocky man she'd noticed on the dirt frontage road in front of Prana Pharmaceuticals. A shapely young woman in a stunning red silk sari walked beside him. Headed toward the lobby entrance, they couldn't miss seeing her and Philip. Before Andrea's horrified eyes, the man shoved his hand in the pocket of a voluminous jacket.

She dropped to the ground. "Philip!" she screamed. "Get down."

Philip darted between the Mercedes and the Ambassador. The Mercedes's rear side window shattered. The concierge yelled again.

The heavyset man turned toward Andrea, a wrathful look on his buttery face. Frantically, she felt in her pocket for the silver pen. Then, with a terrible sinking feeling, she remembered. She hadn't replaced the projector.

She heard the crack of the policeman's rifle. Stone splintered behind the fat man.

Moving quickly for a man of his bulk, her assailant pounded across the driveway onto the patch of grass outside the lighted area. Then he disappeared in the shadow of the hedge along the fence. His female companion had already vanished, probably inside the lobby where she could leave by another exit.

The policeman and concierge ran past Andrea toward the lobby. She leaped up and darted toward Philip.

"Go back," he shouted.

She squatted down beside him. He gripped her arm. No touch had ever felt sweeter.

"Damn it all, Andrea!" he exclaimed. "You should have stayed in the lobby."

She took a couple of deep breaths to regain her equilibrium. "The man who shot at you. He's gone. I'm sure the police are on the way."

"Just the same, you shouldn't have come."

She raised herself high enough to peer into the Ambassador's window. The bright lights over the lobby entrance cast weird shadows over the interior, giving it a surreal appearance.

Two men were inside. Something about the lopsided way they were sitting sent an icy chill shooting through her.

She knocked on the window. Neither man moved.

Her terrified gaze moved from their faces to their sport shirts. Dark stains saturated the cloth.

Blood. It was everywhere—on their clothing, the car upholstery, the dashboard, even spattered on the window in front of her. In the dark, she'd thought it was mud.

Bile rose in her throat, and Andrea swallowed hard.

Beside her, Philip rose so he, too, could see inside the car.

"My God," he whispered. "They've both been shot."

AFTER PHILIP had talked to Ambassador Zimmerman in Delhi on the phone, he sat down next to Andrea on their hotel suite's green brocaded sofa. He was so close she could smell the grease on his shirt from where he'd rolled on the ground outside the hotel lobby.

"With the terrorists still on the loose," he told her, "Ambassador Zimmerman's requesting the Air Force C-12 from Islamabad to take us back to Delhi and from there to Ganthaku. The local police will escort us to Agra's airport."

Andrea's eyes widened. The Air Force plane was used on the subcontinent mainly for emergencies. It had flown the former attaché, Colonel Butler, and his family out of Tisara.

"Then Ambassador Zimmerman thinks we're still targets?" She spoke in a suffocated whisper.

Philip caught her hands. "Whoever's after us means business. Zimmerman thinks the men in the Ambassador were killed because somebody thought they were following the bus to protect us."

She let her breath out in a long sigh. "Then those men *were* CIA?"

Philip grunted his acquiescence. "Zimmerman claims to know nothing about the Agency's surveillance operation on us, but he recognized the men from my description. They worked out of the embassy in Delhi."

"Little did the bad guys know the CIA was after us, too." Andrea heard her bitterness spill over into her voice. "Instead of killing those men, the terrorists should have recruited them to help catch us."

She frowned when she realized how hateful she sounded. "I'm sorry I said that. Those CIA men were only following orders. They didn't deserve to die just for spying on us." Unexpectedly, her eyes filled with hot tears. She bit them back, hoping he hadn't noticed.

He dropped one of her hands and put his arm around her shoulder. "After all that's happened, you've got a right to be upset."

Andrea hesitated, half-afraid to ask the question on her mind. "What happened to Economic Officer White and the drivers of the embassy cars?"

Even before Philip spoke, she knew the answer from the strained look on his face.

"They were all killed?" Her voice trembled.

He nodded. "Shot. Like the CIA agents."

Now Andrea couldn't swallow her bitter tears. She gulped hard, as she felt them slipping down her cheeks. "It's not fair, Philip."

He pressed her shoulder against him. "We'll get whoever did it. With the two of us after them, they haven't got a chance."

Andrea didn't say anything. She knew she didn't have to. Philip would give her time to regain her composure.

They stayed on the sofa until they heard a sharp rap on the suite's door. Philip opened it. Outside stood the hotel manager with two policemen. The manager held a bottle of champagne and two long-stemmed crystal glasses.

"Mr. Ambassador," he began, "please accept this wine with my apologies for your terrible experience. I must assure you that the Taj View Hotel takes every precaution to provide for the safety of its patrons."

Philip stood aside to let them enter. The manager bent down over the apartment-size refrigerator near the door and thrust the bottle and glasses inside.

He smiled at Andrea, sitting on the sofa. "Perhaps you will enjoy the wine before your dinner, madam."

"Thanks. We will."

With a speed very unlike the plodding efficiency of the airport officials, the two police officers completed their questioning in about half an hour. Philip recounted what had happened from the time he and Andrea were attacked in Delhi until their discovery of the bodies inside the Ambassador.

Andrea's interrogation took only a few minutes. The officers didn't press her when she confirmed Philip's statement, indicating she had nothing to add.

After the police had left the suite, Philip studied the room-service menu and, with Andrea's enthusiastic approval, ordered the most sumptuous meal on it—a rice-and-lamb curry with side dishes of cooked vegetables, fresh fruit, sorbet and chewy Indian bread.

"Now, how about some of that champagne?" Philip asked.

Andrea nodded at him from her place on the sofa. "Why not? Since we're still in one piece, we've got plenty to celebrate."

Removing the bottle and glasses from the refrigerator, he performed the small ritual of popping the cork and pouring the frothy liquid. Then he brought the glasses to the sofa and handed one to Andrea.

He gave her a smile that set her heart thudding. "Ambassador Zimmerman thinks we should stay in our suite until the C-12 gets here. It sounds like a good idea to me."

Andrea set her glass on the table without drinking any champagne. She wasn't sure she could handle being alone with Philip in this luxurious suite for the next few hours. A gamut of contradictory emotions raced through her. She wanted him. Body and soul, she wanted him. She was past denying her feelings.

But she wasn't free, not until she knew the truth about Jeffry. She got up and walked to the French doors leading to an outside balcony. Throwing open the doors, she went outside. The cool night air enveloped her like a magic blanket. Looking around, she stared, enraptured, at the spectacle in the distance.

Rising above the dusty trees and grubby one-story hovels at the base of the hotel was the Taj Mahal. It shone whitely in the light of the full moon, its lacy arched walls supporting the graceful marble dome. Andrea stood there, breathless, enthralled by the beauty of the fabled tomb, built by a grieving king for his beloved wife.

Philip followed her out. When he put his arm around her waist, she leaned against him. Until she found Jeffry and solved the awful problem between them, she wasn't free. But she didn't move away from the protection of Philip's sheltering arm.

"I knew the Taj was at Agra," he said. "But until this moment, I didn't really think about seeing it." He sounded as awed as Andrea felt.

"It's a shame we'll be leaving before sunrise," she murmured, and was immediately irritated with herself for saying such a thing. She felt her face flush, thankful the balcony was dark so he wouldn't see.

Philip didn't seem to notice her embarrassment. "That's the artist in you talking. From what I've heard, the Taj is most beautiful at sunrise."

He understood what I meant, she thought, letting herself absorb his warmth. Like the magnificent structure opposite them, Philip projected a compelling sense of power and balance.

"Let's drink a toast out here on the balcony," he suggested.

When she nodded, he went inside and got their filled glasses. Handing one to her, he lifted the other. "Thanks for saving my life again. Twice in one day. That must be some kind of record."

She smiled and raised her glass. "To being alive in this beautiful place."

At her first sip, Andrea suddenly felt very much alive. And very lucky. She took a long swallow of the bubbly liquid. It tickled her throat going down. How good to be drinking champagne with Philip.

"And here's to being *together* in this beautiful place," he added, as though reading her thoughts. He lifted his glass and swallowed.

Chuckling, he glanced at the half-empty glass in her hand. "I was afraid you didn't like champagne."

"I love it," she admitted. "But it makes me sleepy."

"If you get sleepy, you can always lie down." He gestured inside the suite. "We've got plenty of beds at our disposal."

"I know." Andrea ignored the caution light that clicked on in her mind. She couldn't believe how relaxed she felt. With a quick sip, she finished her champagne.

Philip took her glass and went inside to refill it. She followed him and sat down on the sofa. Handing her the glass, he eased himself down beside her.

She half turned to see him better. At the same instant, he swung around toward her. She saw an intense yearning in his eyes that frightened and excited her at the same time.

In that perilous moment, everything around Andrea whirled off into a void. Nothing was left but Philip's tanned face, his eyes searching into her soul. She heard her heart hammering noisily, and took a deep breath to quiet it.

As though he sensed her awareness, Philip drew her toward him, pulling her into his arms. Again Andrea smelled the grease on his shirt, but she didn't care. Philip was wearing the shirt. That was the only important thing. Nothing else mattered.

Her lips parted. His mouth descended toward hers and suddenly, he was kissing her with the passion of a starving man. Andrea felt a flood of warmth gush through her and reveled in the feel of his lips, in the hard strength of his chest, pressed so urgently against her.

The green satin room swirled around them. Beneath her back, the luxurious sofa cushions welcomed her as she sank down against them.

Raising himself a few inches, Philip undid the buttons of his shirt and flung it open. Beneath was a curly mat of dark hair.

Then, very carefully, he lifted her blouse from her skirt and pushed it above her breasts. Andrea felt him fumbling with her bra straps and then he eased the lacy cups aside. Andrea felt his mass of chest hair rubbing against her sensitive skin. Her breasts surged at the feel of him against her.

"I want you so much," he whispered, cupping his hand around her bare breast.

Andrea wanted him, too. Lord in heaven, how she wanted him.

But like this? On a sofa in a hotel room where they were spending a couple of hours? Did she want to feel guilty about loving him? Guilty, maybe, for the rest of her life?

Philip must have sensed her inner struggle.

"What's wrong?" His voice was hoarse with longing. "Why did you turn away?"

She hadn't been aware that she'd moved.

"Is it your husband?" When she still didn't answer, he took a deep breath. "Why can't you face the truth? The man's dead."

"He can't be dead," Andrea cried. Philip's face blurred, and her eyes filled with tears.

Philip's heavy sigh sounded like a groan. "You loved him so much that you still can't accept his death?"

"Jeffry can't be dead," she repeated. Her voice seemed reedy to her ears. "If he's dead, I'll never be able to..." Abruptly, she stopped speaking. This was something she'd never told anybody. Did she really want Philip to know?

Slowly, reluctantly, he pulled her blouse down. Then he helped her sit up. "You'll never be able to do what, Andrea?"

He studied her face, watching her intense blue eyes sparkle with unshed tears. The tears weren't for Jeffry, he realized suddenly. They were for something else, something happening now.

Much as he wanted her, Philip knew this wasn't the right time or place. Andrea was still in semishock from what had occurred today. She needed to sort out her feelings.

He put his arm around her and hugged her. The mere feel of her shoulder and hip against him reignited the heat inside him. Ignoring it was impossible. Somehow he forced himself to kiss her lightly on the forehead.

"Now, what is it you'll never be able to do?" he kept his voice smooth but insistent.

Finally, she spoke. "Forgive him. I'll never be able to forgive him." There was a sob in her voice. "The night he left, I'd asked him for a divorce."

Philip waited patiently for her to go on.

"He begged me to reconsider, but I wouldn't. I threw him out of the house and said I never wanted to see him again."

"You must have had a good reason."

She hesitated. The silence grew between them like a tangible, living creature.

Finally, Philip broke it, knowing she had to get it out or continue to suffer. "What was the reason? You can tell me."

Staring down at her hands, she avoided his eyes. "I caught him in bed with a secretary who worked at the base."

"That's a damn good reason. No woman should have to put up with a cheating man."

She looked him straight in the eye. "I accused him of having an affair with her. He claimed this was the first time and begged me for a second chance. God help me, I wouldn't listen. If he'd gotten a good night's sleep in his own bed, maybe the accident would never have happened."

He heard the guilt in her voice.

"The accident had nothing to do with being tired," Philip pointed out. "Where he slept two or three days before simply isn't relevant."

Her lower lip trembled. "If you'd seen how shaken he was when I threw him out of the house, you wouldn't say that."

She seemed determined to take the blame. Philip tried not to show his frustration. "You had the best reason in the world to ask him for a divorce, especially in this day and age when infidelity can mean death."

"Did I?" Her words were clipped.

He could see that she hated herself for what she'd done. But why?

"In many ways, Jeffry was a good husband to me," she went on. "He was considerate and movie-star handsome.

He'd had lots of women before he married me but swore his free-living days were over."

Philip held back the disparaging comment that came to his mind. "How did you find out?" he asked, instead.

From the way she tensed, he could tell he'd hit a nerve. When she didn't answer right away, he asked, "Surely your husband didn't have his liaison right in your home?"

"No." She paused. "Nobody else knows any of this," she cautioned. "Especially not the Air Force or Jeffry's parents—not anybody."

"I understand."

She looked down at her hands again. "I'm ashamed to tell you this." She had to force the words out. "From the way he was treating me, I thought he was having an affair with someone, so I had him followed." She was whispering now, as though afraid someone might hear. "That's how I found out. And that's the main reason I feel so guilty about the whole thing."

In spite of her harsh words about herself, she sat up straighter, and he sensed a lessening of her burden.

Philip shook her gently. "Maybe you were right, and he *was* having an affair with this woman, or with someone else. How long did you have him followed before you found out?"

"Only a day or two," she admitted. "At first, I was absolutely positive he was lying about this being the first time. After I cooled off, I decided to believe him. But then it was too late."

"Your former husband wouldn't be the first man to lie to his wife about an affair he was having." Philip spoke in an authoritative yet gentle tone. "Or about this woman being the only one."

Andrea snuggled against him. He felt the tension draining out of her.

"I wonder if I'll ever find out the truth," she whispered.

When room service knocked at the door ten minutes later with their dinner, she was curled up with her head on his shoulder, fast asleep.

ANDREA FLOATED through the next few hours as though in a dream. A candlelit dinner in their luxurious suite...a sedate ride to Agra's airport with a six-car police escort... the short flight from Agra to Delhi on the Air Force C-12...an escorted ride from Indira Gandhi International Airport to the Taj Mahal Hotel in Delhi.

When she and Philip finally reached the beds in their adjoining hotel rooms, she slept better than she had in more than a year.

The next afternoon at the U.S. Embassy in Delhi, they faced a barrage of questions, both from embassy officials and the local authorities. As in Agra, they provided specific details about the incident but not about the real reason for their visit to Prana Pharmaceuticals.

That night they went to an embassy dinner in their honor at Ambassador Zimmerman's residence. Afterward, at their hotel, Philip opened Andrea's door for her but remained in the hall outside.

"You were the most stunning woman there." He ran his finger down her cheek.

"And you were the handsomest man." She meant it.

He grinned at her, his teeth white against his tanned skin. "Now that we've got the compliments out of the way, I'll apologize. I should have insisted on dinner in our rooms tonight."

"The party wasn't that bad," she lied.

A quiet dinner with Philip in his hotel room. How would it have ended? Not with him standing in the hall outside her door, his eyes burning with desire.

He stepped toward her, into the room. "Just let me hold you for a few minutes." He took her into his arms.

She rubbed her cheek against his, and felt his emerging beard. A familiar warmth gushed through her. Was she feeling physical need or was she in love with him? Andrea wasn't sure.

"I don't want to disappoint you again," she whispered.

He tightened his arms around her. "I know. I understand."

"Things are clearer than they were," she began, "but they still aren't . . ." She hesitated, torn by conflicting emotions.

He brushed his mouth against her forehead. "Don't apologize. Just let me hold you."

Then his lips, warm and sweet, met hers.

Somewhere down the long hallway, a door opened. The muted sound of voices mingled with the high-pitched tones of an Oriental song. The door slammed shut, and the music stopped.

Reluctantly, Philip released her. "If I don't get out of here, I'll be in trouble."

She clung to him, unwilling to let him go. He kissed her again, hungrily, shattering her calm. This time, when he drew back, he caught her chin in his hand.

"Are you sure you want me to go?"

Andrea wasn't sure. She wanted him so badly she ached all over. "I don't know," she whispered. "I'm not sure of anything anymore."

Slowly, his eyebrows set in a straight line, he turned away from her. "You'll be sure when we find out the truth about Jeffry. Then you'll be able to get on with your life."

For a long time that night, Andrea lay awake in her king-size bed in Delhi's luxurious Taj Mahal Hotel, listening to rustling sounds from the room next door and trying to blot out erotic images of her and Philip lying together, their bodies entwined in an intimate embrace.

Come to terms with Jeffry, she told herself, remembering Philip's words. *Then everything will be clear. Then you'll know what to do.*

ANDREA ARRIVED at the house off Mazipat Street in Ganthaku after Jan had left for work. Though it was Saturday, Philip had asked the older woman to come in and help him catch up with paperwork.

Chandra, the housegirl, was working in the kitchen. She gave Andrea a delighted smile.

"Did you have a pleasant trip?" she asked in Tisaran.

Andrea had been practicing the language with the woman, who was visibly impressed with her pupil's rapid progress. Andrea kept reminding herself to go slow.

"Very nice," Andrea replied.

"There is a note for you on the table." Chandra pointed to the coffee table in the living room.

"Welcome home, stranger," it read. "Thanks for bringing the boss back all in one piece."

Smiling, Andrea laid down the note. It was one of the few welcoming things Jan had done since Andrea had arrived. Lord, had it been only twelve days ago?

Leaving the unpacking to Chandra, Andrea showered and changed into one of her low-visibility outfits. She intended to put this Saturday to good use.

On Mazipat Street, she flagged a cab, giving an address close to the jewelry shop where her source worked. She needed to find out exactly what was going on at Dhara Village. If Tulak had been right, Jeffry disappeared near there.

Tulak. With a tightening in her throat, she remembered the man's proud bearing. What had her new source found out about his accident? And what about the strange mussenda plants? Could the clerk tell her anything about them?

After she got out of the taxi, Andrea hurried toward the jewelry store in the next block. A car stopped ahead of her. Two men in the khaki uniforms of the Tisaran army got out. When Andrea tried to pass them, they grabbed her arms, one on each side.

Her heart dropped to her shoes, but she didn't struggle. "What's wrong?"

"So sorry," one of them said in English. "You will please come with us."

Andrea refused to believe this could be happening. "What have I done?" She struggled to keep the fear from her voice. "Where are you taking me?"

Her captors ignored her questions. Roughly, they thrust her into the car's back seat and slammed the door. There were no inside handles. A fencelike barrier separated the back seat from the front. She was caged in, like a common criminal.

The two men got in front.

"Where are you taking me?" she asked again.

The soldiers ignored her.

Forcing herself to sit calmly, she clenched her hands so tightly that her fingernails pierced the skin. This was the nightmare every intelligence agent feared. The hand on the arm. The ride in the official car. To where? Slonpo Prison?

No, not Slonpo. At least, not yet. Looking out the window, Andrea recognized the route they were taking. It led to the army base where Colonel Khadka had his headquarters.

A short time later, she faced the big man. Standing, he eyed her up and down from the opposite side of his massive desk. His odd bicolored eyes seemed to see right through her.

"Ah, Mrs. Mitchell, we meet again." He took a huge puff of his cigar. The smoke smelled acrid and nauseating.

"Why am I here, Colonel?" Andrea managed to keep her voice reasonably steady.

"You're under arrest, Mrs. Mitchell."

Andrea felt the blood drain from her face. "What for? Why am I under arrest?"

He smiled slyly, showing blackened teeth. "For being a spy, of course. You're under arrest for committing espionage against the sovereign Kingdom of Tisara."

Chapter Twelve

He's caught me. Andrea's insides turned to a swirling mass of jelly. *God knows how, but he's found out what I'm up to.* From the derisive smile on Khadka's face, Andrea could tell she was reacting exactly the way he expected her to: scared and guilty.

Deny everything and play innocent, she reminded herself, remembering the lessons drummed into her at the espionage school.

Folding her arms across her chest, Andrea looked the big man straight in his bicolored eyes. "I'm not a spy, and you know it, Colonel." She willed her shaking knees not to buckle, her voice not to tremble. "Why don't you tell me the real reason you've brought me here?"

An appreciative expression flashed across his swarthy face. "Very good, Mrs. Mitchell. You are an excellent actress."

Andrea didn't like the cynical way his eyebrow lifted. This man was dangerous. She had to get out of here, back to the safety of Philip and the embassy.

"I am a citizen of the United States," she repeated stoically, the same way she had in the school exercise. "I demand you notify the embassy of my arrest."

Khadka stopped smiling. "You are not in a position to demand anything, Mrs. Mitchell." His voice was low-pitched, like the ominous rumbling of an approaching cyclone. "When your embassy hears my evidence, your people will be happy to leave you here to rot for the rest of your life."

The mass of quivering jelly in Andrea's stomach turned to lead. Nobody knew about her assignment here except top-level U.S. officials. Had there been a leak somewhere?

Impossible. The story was too tightly held.

Then how about her and Philip's visit to Prana Pharmaceuticals? Could it have triggered Khadka's action?

Not likely. Even if Prana was tied in to whatever was going on in Tisara, an ambassadorial visit could hardly be construed as evidence that the ambassador's secretary was a spy.

Opposite her, Khadka sat down, his face as hard as granite. He waved toward one of the two upholstered chairs facing his desk. "Please sit down, Mrs. Mitchell. We might as well be comfortable while we talk."

The leaden knot in Andrea's stomach threatened to strangle her insides. She wanted to bolt from the room. Instead, she lowered herself to the chair and leaned back against its upholstered cushion, striving to appear as relaxed as possible.

"What evidence are you talking about, Colonel?"

"I'm sure you know, Mrs. Mitchell. You're much more familiar with your military background than I am."

Andrea froze. *Military background.* Fat drops of perspiration rolled down her back, leaving cool trails on her skin.

Khadka stared at her. Waiting. "So you aren't denying you spent years in the Air Force?" he asked finally. "Your silence tells me something, Mrs. Mitchell." Though his expression was smug, Andrea sensed he was probing for information.

Maybe the situation wasn't as bad as she feared. If he wanted her to confirm what he'd said, that meant he wasn't positive. Besides, he could easily have found out about her

Air Force career. Since it was part of her background cover, it was certainly no secret. The secret was that she was still in the Air Force. Andrea maintained her poise by telling herself that Khadka couldn't possibly know.

She forced a smile. "Of course I'm not denying my Air Force service. I'm proud of it. But now I'm Ambassador Dorough's secretary." She stared straight at him. "You'd better let me call the embassy, or there's going to be trouble."

"Trouble? I think not." Khadka's mouth curved in a sarcastic smile. "Does the ambassador know you're an Air Force intelligence officer who's an expert on this country? Does he know you were assigned to the Pentagon, that you are the most knowledgeable military authority on Tisara?"

Khadka knows. Andrea felt her blood roaring in her ears. She gripped the chair arms so tightly her knuckles turned white.

Control yourself, she ordered. *Your life depends on it.* Only by taking a deep, careful breath was she able to assume a semblance of calm.

She shrugged. "Tell the ambassador anything you like."

Khadka put his elbows on the desk and leaned toward her. "If he knew you were an intelligence agent and still permitted you to come here, that means your government authorized you to spy on us. King Shrestha would have no alternative. He would have to terminate Tisara's relationship with your country."

He smiled sarcastically. "No, I rather doubt your ambassador will do anything to help a condemned spy."

Speechless, Andrea sat frozen in her chair. Khadka was repeating what Philip himself had said when she'd first arrived. It was the same warning the instructors at the school had voiced time after time. *If you get caught, there's nothing your government can do to help. Nothing. Absolutely nothing.*

From Khadka's mouth, the words sounded deadly.

A frightening powerless feeling washed over her. She'd been found out and nobody could help her. Philip would rant and rave and demand she be freed, but it would do no good. Khadka knew the truth about her, the truth that would send her to a wretched Tisaran prison.

Andrea's mouth tasted like old paper, dry and dusty. She licked her lips, but that didn't help. A suffocating sensation tightened her throat.

Colonel Khadka was watching her closely, like a cat stalking a crippled bird. He was ready to move in for the kill.

"Why don't you tell me everything, Mrs. Mitchell? It will make things easier for you." He smiled, his stained teeth even more prominent in the sunlight from the window. "I'll use my influence with the king. Maybe he'll agree to send you home without your going to prison, the way we expelled your former attaché."

Something about his smug expression irritated Andrea. So he wanted her to tell all, did he? Maybe he had just been guessing when he implied she was still in the Air Force.

She sat straighter, the seed of a plan germinating in her mind. It was risky because it meant confirming information Khadka might not be sure of. But her plan just might work. If nobody could help her, she'd simply have to save herself.

"Do you really think you can keep me out of prison, Colonel?" She let her fear show. For her plan to work, he had to be convinced she was ready to confess because she was scared.

His expression turned conspiratorial. "I can't guarantee anything, of course. But if you cooperate, I'm almost positive you won't have to go to prison."

"In that case . . ." She leaned toward him.

Khadka rose from behind his desk, and sat down in the chair next to her. "Now, Mrs. Mitchell. Tell me exactly what you're doing here."

Andrea lowered her voice. "I'm looking for my husband."

"Your husband?" His eyes narrowed, and scowl lines appeared above his bushy black eyebrows. "You expect me to believe that?"

"It's the truth." Andrea found herself gripping the chair arms again and forced herself to relax. "My husband disappeared in a trekking accident a little over a year ago. His body was never found.'

Andrea didn't have to remind herself to be convincing. "I'm sure he's still alive, Colonel. Even climbing the highest mountains in the world, a party of ten people doesn't just disappear from the face of the earth. I have to find him." Tears rolled down her cheeks. Andrea let them flow. Though they were born of fear and tension, Khadka would think they were for her husband.

He took another long puff on his cigar. Now that he was sitting close to Andrea, the smoke was even more sickening. She could feel it stinging her eyes and burning her throat.

"Your husband was Captain Jeffry Mitchell?" he asked.

Andrea's mouth dropped open. She snapped it closed. "Then you know the case?"

His scowl deepened. "Of course I know the case. So Captain Mitchell was your husband?"

"Yes," she replied, nodding. "I resigned my Air Force commission so I could take this embassy job and find out what happened to him." She leaned toward Khadka with what she hoped was a pleading expression. "If the ambassador learns I'm here looking for my husband, I'll probably lose my job. Please don't tell him, or anybody else from the embassy."

Did Khadka believe her? More tears slid down her face. She couldn't stop them now if she wanted to.

Khadka didn't seem to notice her tears. "How does Ishwaranath and the Temple to Ishwara fit into this hunt of yours for your dead husband?'' His smile was more like a sneer. ''You went there deliberately, after secretly plotting to disobey the orders of your ambassador. When I found you, you were spying in a guarded area.''

Andrea's blood ran cold. Nobody knew she went to the temple with a deliberate plan in mind. Or that she'd plotted several days ahead to circumvent Philip's order. Except Philip. And Tulak.

The horrible truth dawned on her. Tulak had betrayed her. No wonder he was so curious about what she knew. He'd been informing to Khadka all along. That's how Khadka had caught her in the temple garden. That's why she was under arrest right now. After the temple incident, he'd checked into her background.

So why hadn't Khadka arrested her then? And why was Tulak dead?

Khadka wore his stalking-cat expression again. ''Did you expect to find your missing husband in Ishwaranath, Mrs. Mitchell?''

Andrea's mind whirled frantically, searching for convincing reasons for being in the temple compound with Tulak.

''It's sort of a long story,'' she said, stalling for time.

Khadka walked to his desk and stubbed out his cigar in an ashtray. Then he returned to the chair next to hers. ''Get on with it, Mrs. Mitchell.''

Andrea took a deep breath. ''The taxi driver who took me to the temple was recommended by an associate in Washington as a good...''

''Who?'' Khadka spit out the word. ''Who is your associate?''

Andrea knew he was probing for the identity of her controller. She gave him a fictitious name.

''According to my associate, the taxi driver was supposed to be a good source of information,'' she went on. ''So I called him and asked about Jeffry. The driver said my husband's accident had been seen by a wandering sadhu.'' She paused, letting Khadka make the connection between the sadhu and the temple. ''I thought one of the priests might be able to tell me about this holy man.''

''You told me you were only a tourist, looking around the garden.'' His words were accusing, but he'd lost most of his belligerence.

''I was trying to find the priest who talked to the holy man,'' Andrea insisted. ''The taxi driver said he was in charge of the temple garden.''

For a long minute, Khadka stared at her. Then, unbelievably, he nodded. ''The temple gardener saw the Americans fall. It wasn't a wandering sadhu.''

Andrea heard ringing in her ears. The room spun around her. She leaped to her feet and faced Khadka.

''Why weren't the Air Force inspectors told? Why wasn't I told? Good Lord, Colonel, I'm his wife!''

Khadka seemed unphased by her outburst. ''You *were* his wife, Mrs. Mitchell. Captain Jeffry Mitchell is dead.'' He paused. ''The inspectors weren't told because I didn't know. The truth was not revealed to me until several months after their departure.''

She balled her hands into fists. ''In God's name, why didn't you notify them?''

''Because such a notification would have accomplished nothing.''

Andrea felt the blood rush to her face and knew she was losing control. She didn't care. ''By interviewing that priest, they could have found out the truth.''

''They already knew the truth. The party fell and was buried under the ice.'' He rose and stood in front of her, his arms folded. ''Please return to your chair.'' he looked as big as a bull elephant.

Numbly, Andrea sat down.

"The priest did not want to be interviewed," Khadka's words were clipped. "In Tisara we respect the desires of our religious leaders."

Fighting her anger, she let the matter drop. The important thing now was to get out of here. She assumed her pleading expression. "If anybody at the embassy finds out I took this job to locate my husband, I'll be fired."

"Better to lose your job than your life." Khadka picked up the phone on his desk. "Get me Ambassador Dorough at the American embassy or his residence. Tell him it's urgent that I talk to him."

A moment later, he spoke into the instrument again. "I'm so sorry to bother you, Mr. Ambassador. I have arrested your secretary, Mrs. Andrea Mitchell, as a spy."

From her chair, Andrea could hear Philip's profane exclamation. She felt a crazy mixture of hope and fear. Khadka had just called her a spy, so he must not believe her story. But then why had he contacted Philip?

"We need to talk about this situation," Khadka declared. "Would you like me to come to your office or would you prefer to meet here?"

Khadka paused, listening. "The woman stays here." Another pause. "All right then, I'll expect you in about an hour."

Suddenly, Andrea's whole body turned limp. Philip was no trained espionage agent. Could he convince the wiley Khadka that she wasn't a spy?

ANDREA SPENT the next hour in an eight-by-ten room with no windows and a hole in the floor for a toilet. A single light bulb suspended from a cord cast dim shadows on walls stained with dirty brown streaks. The room smelled like an open latrine. Combined with the suffocating heat, the unbearable stench almost made her gag.

At least there was a chair—a straight-backed wooden affair with one short leg. Gingerly, Andrea wiped it off with a tissue from her pocket before she sat down. Khadka had confiscated her shoulder bag. She had only one tissue. Grimacing, she threw it in the latrine hole.

"Be thankful if the king agrees to let you go and your ambassador sends you home," Khadka had advised before locking her in.

After spending a few minutes in this horrid place, Andrea knew what he meant. Being sent home in disgrace was infinitely better than staying here under these hellish conditions. And this cell, located in the military headquarters, was probably better than the cells in Slonpo Prison.

For the first time in her life, Andrea felt totally alone and abandoned. Was this the way Jeffry had felt when she threw him out of the house that terrible night? Where had he spent his remaining hours until his flight left for the subcontinent? Had he cried for her and for the married life she'd denied him?

Lord, she wished she'd acted differently—been kinder, more understanding. Was her arrest a cruel punishment for abandoning her husband because he'd made a single mistake?

One hour stretched to two. It was already nearly three o'clock in the afternoon. Andrea tried to fan herself with her hand and succeeded only in making herself hotter.

With each minute, she became more convinced that Philip had failed. When she finally heard the latch turn, she nearly fainted with relief.

Philip stood there in the open doorway with Khadka's enormous frame towering behind him.

"Come along, Mrs. Mitchell," Philip said. "The colonel has agreed to release you to my custody with the understanding that you're on the next plane home.'

Andrea's heart sank. Instead of the welcoming smile she'd expected, Philip was frowning. His voice sounded cold.

Because of Khadka, she told herself. Philip had managed to get her released. That's what was important. But, looking at the two men in the doorway, she got a distinct feeling of camaraderie between them. She shrugged the feeling off. Philip couldn't be friends with this awful man. He was just acting friendly to get her out of here.

Her legs felt wobbly when she stood up. Why had she expected Philip to complain about her wretched circumstances? He didn't even seem to notice the awful smell. Somehow she made it to the door.

In the hall outside the rancid cell, Andrea took a deep breath of fresh air. It tasted so good she almost cried. Never again would she take clean air for granted. Or the freedom to walk in and out of a room.

Khadka returned her shoulder bag and shook hands with Philip. During the long walk out of the headquarters to the waiting embassy car, Andrea and Philip didn't speak.

Finally, safely inside, with the sound of music from the car radio surrounding them, she studied his somber face. He didn't smile at her, hadn't since she got her first glimpse of him in the cell doorway. She took in his firmly pressed lips, his narrowed eyes. Something was wrong.

"I thought I told you to stay home and get some rest this afternoon," he growled. "What the hell were you doing out wandering around near that damned temple again?"

She shrank away from him. "I wasn't near the temple. I was just walking down the street when they arrested me."

He took a deep breath. "Khadka says you were headed toward the temple."

"I was in old Ganthaku, nowhere near the temple."

Philip grunted. "Khadka knows about your military career and your intelligence work at the Pentagon."

"He told me." Andrea felt her eyes filling with tears. "He thought I was a spy until I said I was here hunting for Jeffry."

She reached in the pocket of her skirt for a tissue but remembered she'd thrown her last one down the latrine hole. The stench of the cell still filled her nostrils, penetrating her clothes, her hair. And now Philip was blaming her for something that wasn't her fault. To her annoyance, her tears spilled over and trickled down her cheeks.

Before she could reach into her bag, he handed her a handkerchief. She wiped her cheeks with it. "Khadka would have arrested me even if I'd stayed home." She sniffed moistly into the handkerchief. "His men must have been waiting for me and followed me to old Ganthaku from the house."

"Just where *were* you going?"

Andrea hesitated. She'd never told Philip about her second source.

"I thought so." He sounded bitter. "You were out snooping again."

"I wasn't going to the temple." She tried not to seem defensive.

With a sigh, he took her in his arms. "Andrea, Andrea. What am I going to do with you?" He nuzzled her hair. "I've been going crazy the past few hours. If he hadn't let you go, I don't know what I'd have done."

She pushed herself away. "After hours in that filthy place, I must smell terrible."

He pulled her close again. "I don't care how you smell. All I know is that I almost lost you. I never want that to happen again."

His nearness made her senses sing. A delightful moist warmth gushed through her. She closed her eyes and pressed herself against him with an eagerness that shocked her. Then she felt his lips crushing hers, hard and demanding. The blood surged in her ears.

Philip would be a passionate lover, she thought, a lover who desired every part of her. He wouldn't be nonchalant and matter-of-fact, the way Jeffry had been when they were intimate. No, Philip would take her with the hunger of a primitive.

Is that what she wanted? Yes, yes, yes! her heart shouted. She wanted him with her mind, her body and her soul.

But something was wrong. Philip drew back, away from her.

"Turn up the radio, please, Mohan," he said.

Instantly, the volume increased, reminding Andrea that they weren't alone. The added noise also made their voices difficult for the chauffeur to hear. The surroundings shifted back into focus. They were in the embassy car with its rubbery new-car smell and its tinted windows; Mohan, in uniform, was in front.

"I'm going to have to send you back to Washington." Philip's voice was husky. "I'm sure you know that."

She nodded, her eyes suddenly blurring with tears again.

"Khadka checked the Air India schedule while I was there. There aren't any flights on Sunday. The next one is Monday, day after tomorrow. You've got to be on it. We can't play games here, or you'll end up in another cell."

Remembering the stench of the one where she'd spent the past few hours, Andrea swallowed hard.

"Incidentally," Philip added, "Khadka told me about the priest who witnessed the accident. There's no doubt Jeffry's dead."

"I know." So her long search for Jeffry was finally over. He wasn't suffering in some miserable Tisaran prison as she'd feared. No, the reports of his death were true. In her heart, Andrea knew Philip was right when he said that Jeffry had probably had other affairs, that the time she'd caught him hadn't been the first time he'd been with another woman. Her guilty feelings had stemmed from her sense of loss at her failed marriage. Now she was about to lose again. Holding back her tears, Andrea knew they weren't for her dead husband. They were for her and Philip because they'd soon be parted.

He took her hands and held them. "I swear this to you, Andrea. I'll talk to that priest myself and find out exactly what happened."

"And what's going on at Dhara Village?"

He squeezed her hands. "You bet. I'll give you a full report at the Pentagon." He paused. "Delivered personally."

She searched his face and saw he meant it.

They approached the house. Andrea looked at her watch. "Jan should be home if she left when you did."

With a slow smile, Philip shook his head. "She has a date with Sam Connelly. He picked her up at the office."

They stopped in front of the house and Mohan edged the big car onto the dirt margin.

"Would you like to come in for some coffee?" Andrea asked, feeling terribly bold.

"Yes," Philip answered, as solemnly as though he were in church. "Should I have Mohan wait or come back for me?"

Andrea felt the blood rising to her cheeks and was annoyed with herself for reacting like a schoolgirl.

"Have him come back."

THE HOUSE was pleasantly warm in the late afternoon. Splashes of sunlight brightened the living room's drab upholstered sofa and chair, and intensified the color in the Tibetan area rugs. The smell of a tuna casserole lingered in the air. Chandra must have prepared it before she left for the day.

Andrea had barely closed the door behind them when Philip swept her into his arms.

"For the past few weeks I've thought of nothing but you," he murmured. "Feeling you this close to me." He held her snugly. "Touching you this way." His large hand took her face and held it gently. "Having you want me the way I want you."

His lips pressed hungrily on hers, and Andrea let the familiar warmth melt through her. This time there'd be no resisting. No letting him go when she had an aching need that made her hurt all over. Throwing her arms around his neck, she leaned against him.

Then, somewhere in the back of her nostrils, she smelled the rancid stench of the filthy cell. She couldn't come to him like this, unclean and tainted. She drew back.

As though he could read her thoughts, he swung her around. "Do what you have to do." His voice was a husky whisper.

Andrea's body felt heavy with need. "What I have to do is take a shower."

He went with her to the foot of the stairs. "I'll be out here when you're ready." Grateful that he understood, she went up the stairs to her room.

The house had two bathrooms, but the shower in the one upstairs wasn't working. Donning her favorite red satin bathrobe, she glided through the living room toward the one downstairs.

Philip was sitting on the sofa, his jacket off, his tie loosened. Andrea could feel him watching her, could sense his excitement. It made her own even stronger. She turned and smiled at him as she closed the bathroom door. Trembling in her haste, she flung her red bathrobe across a wicker chair on the far side of the big room, opposite the shower.

She turned on the water, sighing with relief when she felt the drops wash warmly against her hand. Shampoo in hand, she stepped into the hot spray.

There was no curtain. Water from the spigot splashed against white tile walls into a drain in the floor. By now, Andrea had gotten used to drying the toilet cover and European-style basin after she showered.

She was rinsing her hair when she heard a rap on the door. It opened a crack. "Need somebody to scrub your back?"

"Desperately," she called, her voice a paean of joy.

"Just a second."

Andrea knew what he was doing. A surge of anticipation jolted through her. Stark naked, he strode into the room, as unselfconscious and confident as if he'd been entering a staff meeting at the embassy. Andrea drank in the sight of him. From her glimpse of him at the hotel in Delhi, she'd known he was massively built from the waist up.

Now, seeing him like this, she felt a kind of awe at his masculine strength, at the sheer clean beauty of him. The mat of dark hair on his chest angled down to join the crisp mass above his groin. His hips were lean, but rounded, too, emphasizing the strength in his thighs. His legs, sturdy as a stallion's, rippled with muscles. Like his hands, his feet were big and square.

The room swam out of focus as he came toward Andrea, fully aroused. Water was gushing over her face, into her eyes, making everything blurry. She shook her head.

Philip stood facing her, water splashing over him. "Do you like what you're seeing?" His deep voice rumbled with barely controlled passion.

"You're so beautiful," she breathed. "I had no idea a man could be so—so—"

He didn't let her finish. "You're the beautiful one, my darling."

Through the shower's spray, she saw the longing in his eyes. Seductively, his gaze slid downward, a gaze as soft as a caress.

Taking the soap from her, he began lathering her all over, lingering on her pleasure points. His gentle massage brought her to the edge of ecstasy. When Andrea thought she could stand no more, he moved behind her and held her back tightly against his front. She felt his wiry chest hair stimulating the bare skin on her back, his hands sliding magically over her slippery breasts until the nipples were firm and hard.

He groaned thickly. "I'm sorry, darling. I can't wait any longer." He swung her around and drew her close.

She parted her lips. He kissed her deeply, violently, as if his life depended on it.

Finally releasing her, he moved her back, standing against the tile wall, out of the steady stream of the shower. Instinctively, Andrea arched her hips toward him. Taking her in his arms, he entered her.

At first, his movements were cautious and tentative. Andrea pushed toward him, forcing him deeper inside her. The feeling was indescribable. She'd had no idea making love standing up could be so erotic. She moaned in pure ecstasy.

Hearing her, Philip could no longer hold himself back. He let himself go as never before. He was a man in love with a woman, a woman who was his match in every way. With thrust after thrust he brought them to the edge. They hung there for a moment and then exploded in a downpour of fiery sensations.

Gradually, Philip became conscious of the spray from the shower. It was splashing on the wall behind them, trickling over Andrea's face, and running down his back.

In his arms, she quivered. He stared into her eyes.

"Did I hurt you?" His voice was concerned.

"A little." She rubbed against him. "But it was a good kind of hurting."

"I'll be more careful next time," he whispered.

"Don't you dare." He felt her breath in his ear. "I loved it."

Stepping backward, he turned off the shower. He took a towel and dried her off, paying special attention to the private places he knew brought her pleasure. His gentle petting aroused his own hunger.

He wanted her again. Was this what it was like to be in love? Always wanting a woman even after just making love to her? Taking her hand, he led her upstairs to the bedroom.

Philip was more gentle this time, less urgent in his demands. Once again he brought them to their special Eden, with its sweet taste of forbidden fruit.

Afterward, he lay beside her, stroking her hair. It felt damply soft beneath his palm.

"I've got to get back to the embassy," he whispered, breaking the long silence between them. "When I left to get you, I was involved in a three-way negotiation between the secretary of state in Washington and Interior Minister Nakarmi. When we get things settled, we're getting together with the prime minister for a dinner meeting."

"It sounds important." Her voice was muffled as she buried her face in his shoulder.

Gently pulling her head back, he cupped her face in his hands. There were tears in her eyes. "What's wrong, darling?"

"We're what's wrong." Teardrops spilled over her lashes and ran down her cheeks. "It's not fair that we've just found each other and now I've got to go home."

He kissed her wet cheek. "I'm not letting you get away this easily. In another month or two, I'll arrange to be ordered to Washington for a debriefing at State. I'll see you then."

"That's not the same."

She was right, of course. A week's visit to Washington every couple of months was hardly equivalent to having her with him every day and night of his life.

He ran his finger down her cheek. "Sleep in tomorrow morning, and I'll see you around one for lunch at my place."

She nodded and said she'd be there.

Not until Philip was in the car, on his way back to the embassy compound, did a disturbing thought occur to him. From the moment he heard Andrea was coming, he'd done everything in his power to be rid of her. When she left for home the day after tomorrow, he'd be getting exactly what he asked for.

But now it wasn't what he wanted.

Chapter Thirteen

At six-thirty Sunday morning, long before Jan got up, Andrea walked the two blocks from the house to Mazipat Street. There she caught the first three-wheeled tempo that came by. Though she told the driver to take her to the embassy's staff entrance, she did not intend to spend her last day in Tisara anywhere near the office.

Once inside the embassy compound, Andrea headed across the grounds to the front entrance. On the busy street outside, she flagged down a taxi. If Colonel Khadka was having her followed, she'd probably lost the tail at the staff entrance. But she took no chances. She changed taxis twice more before climbing into one near the Everest Hotel.

The driver wore a dirty yellow shirt and smelled of garlic and sweat, but he had a congenial smile and unstained teeth. Apparently, he was one of the few Tisarans over thirty who didn't chew the addictive betel nut leaves.

Peering inside his car, Andrea saw it was relatively clean. After a few minutes' haggling, he agreed—for eight hundred rupees—to take her to the terraced hillside in the shadow of Laigsi Peak.

No matter what the risk, she had to talk to the priest again before she left the country. He was her last chance to find out what had really happened to Jeffry.

He was also her last chance to learn the truth about Tisaran involvement in the production and black market sale of germ warfare weapons. Was the terraced hillside, with its exotic orange blossoms, somehow connected to the strange events in and around Ganthaku during the past year? The priest and his odd mussenda bushes were common threads tying Dhara Village to the temple compound.

Andrea glanced nervously at her watch. Seven-thirty already. Five and a half hours to get to the village, talk to the priest and return in time for lunch with Philip. She didn't dare tell him where she was going. After yesterday, he'd try to stop her. On their last day together, Andrea wanted no arguments.

In preparation for her coming hike across the hillside, she had dressed in rugged twill pants and a heavy shirt. Fresh chemical projectors were loaded into her pen camera and the heels of her hiking boots. Her leather bag was slung across one shoulder, her binoculars across the other.

Now, seated in the back of the taxi, she stared at the crumbling brick buildings on the outskirts of Ganthaku and felt her resolve crumbling, the way the buildings were. Was this last-ditch effort worth the risk of ending up in some wretched little cell, exposed to unmentionable horrors?

Andrea had serious doubts. But she didn't tell the driver to turn around. Giving up now, while there was still a chance to learn the truth, would make her sorry for the rest of her life.

As they left the city, the buildings got farther apart. Behind the structures were fields that looked lush and green compared to the packed dirt everywhere else.

Watching from the window, Andrea realized that these buildings weren't falling down, but being constructed. On their heads, women carried big baskets full of bricks from huge central piles. Scores of people shoveled earth that could have been leveled in half an hour by a bulldozer. Seeing their dogged persistence—and the way they'd turned the valley green with their bare hands—strengthened Andrea's resolve.

The taxi seemed to have no shock absorbers. Andrea felt herself fly off the seat into the air, the bumps were so bad. About halfway to the hillside, the narrow road turned even narrower and became almost impassible. Alongside squatted dozens of men and women, just as when she'd come by here with Philip last Sunday. They were still using crude hammers to pound big pieces of stone into gravel. But in the week that had passed, the piles of gravel had doubled in height. Now they were as tall as a man.

For about half an hour the taxi inched along on the rutted surface of road under repair, its speed rarely exceeding ten miles per hour. When they finally reached a relatively smooth section, Andrea's insides felt sore from all the bouncing.

Why hadn't she felt shaken like this when she'd come with Philip? Because the Jeep had springs and shocks, she thought. And because Mohan was trying to make the ride smoother for them. But mostly because Philip was sitting beside her, taking her mind off the rough road.

She smiled wryly, thinking of how concerned he'd be if he knew where she was. When he found out, he was sure to be angry. She didn't like doing something that would upset him, but she had to finish what she'd started.

Finally, she spotted the terraced hillside she was looking for. Sloping down from the road, its banks blazed with shades of orange from the exotic mussenda blossoms. The snow-covered Himalayas loomed over the terraces on the opposite hill.

"Pull over here and wait," Andrea told the driver. When the little car had stopped, she climbed out, her body stiff from nearly two hours' jouncing.

The trail she'd walked with Philip wound across the hillside, with narrow stone steps leading down each of the terrace walls.

Andrea hesitated. Did she really want to go through with this? She smelled tobacco smoke and knew the driver had lit a cigarette. But she didn't turn back toward the car. If she retreated one step, she knew she'd give up. Then she'd hate herself for the rest of her life for not daring to take this one last chance to learn the truth.

Far below, at the foot of the hill, flowed the Bagmati River on its way to Ishwaranath, and from there to the sacred Ganges. In the distance, near the river, she saw the clusters of two- and three-story stone huts with thatched roofs.

Beyond the huts a plume of white smoke billowed skyward. Andrea tensed. What had Mohan said? That the villagers were engaged in a funeral ceremony when he was there? Could it be a coincidence that last rites were again being celebrated today?

She took a tentative step toward the narrow trail. Of course it was no coincidence. Fires burned here much of the time, according to the satellite report she'd received from her controller.

Andrea wrinkled her nose. The acrid odor from the cremation ghats at Ishwaranath still lingered in her memory. In that sacred place, the last rites were performed hour after hour, day after day. But here? In this remote area? How many cremations were needed in a village of two hundred or so people?

There had to be another reason for the smoke. When Andrea talked to the priest, she'd ask him about it. Squaring her shoulders, she started down the narrow trail across the terraced hillside.

ON THE THIRD TERRACE below the road, Andrea passed a group of women working among the mussenda bushes. They were snapping the orange blossoms from the stalks and gathering them into big baskets.

"Where is the priest who tends the temple garden?" she asked one of the women in Tisaran. Since Colonel Khadka knew she was an expert in the area, and since she was leaving tomorrow, Andrea saw no reason to hide her familiarity with the language.

The woman gave Andrea a curious stare. Barefoot, she was draped in a loose-fitting shirt and skirt wrapped at the waist with a wide band of cloth. The other women stopped their work and moved closer.

Andrea stepped toward them and smiled. Even with her hair under a cap, she knew she must look like something from outer space to these people.

"Where can I find your priest?" she asked again, glancing from one unsmiling face to the next. Again she got no answer.

"He's short and fat with a body like Buddha." Andrea made a quick motion with her hands to show what she meant.

One of the women giggled. Then another turned to a young boy standing behind her. "Run and tell the priest a strange white woman has come looking for him."

Andrea watched the youngster take off for the cluster of huts. Anxiety quickened her blood. Would the priest talk to her?

Holding her emotions in check, she addressed the woman who'd spoken. "Does the priest live in the village?"

"Yes, he tends the sick and dying."

The sick and dying? Andrea's eyes widened. "Then this village has a house of death? Like the one next to the Temple to Ishwara in Ganthaku?"

The women crowded around her, their initial hesitation gone.

"Yes," one replied. "This is a sacred place. Like Ishwaranath."

"People come here from India to die," another chimed in. "The priest purifies them in the sacred river, and they are spared another incarnation."

Andrea's mind rebelled. "If this place is sacred, where is the temple?"

"Inside the house of death," the woman replied.

Andrea knew the Hindus in Tisara practiced their religion somewhat differently than those in India. They flavored their worship with animism and Buddhism, and practiced animal sacrifice. But she'd never heard of a Hindu temple in either country without a *vimana,* or spire, over the inner sanctum.

Whatever was going on here probably had no connection to religion, no matter how much somebody tried to package it in holiness. That meant the activity must be illegal. Otherwise, why cover it up?

Andrea bent down to smell a stalk of the orchidlike blossoms. "Are the flowers sacred?" The smell, sweeter than honeysuckle, made her want to sneeze. "Is that why they're grown in this sacred place?"

"Yes." Several women spoke at once. Then, giggling, they looked to one who continued. "From the flowers we make an ointment that is rubbed on those who are dying."

So the flowers were used to produce a drug. Andrea felt a growing sense of uneasiness.

"Do the families come with the people who are dying?" she asked. In the Hindu faith, only sons could perform the last rites. No one would come alone from India to die. If those who died here came alone, perhaps they were not coming willingly.

"No," came the answer.

Andrea's sense of unease increased.

"These are sadhus with no sons," someone said.

A sacred place with no temple where holy men from India come to die? The story made no sense. A cold knot formed in Andrea's stomach. Were these women being told a preposterous lie to hide what was really going on here? That victims were being brought to Dhara Village as prisoners and then killed for some evil purpose?

Andrea didn't let her uneasiness show. "Are the dying sadhus brought here in an aircraft with a wing on top?" With her hand over her head, she imitated a helicopter's rotary blades.

The women nodded eagerly. "Yes, yes." Their voices joined in chorus.

Andrea remembered the increase in small aircraft traffic between Delhi and Ganthaku. She remembered the bars on the windows at Prana Pharmaceuticals. Were victims held captive at Prana until they could be flown to Ganthaku? Then taken by helicopter to the house of death at Dhara Village?

A sense of unspeakable horror wrapped around her like a shroud. What was happening to the victims from India? Why were they being brought here to die?

"The house of death," Andrea asked. "What is it like?"

Their faces sobered. "We do not know. No one goes inside but the priest and those who care for the dying."

"Do those who care for the dying come from your village?"

They shook their heads. "They are strangers from India. They do not speak our language."

Andrea shuddered. Something ghoulish was going on here. Why else would the villagers not be used as caretakers?

"Where do these strangers live?"

Everybody knew the answer to that. "In the house of death," they chorused.

Andrea felt herself shiver. The caretakers, obviously in on the plot, didn't mix with the villagers.

"Which building is the house of death?" Andrea took her binoculars out of their case.

A woman extended her arm, pointing her finger in the general direction of the village. "There. By the river."

Andrea lifted her glasses. "You mean it's the building two stories high, closest to the river?"

"Yes," the woman returned. "Closest to the river."

The building, down a slight hill from the others, was half-hidden behind them and some trees, but Andrea could make out most of the upper story and a small section of the lower. When she compared the building with the others in the village, she noticed it had more windows on the upper floor. Was that where the caretakers lived? She had to get closer for a better look.

After telling the women goodbye, Andrea continued down the narrow pathway. At the edge of the terrace, she had a better view of the building's lower story. She lifted the binoculars again.

The windows on the lower floor were smaller than those above and built high up on the wall. Intently she studied them. They were barred. At first, she thought she was mistaken. Bushes growing beside the building partially obscured the windows.

She walked another quarter mile or so closer and again lifted the glasses. She wasn't wrong. The windows were barred. *Just like the ones at Prana Pharmaceuticals.*

Her heart thudding, Andrea angled the binoculars around. Was there anything else unusual about the building?

It's air-conditioned. Andrea couldn't believe her eyes. But there sat the compressor. It was partly hidden in the brush, but she had no doubt that's what it was. In a village of mud and stone huts, here was an air-conditioned building, or one that held some kind of big refrigeration unit.

Without lowering the binoculars, she turned, scanning the area. A brown blur appeared in front of her lenses. Jerking the glasses away, she saw two Tisaran men heading up the trail toward her single file. Their faces wore the same stoic look Andrea had seen on the women's. And their ragged clothes had the same dusty look. But there was something threatening in the way they stared at her.

Sheer, black fright twisted through her. If something ghoulish was going on at Dhara Village, she was in real danger.

"I've come to see your priest," she began, when the first of the two men reached her. The other was standing behind him.

"The priest is not here today," one of them said.

Turning, Andrea waved a hand toward the women, now hunched over the flaming orange bushes. "They told me he was in the house of death, caring for the dying."

"The women are wrong." His tone carried a note of finality.

Andrea didn't argue. The priest didn't want to see her. Well, that was fine with her. She'd seen and heard enough to know something was terribly wrong here. With what she'd found out, Philip had good reason to ask his friend the interior minister some very direct questions.

The men started toward her. "We will accompany you to your car."

Andrea held up her hand. "I'm going." Turning, she walked away as fast as she could. She didn't hear them behind her. But when she reached the next terrace, she swung around to see if they'd started back toward the village.

No. They were still standing there, watching her. Their hostility stabbed across the distance like an invisible dagger. Andrea could hardly keep from running the rest of the way to the waiting taxi.

WHEN PHILIP TOLD Interior Minister Ganesh Nakarmi about the barred windows and air-conditioning at Dhara Village's house of death, Nakarmi broke into a broad smile.

Philip didn't return it. He could see nothing humorous in this situation. Ever since Andrea, over lunch, had described her trip to the hillside, he'd been seething with carefully controlled anger. Once again she'd done exactly what he asked her not to. What she'd found out made him even more fearful for what might have happened to her.

Now Philip was sitting on an easy chair in Nakarmi's living room. The rest of the house was quiet. Nakarmi's wife and two sons had vanished when Philip said he had important business to discuss on this Sunday afternoon.

"Ah, you have stumbled onto our secret," Nakarmi admitted. "I'm sorry, my friend, I should have confided in you sooner."

Philip frowned. "Confided in me? About what, Ganesh?"

A man about Philip's age, Nakarmi radiated congenial good spirits. The elaborate living room, decorated in shades of yellow and orange, reflected his cheerfulness. Brown and lean, with finely sculpted features, he looked more Indian than Tisaran.

"It's a government secret." Nakarmi lowered his voice. "We're trying to keep it quiet. Only the king and a few other important people know about it."

"Then maybe you shouldn't tell me." Philip pictured Andrea's excitement as she described what she'd seen at Dhara Village. She wouldn't encourage Nakarmi to keep silent. But Philip respected his friend too much to encourage him to reveal confidential government information. Just as Philip couldn't share the Sparrow code with Nakarmi, his friend couldn't tell Philip classified details of the kingdom's business.

"I trust you," Nakarmi confided. "I think it's time for you to know about this matter."

"If you want to tell me, I can't stop you." Though eager to hear his friend's explanation, Philip kept his voice restrained.

Nakarmi, on the sofa, moved closer to Philip's chair. "We have developed a new drug." His voice lowered to a whisper. "Even now, in spite of what you've found out about Dhara Village, I wouldn't tell you about it if you weren't a friend I trusted."

"New drug?" Philip said. "I'm not sure I like what I'm hearing."

Nakarmi laughed out loud. "Oh, no, Philip. Not a mind-altering drug."

Philip waited, trying to be patient. Sometimes Nakarmi's lengthy lead-ins annoyed him.

"What we've discovered is a marvelous hair restoration drug that will . . ."

"A hair restoration drug!" Philip spit out the words. So he'd guessed right when Andrea told him about the odd-smelling flowers. "Are you telling me those villagers are making a product to grow hair?"

Nakarmi nodded sagely. "Yes, but they don't know it. They think they're making a sacred balm to help dying Indian sadhus on their journey to nirvana. The story is part of the deception to keep the drug secret. The stuff's worth a fortune." Nakarmi paused. "That's why we guard the temple garden. The new strains of the plant are being developed there."

Philip pictured Andrea's amazement at the news. And in his head, he heard the objections she was certain to voice. Unable to sit still longer, he rose from the sofa and stood before Nakarmi, his arms folded. "What about the bars on the windows?"

His friend leaned back and clasped his fingers in front of his chest. "The bars are to keep people out."

"The guide at Prana Pharmaceuticals in Delhi said the same thing." Philip studied Nakarmi intently, remembering India, where three Americans had been murdered. Were they killed to protect a secret hair restoration drug?

Nakarmi's face tightened. "Why did you go to Prana Pharmaceuticals, Philip?"

"They make a special type of fertilizer," Philip answered quickly. "I'd heard of it in connection with the garden you showed me at Ishwaranath."

"Prana is working with us on our new drug." Nakarmi chuckled again, but his eyes narrowed with concern. "We're not keeping our secret very well if the U.S. ambassador hears about our researchers in Delhi."

"I've heard some rumors," Philip admitted, "but most of my conclusions seem to have been wrong. What about the cremations at the village? The people who live there think the bodies of sadhus from India are being burned."

Nakarmi smiled more broadly. "The cremations are really brush fires. The villagers aren't permitted near the river during the so-called cremations. The priest told them it wasn't allowed for sadhus. Instead, he burns the mussenda bushes."

"I don't believe it, Ganesh." Philip planted himself in front of Nakarmi. "Those people may not be educated, but I'm willing to bet they know the difference between a brush fire and a cremation, even from a distance."

"What are you saying?' Nakarmi wasn't smiling now. "That the priest is really burning bodies?"

"That's what I'm saying." Philip's tone was accusing.

Nakarmi stood up and looked Philip straight in the eye. "Do you want to see Dhara Village for yourself? I'll take you."

Philip remembered Andrea's warning that, with a little time, an area could be sanitized. "If it isn't soon, there's no point."

"How about right now?" A slow smile slid across Nakarmi's lips.

Philip dropped back into the easy chair, his mind reeling. If he could get a look at the village with no warning to the inhabitants, he'd see exactly what was going on. Whoever was in charge would have no chance to clean up his "ghoulish business," as Andrea called it.

But Philip had planned to spend the night with her. Now that he'd found her, he couldn't let her leave tomorrow without being with her this last night.

Reluctantly, he shook his head. "We'd have to stay there all night. Much as I'd like to go, I've got to turn you down. I've got something planned this evening that can't be put on hold."

Nakarmi examined Philip's face through narrowed eyes. "I want you to see the village for yourself so you'll have no more doubts." He paused and smiled. "I, too, have something planned for tonight and must return. So, we'll take the helicopter. Figuring a half-hour ride to the airport, twenty minutes over and twenty back, we should be home before dark."

A sense of triumphant elation surged through Philip. "I'll have to call my secretary and let her know where I've gone."

Nakarmi gestured toward the nearby phone on a table in the front hallway. "Please."

Philip called Andrea at the house. He knew she'd be waiting for his call. "Mrs. Mitchell?" he asked, letting her know he wasn't alone.

"Yes." She sounded breathless, the way she always did when she was excited about something. He pictured her intense face with its frame of platinum-blond curls. He missed her already, though only an hour had passed since he'd seen her for lunch. How he wished she could come with them.

"The interior minister is taking me on a visit to Dhara Village." Philip spoke quickly, without pausing. "We're flying there in a helicopter and should be back in Ganthaku before dark. Will you tell the duty officer, please?"

"Yes." She hesitated.

"Don't change your plans." Philip emphasized the words. He was going to be with Andrea tonight. He wanted to be sure she knew it. "I'll call you as soon as I get back."

Philip hung up the phone and turned to Ganesh Nakarmi. "Is there a chopper pilot on standby at the airport?"

His friend's chest swelled visibly. "I myself am the pilot."

Philip eyed Nakarmi with astonishment. "You are a man of many talents, Ganesh. Why didn't you tell me before?"

Smiling, Nakarmi lifted a thin eyebrow. "It was part of the government secret. Soon you will know everything. You can see how much I trust you, Philip."

WHEN THE SETTING SUN reflected on the tip of Liagsi Peak, Andrea settled herself on the living-room sofa, close to the phone. She knew Philip would call her as soon as he got back. What would he find out? She couldn't wait to hear.

Unlike Philip's tour of Ishwaranath Temple with Nakarmi, this visit to Dhara Village was unannounced. The priest wouldn't have a chance to clean up his operation before Philip saw it.

Did that mean the interior minister knew what was really going on there? He must think so, or he wouldn't take Philip to see it.

Could Nakarmi be wrong? Andrea's nerves tightened. Could something sinister be happening there without his knowledge? If so, by arriving at the place unannounced, Nakarmi and Philip were in real danger.

Frowning, she shook her head. Nakarmi must have given Philip a reasonable explanation for what Andrea had seen. Otherwise, Philip wouldn't have agreed to go.

But Nakarmi had insisted nothing suspicious was going on at Ishwaranath, too. Andrea suspected a communications network originated there—or had when she was at the Pentagon.

Ishwaranath. What she wouldn't give to spend a couple of hours combing through the temple complex.

The room darkened rapidly. Andrea pulled the chain on the floor lamp behind the sofa. A pool of light flooded the space where she was sitting, but the rest of the room remained in shadow.

Her anxiety mounted as the minutes passed and the phone didn't ring. *Where is Philip? He said he'd be back in Ganthaku by dark.* She picked up the newspaper but was too worried to concentrate on what it said.

When forty-five minutes had passed, she called the residence. He wasn't there. Then she called the duty officer to see if he'd heard anything. He hadn't.

With a choking sense of disaster, Andrea knocked on Jan's bedroom door. It opened.

"I think the ambassador's in trouble." Andrea couldn't keep her voice from quivering.

Jan reached for Andrea's hand and pulled her inside. Since Andrea's return from India, there'd been a three-hundred-sixty-degree change in Jan's attitude. She actually seemed sorry Andrea was leaving.

Plopping down on the bed, Jan gestured toward one of the room's two chairs. Andrea sat down.

"What do you think's happened to him?" There was real concern in Jan's voice.

"I only know he said he'd be back before dark. I just called the residence, and he isn't there yet." Andrea felt as though a giant hand had closed around her throat. "We've got to do something. Maybe the helicopter's crashed. Maybe somebody's taken him hostage."

Jan touched Andrea's arm. "Sam will be here in a few minutes to pick me up for our date. He'll help us."

WHEN SAM CONNELLY arrived, he listened to Andrea's story; then he made some phone calls. Andrea paced nervously as she heard Connelly's end of the conversation. The first two calls, to the residence and then to the duty officer, confirmed that Philip had contacted neither.

Something was terribly wrong. Philip would never be gone this long without getting in touch.

Connelly's third call, to the Tisaran Ministry of Interior, got no answer. His fourth was to the minister's home. Andrea saw relief on Connelly's face as he talked to the minister's wife. When he'd hung up, he faced Andrea and Jan.

"They decided to spend the night in Dhara Village." He flashed a triumphant smile. "They'll be back tomorrow morning."

After I've gone. Andrea felt an instant of squeezing hurt.

Jan took her hand, her face drawn down with concern. "I'm sorry. I know you were planning dinner together tonight."

Unable to speak, Andrea squeezed Jan's hand.

"The delay must be something he couldn't help," Jan sympathized. "Would you like to have dinner with Sam and me?"

Swallowing the lump in her throat, Andrea shook her head. She didn't try to smile when she thanked them.

After they'd left, she sat in lonely silence. Her throat ached with sick yearning. If the interior minister had reached his wife, why hadn't Philip called her? He had intended to be with her tonight. He'd made that very clear.

Her earlier fears returned. Maybe he was in some kind of trouble and couldn't call. Was there a way to find out?

Andrea picked up the telephone receiver. Dhara Village must have at least one phone or Nakarmi couldn't have gotten through. She spent half an hour trying to reach a working number. Finally, she hung up, convinced there were no phones within miles of the village.

Then how had the interior minister reached his wife? The answer was obvious. Over the communications network, of course, the one Andrea had read about at the Pentagon. From Dhara Village, the minister—or someone claiming to speak for him—had radioed the network's element at Ishwaranath. Somebody at the temple compound had relayed

Nakarmi's message to his wife over the telephone. With the minister and the ambassador accounted for, nobody would start looking for them.

If Nakarmi had arranged for a message to his wife, why hadn't Philip done the same for Andrea? *Because he was being held prisoner.* The thought wouldn't go away.

The gilded three-tiered roof of the Temple to Ishwara appeared in Andrea's mind. The image brought back a loathsome memory of Colonel Khadka and his wretched cell. She didn't dare go back to Ishwaranath again. Not ever.

But now Philip was in trouble. She had to do something to help.

Ishwaranath. From the very first, the temple compound had played an important part in this murderous game. But what part? Intuitively, Andrea knew that somewhere inside she could learn what had happened to Philip, and why.

She had to go there again.

Tonight.

Chapter Fourteen

Changing quickly into the twill pants and heavy shirt she'd worn that morning, Andrea draped the gray wool shawl over her shoulders and around her waist. As she hurried toward Mazipat Street to flag down a taxi, she calmed her apprehension by downplaying the risk. After the way Colonel Khadka had frightened her, he was unlikely to suspect her of venturing onto the temple grounds again. And tonight there would be no treacherous guide along to betray her.

Andrea frowned, remembering how she'd trusted Tulak. If he'd been reporting to Khadka, why had he been killed?

Because he was probably working both sides of the street and being loyal to neither, she thought grimly. Clearly, the guide had played a dangerous game and lost. With sudden insight, she realized why Tulak had known someone witnessed Jeffry's accident. He must have found out in his dealings with Khadka.

Andrea sighed to herself. Tulak had probably informed on Colonel Butler, too. Philip should be told that if— *when*—she saw him again.

As she had that morning, Andrea changed cabs several times, taking special care to avoid being followed. When she finally reached Ishwaranath Village, it was nearly ten. Draping the shawl over her head to hide her hair and then wrapping the cloth around her waist, she started down the dirty stone street toward the temple compound.

There were no streetlights. But on either side of the road, bare bulbs lit the interiors of most of the open shops she passed. The lights cast deceptive shadows on the piles of dirt along the side of the street.

Though nighttime, a multitude crowded the dirt path that passed as a sidewalk. Andrea's heart beat faster. Why were all these people going to the temple?

Instead of heading toward the bridge, she continued down stone steps to the block-wide series of platforms and three-tier stairways leading into the river. Here were the cremation ghats she'd seen before. But ashes from the day's cremations were gone, she noticed, already swept into the river.

Some sort of celebration seemed to be underway. Andrea heard the soft bonging of temple bells. Below the Temple to Ishwara, floodlights mounted on stone buildings shone on an orderly line of the faithful. The line snaked up a steep flight of steps into the temple courtyard. Countless more worshippers thronged the platform and stairs closest to the river.

For a moment Andrea hesitated. A tremor passed through her. How could she bribe the guard with all these people watching? All around her, men and women—some of the men naked except for a loincloth—were drenching themselves in the murky water.

She started with surprise when a woman spoke next to her. "Have you paid tribute to Ishwara?" Water dripped from the woman's clothes. She'd just emerged from the river.

"No," Andrea replied. "I will cleanse myself first." The woman murmured a blessing and moved into the shadows to wring out her garments.

Dismayed, Andrea eyed the line heading upward into the temple. In the shadows she'd been mistaken for a believer, but never under the floodlights. She studied the wall around the courtyard. How could anything secret be hidden in a temple filled day and night with these throbbing hordes? She'd had no idea this many people crowded into the place at any one time.

Staring up the stone staircase at the masses coming and going, Andrea shook her head. No, if something secret was going on in this compound, it would be in a remote place. *A remote place that was guarded.* A burst of adrenaline jolted through her. *A remote place like the temple garden.*

Without hurrying, she retraced her steps up the hill beside the bridge. At the top, she crossed to the river's far side.

Though the hour was late, small bands of tourists watched from the bridge and stone parapet opposite the temple. They stared fixedly, their faces sober, as if trying to understand such devotion.

Her heart in her throat, Andrea turned away, into the darkness. After staring into the floodlights, the blackness blinded her. Was anyone following? She paused, listening. Nothing moved.

Climbing the stone stairs up the hill across from the temple, she reached a place low enough to step onto the series of ledges on the other side. Even here, high above the river, its dank smell hung in the air.

Suddenly, the compound seemed strangely empty. After the multitude near the temple, the emptiness pressed in on Andrea, looming around her like an evil mist. The few lights provided a hazy yellow glow that disappeared within a few feet. Off in the distance, at the compound's highest point, a faint circle of light marked her objective: the walled temple garden.

A cold knot formed in her stomach. She breathed deeply, reminding herself she was a lot safer here than in most cities in the United States. She'd barely started to relax when she smelled cigarette smoke. Her stomach clenched again. Someone was nearby, hidden behind one of the crumbling stone buildings. Was he watching her?

Don't be an idiot, she told herself. *If somebody's after you, they're not standing around smoking.* Her stern admonishment did nothing to allay her fear. Finally, when she climbed more stairs, the cigarette smell disappeared.

Trembling, she made her way through the dark stone maze. She tripped on uneven steps, stumbled over the rocky floors and bumped into small square structures and statues that turned to demons in the darkness. But she didn't dare turn on her flashlight. The guard in the kiosk outside the garden might spot a moving light. She had to get around him and over the five-foot-high wall without being seen.

Breathing in shallow quick gasps, she strove to maintain some measure of control over her fear. One time she took a step and dropped through eight inches of empty space. When she landed, her jaw snapped together so hard her whole head hurt. Another time she stepped in something slippery that felt suspiciously like excrement. The nauseating smell wafted around her like a premonition of impending disaster.

Finally, Andrea climbed a stone staircase, rounded a building and saw the garden wall straight ahead. She stopped and nervously surveyed it. Her heart sank. The lights were brighter than they'd looked from a distance.

She drew close, shrinking into the shadows. The guard was slumped over on a chair in the kiosk. He appeared to be dozing. But there might be another patrolling the area.

Andrea took no chances. For ten minutes, she observed the slumped figure in the kiosk and the stone walkways around the wall. At last she made a dash through the lighted area and around the wall's corner. Once out of the guard's sight she paused, taking deep breaths to control her racing heart.

Had anyone seen her? She stopped, half expecting the guard to come charging after her. But she heard only the sound of her own heavy breathing.

Hunched over, she slipped along the wall, staying in its shadow. Halfway down it, she straightened and peered over. Inside the garden she could see only one floodlight, positioned near a corner. Her heart thudding crazily, Andrea headed for the darkest spot. When she'd reached it, she gripped the top of the wall with her arms. With a mighty heave, she managed to pull herself up and throw one leg over.

Hoisting the rest of herself up and over, she dropped lightly to the ground. Then she ran through the mussenda bushes to the small brick building behind the greenhouse and pressed herself flat against it.

Lights were on inside, but the windows were covered with dark curtains. She moved close to the glass, hoping to see through a tiny hole or split in the fabric. Nothing.

Moving out of the shadows, she inched along the building to the next window. Her heart surged with hope. The curtains didn't quite meet in the center.

Andrea peered inside. A heavy black-haired man was seated, his back to her, in front of what appeared to be a broadcasting console. Next to it was a computer data display terminal.

A sense of great excitement swept over her. She'd found it—the communications station on whose messages she'd based so much of her analysis. Since the minister of interior knew nothing about the station, it must be operating outside of government authority. And that meant something clandestine was going on here. If not biological warfare, what?

She heard the voice of the man at the console. Was he sending a message? She pressed closer to the window, trying to make out the words.

Another man spoke. He sounded so close that Andrea froze. He must be standing inside, right next to her window. She had no trouble hearing him.

"The minister's no fool, Dass. With the right incentive, he was overjoyed to join us." He laughed raucously.

Dass? He'd called the man at the console *Dass.* She'd been right about somebody taking Dass Verma for a code name. That's why it had appeared on the intercepted messages.

She felt a terrible tenseness in her body. But what did the unseen speaker mean about the "minister" being "overjoyed" to join them? Could the minister be Ganesh Nakarmi, the interior minister? The friend Philip had gone to Dhara Village with?

The pudgy man sitting at the console swung around. Stark terror swept through Andrea when she glimpsed his buttery face. There was a satanic smile on his swollen lips.

Dass Verma was the assassin, the man who'd come close to killing her and Philip in India, who'd murdered the two CIA agents in Agra and Economic Officer White in Delhi. She gripped the window ledge to steady herself.

"It's a nasty business, but lucrative." His voice was high-pitched with nasal tones.

A split second later a heavy hand tightened on her shoulder. Andrea's heart dropped like a stone. She jerked her head around.

The guard. "You are prisoner, madam." He spoke in broken English. "Please to come with me."

"I WAS ONLY TRYING to find my husband," Andrea told a wrathful Colonel Khadka in his office at army headquarters. This was at least the tenth time she'd said the same thing. Though her insides were in knots, she remained outwardly calm, insisting she'd done nothing wrong.

Roused from his bed, the colonel glowered at her, cold fury in his bicolored eyes. He didn't let Andrea sit down.

"I tried to be lenient with you, Mrs. Mitchell. But you've deliberately disobeyed me." He scowled at her. "Disobeying me carries a much stiffer penalty than disobeying your ambassador.''

Andrea sucked in her breath. She remembered Khadka's treatment of the young guard who had accepted her baksheesh.

Take the dog to Slonpo and shoot him. Just remembering the words made her feel sick. Thank the Lord she hadn't had dinner. Nothing was inside her stomach to come up.

She forced herself to stand erect, not to tremble. "I'm a citizen of the United States, and I've done nothing wrong." She paused, remembering the throbbing hordes around Ishwaranath Temple. "On this sacred night, I thought the priest would be in his garden. Since this is my last night here, I wanted to talk to him, to find out what happened to my husband.''

"You're a liar." He spoke the words flatly, without emotion. "You are a spy and will be treated as a spy."

He looked past her toward a uniformed captain behind her.

"Search her," he ordered in Tisaran.

Andrea let her breath out in a long sigh. Being searched was humiliating but better than getting shot or turned over to the assassin.

The captain's hands were on her, patting at her shirt and pants pockets, stroking her legs and back and stomach. Andrea submitted stoically, fighting her revulsion. She felt her face flush with resentment.

Khadka dumped her shoulder bag bottom-up on his desk, poking among the contents until he found what he seemed to be looking for. *Her pen camera.*

"Ah, the famous pen that sprays tear gas." Holding the pen in two fingers, he waved it in front of her. "You'll have no need of this where you're going."

The room swayed dizzily around Andrea. If Khadka knew about the weapon, he'd had a firsthand report from Dass Verma, the fat assassin. That meant he knew about the broadcasting terminal at the temple complex, about the strange goings-on at Dhara Village.

Andrea felt momentary panic as her mind leaped ahead. Colonel Ratna Khadka, the most powerful man in the Tisaran army, must be part of this horrible plot. She'd probably be taken to Slonpo Prison and shot. *The way the young guard was.*

It was her last thought before everything turned black.

WHEN ANDREA CAME TO, she was lying on the floor of Khadka's office. The captain was tying her hands behind her back. She felt his fingers crawling on her wrist.

How long had she been unconscious? Probably only a few minutes. Her cheeks burned with shame that she'd fainted.

"Ah, you're with us again, Mrs. Mitchell." Khadka's mouth twisted into a thin-lipped smile. "Let's see if you can walk."

He thrust a big hand under her arm and jerked her to her feet. His swarthy face was set in a vicious expression. Andrea swayed precariously, afraid she was going to faint again.

"She's faking, my colonel," the captain said.

"Watch what you say," Khadka returned. "She speaks our language."

With one on each side of her, they half carried, half dragged her to a waiting sedan. Andrea felt hands fumbling at the top of her boots, pressing her legs together, tying them with a strap. Then she was dumped on the car's back seat on her side.

The seat felt hard. Facing front, Andrea had to bend her legs. Her knees, extended over the seat edge, were jammed against the back of the front seat.

"Where are you taking me?" In spite of her ignominious position, Andrea tried to sound indignant. But she could hardly lift her voice above a whisper. She turned her head toward Khadka, standing outside the car's open door.

He smiled sarcastically, showing stained teeth and reddish-black gums. "You'll find out when you get there." He threw the captain a warning glance. "She fainted and may be too ill for our plans. The doctor will have to examine her."

Plans? Doctor? Sheer black fright twisted through Andrea. What plans did Khadka have for her? Why did they involve a doctor's examination? Were they going to use her as a guinea pig for some awful germ warfare experiment? Since Khadka and the fat assassin were in this together, no horror was beyond her imagining.

When the car left the army post, Khadka stayed behind. An enlisted man drove. The captain sat beside him.

Lying in the back of the moving car, Andrea tried to think of some way to escape. She was no good to Philip—or to herself—trussed up like a stuffed turkey.

But try as she would, she couldn't think of a viable plan. Her attempts to work her hands free failed. The captain had done a good job tying them. The rope was just tight enough to keep her from getting loose without cutting into her skin.

The captain and his driver spoke little. When they did talk, their voices were so low she had to strain to hear them over the vehicle's engine and the sound of the tires on the road.

Andrea's blood froze when the enlisted man said something about "having a little fun along the way."

The captain grunted his response. "Impossible. You heard the colonel. She will be examined by the doctor soon after we arrive."

Stark terror tore at Andrea's insides. She'd been saved from violation at the hands of these two soldiers only to be exposed to something far worse. Thinking about the doctor and what he might do to her brought her to the edge of panic. She tore at her bonds with the fury of one condemned.

What would Philip do if he knew what was happening to her?

Philip. She didn't dare think of him. His image in her mind made her turn soft, regretful. If there was one time she couldn't afford to feel sorry for what might have been, this was that time. As the car rattled on in the night, she kept trying to untie her hands. But the stubborn knots refused to yield.

Some time later, they entered an especially rough section of road. Immediately, Andrea began counting so she could tell how long they were on it. The seconds she counted off added up to about thirty minutes—almost exactly the time required to get across the section of road under construction en route to the terraced hillside near Laigsi Peak.

That's when she guessed where they were going on this midnight ride. To Dhara Village. Would she find Philip there?

THE PHYSICIAN WORE a blue mask over his nose and mouth. His hair was covered with a green cap.

Dressed only in a flimsy cotton robe, Andrea sat on the edge of a metal examining table. Fear of what this ordinary-looking man was going to do to her chilled her more than the room's sixty-eight-degree temperature. The air-conditioned chamber appeared to be an operating room. Though crude by the standards of modern Western hospitals, it had the bright lights and hanging tubes Andrea associated with operating rooms.

"What ... are you ... going to do to me?" Her voice was halting.

"Tonight we give you a thorough physical examination." he had a distinctive accent that wasn't Tisaran. His words, spoken through the mask, were blurred. "You fainted before you came here. We want to be certain you are well enough to perform certain tasks tomorrow."

Andrea shuddered inwardly. What kind of sadistic *tasks* did Colonel Khadka have in mind?

The doctor's eyebrow lifted. "After the examination, you will eat. Get a good sleep."

Andrea had no illusions about where she'd be sleeping. While an Indian woman watched, she'd changed into the flimsy robe in a room with bars over its one window.

"If I'm going to be spending the night in a cell, why bother with a physical exam?" She spat the words out, hoping to catch him off guard.

Apparently she did. He lifted the mask to speak more clearly.

When Andrea saw his face, her breathing stopped. She forced herself to inhale, struggling to regain her composure.

This man was the Middle Eastern physician specializing in biological warfare whose picture she'd seen in Pentagon reports. She had come up with her germ warfare conclusions only after reading his name in intercepted messages.

What was he doing here? Worse, what awful experiment was he going to perform on her? Gut-wrenching horror assailed her. Would she leave this operating room with her body and mind intact? Without being lobotomized or otherwise mutilated?

In spite of her efforts to hide her horror, the doctor noticed it. "I am an authentic physician, Mrs. Mitchell," he declared, misunderstanding her fright.

"Y-yes, of course," she stammered, still too terrified to speak clearly.

Pulling the mask over his head, he laid it on a desk. "So many of these people have tuberculosis, we are forced to wear protection." He sighed. "It is too bad. Their lungs are always damaged."

Why does he care? she wondered. But she didn't let herself dwell on the question. She had to get out of here before he did something dreadful to her. She had to escape.

Andrea considered hitting the doctor with her fist and making a run for the door. But there was an armed guard outside. She considered putting up a fight so he couldn't examine her. But that meant they'd restrain her forcibly, the last thing she wanted. She considered screaming at the top of her lungs. But who was there to hear? Finally resigned, she offered no resistance when he began the examination.

He took her pulse and blood pressure and temperature, listened to her heart and thumped her a couple of times on the back. He looked down her throat and into her eyes. Then, to Andrea's astonishment, he said she could go. Her health was fine. His "complete physical examination" had amounted to nothing more than a check of her vital signs.

After the doctor had released her, the guard took her back to the small bare room where she had changed into the cotton robe a half hour earlier. He closed the door, leaving her alone.

For a moment, Andrea stood there, feeling the cold stone beneath her bare feet. Was this how she was going to spend her last night on earth? In a tiny room with a steel cot for a bed and a hole in the floor for a toilet?

Where was Philip? she wondered, acutely conscious of her yearning for him. Was he somewhere nearby, in a tiny cell like this one, expecting her to be safely on her way home tomorrow?

Andrea forced the image of his face from her mind. She couldn't bear to think about him. She gazed slowly around her small prison. On the steel cot was a tray filled with curried meat and rice. The spicy smell permeated the air. To her surprise, her mouth began to water.

Andrea hadn't eaten since lunch. That's probably why she'd fainted. She took a tentative bite. To get out of this mess alive, she needed all the energy she could muster. The food tasted as good as it smelled. She took another bite and tried some of the unleavened Indian bread. In no time, she'd finished everything on the plate.

And the condemned woman ate a hearty supper, she thought grimly. The doctor said she'd be doing "certain tasks" tomorrow. Whatever the tasks were, at least she wouldn't have to face them half-starved. And if she could get out of here, she wouldn't have to face them at all.

She put the tray in the corner by the door and pulled the chain on the bare bulb dangling from the ceiling. The room was plunged into darkness. After her eyes had adjusted, Andrea examined the barred window. Could she get out through it? Even standing on her tiptoes, she could barely see over the sill.

If she broke the glass, was there a way to remove the bars? Maybe the mud mortar holding them would crumble under pressure.

Andrea crossed to the bed, planning to shove it under the window. But it was bolted to the floor and wouldn't budge.

After scrutinizing the window again, she decided not to try anything tonight. Even if she managed to escape, how could she find Philip without weapons, barefoot, dressed only in a flimsy cotton robe? Where could she run for help?

Chagrined, Andrea crawled between the sheets. They felt coarse and stiff against her skin. But for a wonder, they were clean. Her tired body welcomed the hard mattress, but her busy mind wouldn't stop working.

Why were people locked up in cells, both here and at Prana Pharmaceuticals in Delhi? What was going on in this gruesome house of death? She closed her eyes and tried to sleep, but the questions wouldn't stop. If sadhus came here expecting to die, as the village woman said, why was a physician here? Why an operating room?

She went over the scene with the doctor again. Had he revealed any clues? She remembered what he'd said almost word for word. Except for mentioning "certain tasks" she'd have to perform, and tuberculosis, most of his conversation was in connection with his examination. What had he said about TB?

All these people have tuberculosis, he'd declared. All what people? She remembered Tulak's hacking cough; the cough of the embassy gardener. The disease was epidemic in this part of the world. And the doctor had sounded upset because their lungs were damaged by the disease, as though the lungs were valuable.

But Andrea didn't have TB so he had taken the mask off. Had he examined Philip, too? Probably not, since Philip didn't faint in Colonel Khadka's office the way Andrea had. Wasn't that the reason Khadka gave for the physical?

She sensed she was overlooking something important. But after all that had happened today, she didn't have the strength to dwell on it. Tomorrow she'd put everything together and figure out what to do.

Tomorrow.

THE SOUND OF A KEY turning in Andrea's locked door brought her instantly awake. Someone was coming into her cell. She sat up and pulled the sheet around her.

The plump Indian woman who'd guarded Andrea yesterday entered. She was wearing the same green sari. Under one arm she carried a bundle of clothes. In her other hand were Andrea's hiking boots.

Andrea's heart gave a thankful leap. The hiking boots had tear gas weapons in the heels. Or did when she took them off yesterday. During the night, her clothes had probably been searched. Without physically checking the heels, she couldn't tell if the chemical had been discovered and removed.

The woman dropped the bundle on the bed and the boots on the floor. Then she positioned herself solidly in front of the door.

Quickly, Andrea searched through the bundle. Everything she'd worn yesterday was here. But something had been added: a lined woolen jacket, the kind trekkers wore. Andrea's breath caught in her throat. Colonel Khadka expected her to climb a mountain today. That was the "little task" he had planned for her. And he wanted her to be suitably dressed when she was found.

Her blood froze in her veins. *When my body's found,* she amended. *Khadka wants my death on the mountain to look like an accident.*

Jeffry's death had seemed like an accident, too. Had it been planned? Andrea remembered her conversation with Khadka. He knew all about Jeffry's accident—he'd told her the priest had witnessed it, and that there was no doubt Jeffry was dead.

He was behind Jeffry's accident and wanted me to stop my investigation, she concluded grimly. *When I wouldn't, he had to send me home.*

She laid the jacket on the cot. *And when he caught me at the temple last night, he knew I might have seen something important. So now he's got to get rid of me for good.*

The woman in the green sari was watching her. Deliberately, Andrea turned her back toward the door and started dressing, as slowly as possible to give herself time.

If Khadka had his way, Andrea was going to die today in a trekking accident because she knew too much. But too much about what? What ghoulish business was behind all the odd happenings during the past year? She finished putting on her bra and panties and slipped into her shirt, buttoning it slowly.

As she'd done last night in bed, she reviewed everything that had happened, beginning with Jeffry's accident and the disappearance of his body, and ending up in the little doctor's operating room.

She remembered the cells at Prana Pharmaceuticals in Delhi and here in the house of death in Dhara Village. In her mind, she heard the heart-wrenching cry at Prana Pharmaceuticals and knew—as Philip had said—that it came from a victim imprisoned there. She remembered the increased air traffic between Delhi and Ganthaku, the communications network at the temple compound, the helicopter hovering over Dhara Village.

But what did these happenings have in common?

The plume of cremation smoke rising over the river appeared in her mind. At the memory, an awful suspicion arose deep within her. Were the victims brought here, killed, and their bodies burned? Is that why no trace had been found of Jeffry's trekking party? Had they, too, been victims? Their bodies burned?

But why, for God's sake?

Andrea pulled her pants up and threaded the belt through the loops around her waist. Then she sat down on the steel cot and put on first one sock and then the other.

The doctor appeared in her mind again. Khadka was doing something to the bodies that required a doctor. And an operating room. And refrigeration. What had the physician said about the victims? That "many of these people" had TB and their lungs were bad. Why would he care if their lungs were bad? Unless he planned to make use of the organs in some way.

The awful truth exploded in Andrea's brain like a grenade. The people in Jeffry's trekking party had been taken prisoner and killed for their lungs—lungs that were needed because the lungs of the victims from India were all diseased. She added everything she'd found and came up with the only possible solution.

Harvesting body organs and selling them on an international black market. That's what these monsters were up to. Khadka flew in destitute men from India who would never be missed and locked them up until they were killed and their organs removed. Then their bodies were burned.

Andrea gagged. She had to get out of here and find Philip. He must have stumbled on this plot during his unannounced inspection yesterday, so Khadka's men had taken him prisoner.

She put on her hiking boots with the same deliberate slowness she'd used with her other clothes. Taking each lace out, she pulled the boots on, then painstakingly relaced each one. Lord, but she wished she could check the heels to see if the tear gas projectors were intact. But she didn't dare. The Indian woman was watching her too closely.

Where did the strange mussenda bushes fit in? *They're just a cover,* she concluded. *The villagers—and anybody else who's curious—are told they're for a sacred ointment worth guarding.*

Finally, Andrea stood. She refused to put on the jacket.

"It isn't mine," she insisted when the woman handed it to her. Shrugging, the woman put the jacket over her own shoulders and motioned for Andrea to follow.

Outside, the woman said something to the guard in Hindi. He was Indian, not Tisaran—something Andrea had missed last night. She could hear his boots clicking on the stone floor, could feel him close behind her.

Fearful images twisted in her mind. Images of Philip strapped down on a table, of his body burning on a cremation ghat beside the river. She thrust the thoughts from her mind. Philip was a U.S. ambassador. He couldn't just disappear the way the victims from India did—the way Jeffry had.

But he *could* have a bad accident, the kind of accident Khadka was planning for her. And there seemed to be nothing she could do to help herself. She balled her fists at her sides in impotent fury and guilt. If not for her, they wouldn't be in this mess. Why hadn't she figured out Khadka's plot sooner? The clues had been staring her in the face for days now. Why had she let herself get caught again in the temple garden?

Andrea followed the Indian woman down a long hallway in a direction opposite from the operating room. Breaking through her anger came a familiar smell. *Fresh coffee.*

She shook her head. *I'm imagining it.* But the smell grew stronger. They reached a door. The Indian woman opened it.

Andrea peered into the room, not believing her own eyes. A big rectangular table was set for a meal. A steaming pot at the center provided the enticing odor she'd been smelling.

Seated at the head of the table was Colonel Ratna Khadka. Next to him was Interior Minister Ganesh Nakarmi. Khadka had his arm across Nakarmi's shoulder. Next to Nakarmi was the little Mid-Eastern doctor Andrea had met last night.

Then she saw Philip. His back was to her. There he sat on Khadka's other side, dressed in hiking clothes, a cup in his hand. Why was he having breakfast with Khadka and Nakarmi?

When Philip turned and saw Andrea, the startled expression on his face matched her own shock.

Chapter Fifteen

"What the hell's my secretary doing here, Khadka?" Philip's voice rasped with barely controlled anger.

Stunned into immobility, Andrea stared at the four men seated at the table. To her horrified eyes, they looked like businessmen planning the day's strategy. Her mind jumped to a stupefying question. Could Philip be collaborating with Khadka in this murderous black market operation?

Khadka glanced from Philip to Andrea, his expression taut and derisive. "Why don't you ask *her* what she's doing here, Mr. Ambassador?" His tone bristled with contempt.

Turning toward Andrea, Philip half rose from his chair.

The guard lifted his rifle and pointed it straight at Philip's chest.

"Please remain seated," Khadka ordered, his mouth tight and grim.

Philip lowered himself into his chair. "You bastard. Wasn't catching me prize enough? Did you have to involve my secretary?"

Relief flooded Andrea. So Philip was a prisoner, too, and not part of this horror.

Nudging Nakarmi with his shoulder, Khadka chuckled. It was a dry, rasping sound deep in his throat. "I think the ambassador has more than a casual interest in his secretary, wouldn't you say, Ganesh?"

The interior minister chuckled, too. "It would seem so, Ratna." He avoided eye contact with either Andrea or Philip.

Andrea swept Nakarmi with a scathing look. The brief conversation she'd overheard in the temple garden made perfect sense. The assassin, Dass Verma, had said the "minister"—obviously the interior minister—had "joined" them. After stumbling on the truth in his unannounced inspection with Philip, Nakarmi had joined forces with these killers. Andrea wondered how much he'd been offered to betray his friend.

Khadka turned toward Philip. "Go ahead and ask her what she's doing here, Mr. Ambassador." He leered at Andrea with a twisted half smile. "She'll tell you we caught her spying in the temple garden again, won't you, Mrs. Mitchell?"

A vise tightened around Andrea's throat. Who else in the Tisaran government was involved in this plot? she wondered. The army chief of staff? The prime minister? The king himself? In Tisara, the king was believed to be a god, an incarnation of Vishnu. He was also one of the world's richest men. Would he stoop to dealing in a black market organ donor operation?

Philip looked up at her, his eyes apprehensive. She knew he was waiting for her response to Khadka's taunt.

"I couldn't leave Tisara without talking to the priest," she asserted, repeating the story she'd told Khadka.

Her fear was tinged with humiliation. If she hadn't lingered to eavesdrop in the temple garden, the guard would never have caught her. She'd gone to the temple because she knew Philip was in danger and hoped to find some way to save him. Instead, she'd gotten them both into deeper trouble.

A tight-lipped smile spread across Colonel Khadka's swarthy face. "Why don't you tell him the rest, Mrs. Mitchell? Tell him you discovered our broadcast terminal and eavesdropped on two of my men."

Andrea winced, even more certain the colonel intended to kill her and Philip. With what the two of them knew, Khadka couldn't afford to let them go free.

"For God's sake, Khadka." Philip's mellow baritone was edged with control. "At least let the woman sit down."

Khadka nodded. "By all means." He waved a hand toward the chair next to Philip. "Mrs. Mitchell. Please."

When Andrea hesitated, the Indian woman beside her gave her a shove. But Andrea didn't sit down.

"Please join us for breakfast." Khadka's invitation sounded like an order.

"Breakfast?" Andrea met his eyes without flinching. "You can't be serious." She didn't intend to eat a morsel in this man's company.

After another shove, Andrea sat down. Under the table, Philip squeezed her knee. His touch sent a hopeful tremor through her. They were in bad trouble, but at least they faced it together.

"He's serious, all right." Though Philip addressed Andrea, he didn't lower his voice. She sensed his frustration.

"The colonel wants to be sure our stomachs are full of hearty food when our bodies are autopsied." He glared at Khadka. "That'll corroborate his story that we were in good health when we started out on our morning trek. Am I right, Colonel?"

So Philip, too, had guessed what their fate would be—probably when he, too, was told to dress in hiking clothes.

Khadka's eyes darkened. "Whether you're right or not, you might as well eat."

We've got to get out of here, Andrea thought grimly.

When was the best time to try? She'd have only one slim chance—if the tear gas projectors in her boot heels hadn't been discovered and disarmed. Without the weapons, she and Philip were as good as dead.

Beside her, Philip spoke. "Don't worry, Khadka. If your food's palatable, we'll eat it."

Unobtrusively, Andrea surveyed the room. Sitting opposite her were the doctor and the interior minister. Khadka was at the head of the table. The Indian woman remained standing behind her. The guard stood behind the woman, holding his rifle with one hand. Andrea was certain he'd been ordered not to shoot unless absolutely necessary. Bodies with bullets in them couldn't be considered accident victims.

Three doors led into the windowless room. The one she'd entered, another on the opposite side and a third door behind Khadka that—since this was a dining room—logically would go to the kitchen. There were probably more guards outside the first two entrances.

But maybe not in the kitchen, she thought.

What had her instructor at the espionage school said? *When using the KL-40 chemical weapon to escape multiple adversaries, your chances are best if the scene is confused and there are innocent people in the room.* Like the servant or servants who'd be bringing their food.

She remembered another lesson from school: how to bump into someone and make it look accidental.

Where would she and Philip go if they did escape? The villagers, who obeyed the priest, would try to stop them. And even if they reached the road, they couldn't be sure a vehicle would stop, or that the driver would be friendly.

Andrea refused to be discouraged. She and Philip had to get out of here. If they didn't, they'd die.

Khadka was speaking to her. She focused her gaze on his bicolored eyes.

"I hope you like scrambled eggs and ham, Mrs. Mitchell. It's the only American breakfast my cook prepares well."

She nodded. "I do." If she seemed congenial, he'd be less likely to suspect what she was planning.

Philip threw her a surprised glance. She smiled back at him with a bland expression, avoiding any semblance of communication. Khadka was watching them intently. He'd be sure to spot any signal between them.

Lord, Andrea hoped Philip would follow her lead. If he didn't, her plan would fail. She felt herself begin to perspire when an Indian man in dark baggy trousers and a loose white shirt came through the door behind Khadka and announced that breakfast was ready.

The colonel turned his head toward the servant. "Bring it in."

Andrea stiffened. The moment of truth was upon her. When her plate was served, she planned to bump into the servant's arm so he'd drop it. She'd remove the tear gas projectors from her boot heels while she was bent over, cleaning up.

To her dismay, three more Indians appeared. Two held platters heaped with food. The third carried a stack of plates. They placed the dishes in front of Khadka. Onto the top plate, he spooned a generous helping of scrambled eggs, ham, bread and a spicy Indian breakfast patty made of mashed rice and yogurt.

"For Mrs. Mitchell," he said, handing the plate to Philip.

Andrea thought fast. If she intended to drop the food on the floor, she wouldn't have a better time than right now.

She leaned toward Philip. As he passed the loaded plate to her, she took it with the hand closest to him. The instant he let go, she jerked her wrist, flinging the plate to the floor. Eggs, ham and minced rice cascaded onto the table and floor and all over her and Philip.

Andrea shot to her feet, brushed quickly at her clothes and dropped to the floor, her napkin in her hand. Next to her, Philip jumped up and shook food off himself.

"Sit down, both of you," Khadka thundered from the head of the table. A servant dashed through the door toward him.

On the floor, with her back to the guard, Andrea twisted frantically at the heels of her boots. The false bottoms containing the tear gas weapons came off easily. With one in each closed hand, she crawled from under the table. The guard eyed her with an interested expression, but didn't lift his rifle.

She returned to her chair and dropped the weapons in her lap. "I was trying to clean up," she mumbled, trying to sound apologetic and nervous. The nervousness was no pretense. She'd never felt jumpier or more scared. Anxiously, she fingered the weapons in her lap. Were they armed?

Khadka filled another plate. He handed it to the servant and said something in Hindi. From the way the servant smiled, Andrea suspected Khadka had insulted her.

Good, she thought. *If he thinks I'm a clumsy dolt, so much the better.*

The servant stood well off to one side when he set the heaping plate down in front of her. She waited until everyone had been served and started eating before she made her move.

With a KL-40 in each hand, she leaped up, swung around and sprayed the chemical at the woman and the guard. Thank God the weapon worked. The two Indians staggered backward, their hands in front of their faces. Beside her, Philip jumped out of his chair, knocking it over.

She pointed one of the devices at Khadka and Nakarmi. Both men were on their feet. Nakarmi's back was to her, but Khadka had already taken a stride toward her. She blasted him full in the face. Lunging at her, Khadka grabbed her arm and held on with a madman's strength, his eyes and nose streaming water.

She heard a snarling growl, almost like that of a wild animal. Then Philip smashed Khadka solidly on the jaw. The colonel released her arm, swayed backward and hit the stone floor like a giant tree.

The little doctor hadn't moved from his place at the table. Instinctively, Andrea knew he was no threat. The door behind him opened and two more guards burst into the room. Andrea sprayed them from across the table and watched them turn back toward the hall outside.

Ganesh Nakarmi sprinted toward the kitchen door. "Follow me to the chopper," he yelled at Philip over his shoulder. "We don't have much time. Indian guards are everywhere."

Andrea jerked to a stop, reeling with confusion. Whose side was Nakarmi on? Her eyes were starting to sting and her nose to water. If she didn't get out of here, she wouldn't be able to see well enough to run.

Philip grabbed her hand. "We're with you, Ganesh," he yelled at the minister's back.

Andrea didn't like following the turncoat Nakarmi. But they had no choice. Her heart in her throat, she let Philip pull her through the door.

WITH ANDREA behind him, Philip followed Nakarmi into a huge kitchen area. Steam rose from food cooking in big pots over open fires. The red brick walls were black with soot. The strong scent of curry permeated the atmosphere.

The ragtag crew of a dozen or so kitchen workers stopped their work to watch, their faces glistening with sweat. But nobody tried to stop the three escapees. Outside, in the shadow of the building, Nakarmi stopped and looked around.

Philip gripped his friend on the shoulder. "I knew you were faking."

During the long night in his cell, Philip had never doubted his friend's loyalty. By pretending to join Khadka, Nakarmi was trying to get them out of this mess.

"It was the only chance we had," Nakarmi declared. "Until Mrs. Mitchell came along with her tear gas."

"Her name is Andrea." Philip smiled at Andrea, feeling great tenderness for her. Shading his eyes, he stared up the hill. "The chopper's that way, isn't it? On the other side of the village?"

He felt Andrea stir beside him.

"It's sure to be guarded," she warned. "And we've got no weapons except what's left of my tear gas."

"Then we'll have to bluff our way out of here." He turned to Nakarmi. "The guards think you're working for Khadka so they won't stop you." Holding Andrea's hand, Philip started toward the helicopter. "Let's get out of here. Bad news travels fast."

They walked through the village as quickly as they could without running. They encountered curious looks but no opposition.

The helicopter, painted white and green to look like a sight-seeing craft, was surrounded by four Indian guards. They saluted Ganesh Nakarmi. He said something to them in Hindi.

One of the guards pulled the aircraft's door open and helped Nakarmi inside. Philip boosted Andrea up. As the small craft lifted off, he sat next to Nakarmi, with Andrea behind them. Nakarmi smiled and waved at the men below. They waved back.

An intense relieved feeling swept over Philip. They'd gotten away. And the woman he loved was with him. What better reward could any man ask for?

Turning to Nakarmi, he whistled softly. "You sure got the royal treatment. What did you tell them?"

"That I was taking you back to Ganthaku on Khadka's orders."

"They believed you?" Philip was astounded.

Nakarmi shrugged. "Of course. I was the pilot who picked the colonel up at the army base early this morning. The doctor came with me to make sure I didn't stop and make any unauthorized phone calls." He grinned at Philip. "I can't imagine why, but Khadka didn't completely trust me."

"Why did Khadka pick that particular doctor to do these operations?" Andrea asked. "He doesn't look Indian or Tisaran."

In spite of her matter-of-fact tone, Philip heard more than mere curiosity in her question. Could the physician in the house of death be the Arab biological warfare expert whose name had led to her faulty conclusion?

Ganesh glanced over his shoulder at Andrea. "He is Middle Eastern—Syrian, I think."

So he *is* the man, Philip thought.

"I imagine he is available to the highest bidder," Nakarmi went on. "From what I heard last night when I ate with the physician and the priest, he's a brilliant surgeon. But to be involved in this dirty business, he must have the ethics of a monkey."

Philip turned around to look at Andrea. God, but it was wonderful to have her here with him, to know they were both safe. *Safe.* The word took on a special sweetness with Andrea near.

A disturbing thought occurred to him, and he frowned. "What's going to happen to Khadka?" he asked Nakarmi.

When Nakarmi answered, the anxiety in his tone dismayed Philip. "I'm afraid Colonel Khadka may be a problem."

"How big a problem?" Philip felt Andrea lean against the back of his seat to hear better.

"As chief of intelligence, Khadka has secret files on every officer in the Tisaran security forces. They're afraid of him, even the generals. If he threatens them, they may support him."

Philip heard Andrea catch her breath.

"Are you suggesting Khadka may try a coup d'état?" she asked. "Does he have enough troop strength to take over the government?"

Nakarmi nodded grimly. "I'm afraid he does. But there's not much he can do from Dhara Village. Without the chopper, it'll take him a couple of hours to get back to Ganthaku."

Andrea crossed her arms on the seat behind Philip's shoulders. "From Dhara, he can use his broadcast network to contact troop commanders who are loyal to him." Her voice was urgent. "All they have to do is seize the airport, and three TV stations and the Parliament Building, and they're well on their way to securing the government."

Nakarmi twisted his head toward Philip. "Your secretary seems very well informed." He lifted an eyebrow, and a devilish look appeared in his eyes. "I think she may well be a spy, just as Khadka said."

"Listen to her, Ganesh," Philip urged. "She's a military expert."

Nakarmi nodded slowly. "Somehow that doesn't surprise me." He glanced over his shoulder. "So what does the expert think I should do?"

"If you don't want a military junta to take over your country, you've got to deactivate that broadcasting terminal at Ishwaranath." Andrea's forehead creased with concentration. "Do it before Khadka orders the terminal moved someplace else. I'm sure it's portable. All he has to do is send one message, and his people will take action."

Philip touched his friend's arm. "Is there anyone high up in the army you trust completely? He could take some troops and dismantle the terminal."

Nakarmi nodded. "The quartermaster is a good friend, and loyal."

Philip heard Andrea's sigh of dismay.

"General Joshi's a bean counter," she declared. "How about somebody in operations?"

Nakarmi gave her a surprised look over his shoulder. Philip could tell that Andrea's familiarity with Joshi's name had thrown his friend off balance.

"General Joshi may be a supply officer or, as you say, a bean counter," Ganesh returned, "but he's close to the chief of staff and popular as well as loyal."

"Then General Joshi's our man," she agreed quickly.

Philip admired her ability to make such a rapid-fire decision.

"Can you radio him from the helicopter?" she asked.

"Not directly," Nakarmi replied. "But I can call the control tower and have the operator relay a message." He glanced at Andrea again. "You say there's a broadcast terminal at Ishwaranath?"

"It's in a building behind the temple garden. That's why the place is guarded."

Nakarmi let his breath out in a huge sigh. "And I believed Khadka when he said the troops were posted there to protect the secrecy of our new drug."

"What new drug?" Andrea's words were tense, clipped.

Philip twisted around in his seat to see her better. Her eyes were wide with amazement.

"The Tisarans have discovered a new hair restoration product," he told her. "It'll make them a fortune if they can perfect the process."

Understanding flooded her face. "So you were right about that, Philip."

Philip glowed with satisfaction when he saw her admiring glance.

"Of course, Khadka was using the hair research as a cover to hide his illicit black market in body organs," she said reflectively.

Philip nodded. "And if we don't do something right away to stop his coup attempt, he might get away with it."

"We're going to do something." Nakarmi's expression was grim. He put on his headphones and began talking into the microphone. After he'd identified himself, he dictated a terse emergency message to be relayed to Quartermaster General Hari Joshi.

Meet me at the Palace as quickly as you can. Situation urgent.

"If we're lucky, Joshi will get to the palace shortly after we do," Nakarmi said.

Listening to his friend, Philip stirred uneasily in his seat. "What do you mean, *if we're lucky?*" Why had he felt secure only moments earlier?

His friend's eyes narrowed. "The controller said military security guards at the airport were massing outside the tower."

"We can't land there." Andrea's voice rang with command. "They may seize the helicopter and force you to fly Khadka back to Ganthaku."

"I am in full agreement," Nakarmi returned. "We'll put down on the palace grounds."

AFTER ALIGHTING from the helicopter, they hurried to the suite of palace offices where the king received government visitors.

In the spacious reception area, Ganesh Nakarmi gave Andrea a tight-lipped smile. "After the way you have helped us, I hate to say this, Andrea, but you will have to wait here while Philip and I talk to King Shrestha. I think he would not be as understanding as I about your role as a military spy."

Andrea returned his smile. "I am not a spy, Ganesh. As Ambassador Dorough's secretary, I'll be happy to wait right here."

"We understand each other perfectly."

Philip gave her a sober look. "Keep your fingers crossed," he whispered as he and Nakarmi followed a uniformed officer into the royal audience chamber.

A beautiful Tisaran woman, the king's administrative assistant, showed Andrea to a comfortable leather chair in the reception room.

In less than ten minutes, General Joshi rushed into the king's chamber. Andrea recognized him from her biographic files at the Pentagon. A few minutes later, the chief of staff of the Tisaran army strode by. Next came a television camera crew.

The administrative assistant flicked a switch and teak doors at one end of the reception room parted to reveal a large-screen television. Tisara might be a backward third-world country, but its royal palace obviously contained all the latest technical marvels.

The king's visage appeared on the screen.

"Loyal members of our armed forces and people of Tisara," King Shrestha began. "Forces hostile to your country, your king and your government are engaged in a diabolical plot to overthrow us."

From there he launched into a brief warning of the expected coup attempt. Pinpointing Khadka and several others, he asked the military to follow the orders of the chief of staff. He assured the officers their loyalty would be rewarded.

During the next two hours, military officers dashed in and out of the king's chamber. Andrea suspected that a makeshift war room had been set up inside.

When Philip and Nakarmi finally emerged, they were smiling.

"Khadka is in custody," Philip announced. "Loyal troops arrested him on the outskirts of Ganthaku a few minutes ago."

"What about the Indian guards at Dhara Village?" Andrea asked.

"Probably on their way to Delhi," Nakarmi replied, smiling. "With Khadka gone, I doubt they'll stay in Tisara long."

"Then the coup's over?" A powerful relief filled her.

"Pretty much so," Philip affirmed. "After the king's appeal on television, only two of the battalions in the Ganthaku area sided with Khadka. They held the airport for an hour or so. That was the most threatening situation."

Ganesh flashed Andrea a big smile. "Your spying really turned the trick."

Andrea did not smile back. "I wasn't spying, Ganesh."

"I know, I know," he soothed. "But the coup didn't collapse until we knocked out that broadcasting station at Ishwaranath. With that terminal gone, Khadka and his revolutionaries had no way to keep in touch."

"Did you arrest the men on duty at the station?" Andrea pictured the fat assassin in her mind.

"They are in custody," Nakarmi assured her. "One of them is known as Dass Verma." He turned to Philip. "Wasn't that the name of the gardener you called me about last week?"

LATER, when Mohan drove Andrea and Philip back to the embassy compound, she explained that Dass Verma was the assassin, and as she'd suspected, he'd taken the name of the fertilizer as a cover.

"Thank God you're safe," Philip breathed, his voice rough with emotion. "If Verma had caught you spying on him . . ."

He took Andrea's face in his hands and brushed a gentle kiss across her lips. "When you walked into that room this morning, I felt like the end of the world had come."

"I know." She leaned against him. "Sunday night when I realized you were being held prisoner, I just about went crazy."

Startled, he straightened. "How did you figure that out?"

"Simple. There are no phones in Dhara Village."

Mystified, he stared at her. "So what does that prove?"

"That nobody could have called Ganesh's wife from the village to tell her you were staying the night." She lowered her voice to whisper. "The message had to be sent over the network I'd been reading about at the Pentagon—from Dhara Village to Ishwaranath. Then somebody from the temple compound called Mrs. Nakarmi on the telephone."

He let his breath out in a long sigh. "So that's why you went snooping in the middle of the night."

"I had to start looking for you somewhere. Ishwaranath was the only place I could think of where there might be a clue."

Philip watched her cheeks color and knew she was about to reveal something that embarrassed her.

"Unfortunately," she went on, "I was eavesdropping on Dass Verma and let myself get caught."

He drew her into his arms and held her close, enjoying the feel of her softness against him.

"If you hadn't gotten caught, I'd be lying in some crevasse right now." He whispered the words in her ears. "Now that you've saved my life three times, how would you like to work at keeping an eye on things around here full-time?"

He felt her tense in his arms. She drew back. Her eyes sparkled with what he hoped was happiness.

"What do you mean?"

A truck went by the car, its horn blaring. Philip waited until it had passed before he replied.

"The embassy's got an opening for a defense attaché. I've already cleared it with Ganesh. He says you're the only military officer Tisara will accept as attaché."

"You told him I was in the Air Force?" She didn't sound upset that he might have broken her cover.

"No," he said. "Even though I trust Ganesh completely, I gave him the party line. That you'd been in the service until you came to work as my secretary. But that I was certain you could get your commission back if Tisara accepted you as attaché."

She leaned against him again. "Then I could stay here in Tisara as a bona fide captain?"

"For as long as I'm here." Hope surged through him.

"What happens when you leave?" Her eyes were thoughtful. "Air Force officers don't get transferred along with their bosses."

He grinned at her. "By then I hope you'll have accepted your promotion."

The beginnings of a smile touched her lips. "I'm not due to make major for at least three years."

"I wasn't talking about a military promotion." He studied her face.

Her smile broadened. "What, then?"

Sweeping her into his arms, he whispered in her hair. "Why, your promotion to M. R. S. Dorough, of course." He pressed her lips to his, caressing her mouth more than kissing it.

Finally, when they'd parted, he gazed into her eyes. They sparkled with the vitality he loved so much in her.

"So how about it? Does the promotion sound good to you?"

She drew back. For a heart-stopping minute, Philip thought she was going to turn him down.

Then the corners of her eyes crinkled with mischief. "As long as I can keep on calling you Philip, I suppose it'll be all right for you to call me Mrs. Dorough."

Her teasing words brought a memory of their first night together. He held her close. "You can call me anything you like," he whispered, his voice husky. "As long as I can call you my wife."

Suddenly, the sweet sense of satisfaction that had eluded Philip for so long washed over him. With Andrea at his side, he would always have someone to share his successes and give them meaning. Like the majestic mountains he saw through his office window, he would, at last, find peace.

HARLEQUIN®

I N T R I G U E®

It looks like a charming old building near the Baltimore waterfront, but inside 43 Light Street lurks danger ... and romance.

by

REBECCA YORK

Labeled a "true master of intrigue," Rebecca York continues her exciting 43 Light Street series in July. Join her as she brings back Abby Franklin and Steve Claiborne—whom we met in the first 43 Light Street book, LIFE LINE—in a special edition:

#233 CRADLE AND ALL
July 1993

The birth of their first child should be a time of unparalleled joy, but when the baby is kidnapped, Abby and Steve are thrust into a harrowing ordeal that has them fighting for their lives ... and their love.

"Clever, crafty Rebecca York once again practices to deceive in splendid fashion as she whisks us away for a superlative foray into heart-stopping suspense, daring adventure and uplifting romance."
—Melinda Helfer, *Romantic Times*

Don't miss #233 CRADLE AND ALL, coming to you in July—only from Harlequin Intrigue.

LS93-2

Take 4 bestselling love stories FREE

Plus get a FREE surprise gift!

Special Limited-time Offer

Mail to Harlequin Reader Service®

**3010 Walden Avenue
P.O. Box 1867
Buffalo, N.Y. 14269-1867**

YES! Please send me 4 free Harlequin Intrigue® novels and my free surprise gift. Then send me 4 brand-new novels every month. Bill me at the low price of $2.24 each plus 25¢ delivery and applicable sales tax, if any.* That's the complete price and—compared to the cover prices of $2.99 each—quite a bargain! I understand that accepting the books and gift places me under no obligation ever to buy any books. I can always return a shipment and cancel at any time. Even if I never buy another book from Harlequin, the 4 free books and the surprise gift are mine to keep forever.

181 BPA AJJE

Name	(PLEASE PRINT)
Address	Apt. No.
City	State Zip

This offer is limited to one order per household and not valid to present Harlequin Intrigue® subscribers.
*Terms and prices are subject to change without notice. Sales tax applicable in N.Y.

UINT-93R

©1990 Harlequin Enterprises Limited

HARLEQUIN®
I N T R I G U E®

Hop into a pink Cadillac with the King of Rock 'n' Roll for the hottest—most mysterious—August of 1993 ever!

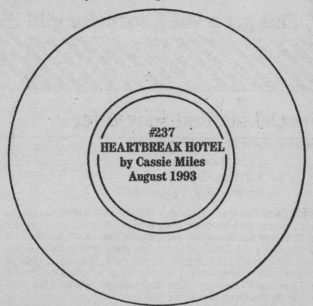

#237
HEARTBREAK HOTEL
by Cassie Miles
August 1993

All Susan Quentin wanted was a quiet birthday, but she got lots more: sexy greetings over the radio, deejay Johnny Swift himself—and a dead Elvis impersonator outside her door. Armed with only sunglasses and a pink Cadillac, could they find the disguised "King" killer amid a convention of impersonators at the Heartbreak Hotel?

Don't be cruel! Come along for the ride of your life when Johnny tries to convince Susan to love him tender!

ELVIS